PLOVER LANDING

Also by Marie Zhuikov

Eye of the Wolf

PLOVER LANDING

MARIE ZHUIKOV

Marie Zhuikov (signature)

NORTH STAR PRESS OF ST. CLOUD, INC.

St. Cloud, Minnesota

ISBN: 978-0-87839-727-3

First edition: June 2014

Printed in the United States of America

Published by North Star Press of St. Cloud
PO Box 451
St. Cloud, MN 56302
www.northstarpress.com

Acknowledgements

I would like to thank a good dose of "butt glue" and focus for helping me finish this novel in only two and a-third years instead of the seventeen it took for my first book. It also helps knowing that a publisher like North Star Press is waiting for it.

This story would not be what it is without the help of my steadfast (and merciless) writer's group: Lacey Louwagie, Linda Olson, and Jim Phillips; also BFF and fellow writer, Sharon Moen. Douglas Aretz, thank you for your review and answering my strange sailing questions, like, "Are toilet seats on sailboats kept open or closed?"

For information related to violas, I thank Judy MacGibbon. For information related to the Duluth-Superior Symphony Orchestra, I thank Rebecca Peterson and Jessica Leibfried. For information about what it's like to be a plover monitor, I thank former University of Minnesota Duluth biology student Kiah Brasch. I thank Mike Furtman for the wild plover chase, Tom Betts for all things airplane, Island Man Potilla for his review, Martha Dwyer for Native American insights, Carrie Lane for sharing her airedale with me, Janine and Kelly Olsen for logging equipment information, former Kansas Poet Laureate Caryn Mirriam-Goldberg for helping me get unstuck, and Lake Superior Writers for their support.

Thank you, dear reader, for reading. Please do what you can to mitigate the effects of climate change. This novel reflects knowledge and attitudes about the climate from 1995. We know a lot more now. And please support any shorebird restoration efforts going on near you!

Listen, the only way
to tempt happiness into your mind is by taking it
into the body first, like small
wild plums.

From *The Plum Trees*
Mary Oliver

Prologue

THE PIPING PLOVER rode the high breezes over the beach. He scanned the dunes, looking for a wide stretch of sand—better yet, a wide stretch scattered with cobble stones. Building a nest required stones.

Ahead, the little bird saw a promising expanse. His heart, already beating fast from flight, began to pump faster. He flapped his wings, and called, "Peep-lo, peep-lo."

He had flown long and far from the tropical beach where he wintered to this cold freshwater lake in search of a nesting site and a mate. He was tired and hoped this would be the end of his journey.

Turning his head landward, the bird surveyed the tree line. The pines were a dozen wing beats away from the beach—just how he liked it. The farther away the trees were, the farther away the predators were. If anything came out of the trees to harm his nest or his mate, he would have time to react, dragging a wing to feign injury and lure the predator away.

But he knew that sometimes a far tree line did not help. He gave another cry as he remembered his mate from last spring—the first time he had nested. In spite of the open space around their nest, a cat caught her while he was watching the chicks. By the time he heard her cries, it was too late.

Their three chicks had survived in his care, but it had not been easy to watch over them alone—catching the bugs they needed to eat, on guard for other predators.

The breeze off the lake blew him toward the trees. The plover pumped his wings to regain his course. He circled the beach, once, twice, and then landed.

He skittered across the wet sand at the water's edge, his orange legs trembling. This place might do. He hoped a female plover would like this spot, too. But would she travel far enough to find him?

The bird stopped to snatch an iridescent green beetle from the sand. As he swallowed, he felt some of his fatigue slip away. He'd had to fly farther than last year. All the nesting sites on the south shore of the lake were taken. More plovers meant his kind was doing well, but it also meant a longer search into new lands for his own nest.

A dog barked, racing down the beach toward him. A human followed, calling. The bird burst up in flight out of reach. This would not do. People could step on eggs laid here, and the dog could eat his young, or his mate.

Gathering his strength, the plover continued flying down the beach.

Chapter One

THE TAN-SKINNED MEN sat in a circle, beating rawhide drums in unison. Their voices, soft and low at first, rose in pitch and intensity, calling out to earth and sky in time to the pulsing beat. Although they were dressed in street clothes—the jeans and plaid shirts common to northern Minnesota—the ceremony they conducted was far from modern.

Melora St. James stood on the beach, part of the crowd that had gathered to watch. Moved by the nature of the men's singing, it didn't take much for her to imagine them in an earlier time, wearing skins, with moccasins replacing their shoes.

She wiggled her toes in her tennies, trying to move the sand inside them to a more comfortable spot. It made her wish she had worn sandals, or better yet, gone barefoot. The tentative sunlight of a mid-April morning glinted off a small group of television cameras filming the event. Several reporters were clustered to one side, notebooks and microphones in hand.

Standing beside Melora, her co-worker Trevor Aston whispered, "Looks like we'll be getting good media coverage. The project funders will be happy . . . and it gets the tribe involved."

A lock of Trevor's black hair fell across his glasses. Melora looked through his hair and into his sea-blue eyes. She smiled, remembering how uncomfortable she had been approaching him with the idea. It wasn't every day that a Native American drum ceremony served to dedicate a piping plover nesting site. "So you don't think I'm some nutso hippie for arranging this?"

"No," Trevor said. "It's a great move."

Melora knew the endangered birds hadn't nested in the Duluth-Superior area for twenty-five years. As part of her work as an environmental project manager for The Nature Conservancy, she had, with advice from Trevor, written a grant for five years of funding to develop an area of beach so it would appeal to the birds for nesting.

The site she had chosen along with federal and state wildlife officials was on Minnesota Point, a seven-mile-long natural sandbar on Lake Superior that stretched between two towns and two states: Duluth on the Minnesota side, and Superior on the Wisconsin side. The point protected the harbor from the strong waves of Lake Superior. Its beaches offered a playground for residents and tourists seeking relief from the summer heat that was far too fleeting at this northern latitude.

Melora often thought of the sandbar as a dividing line separating two sisters who could not be more different. The harbor was home to an estuary, fed by rivers and streams; it turned brown from the dirt and vegetable matter picked up along the way. The estuary was warmer than the lake and provided a home to many fish, ducks, and other animals. This was the quiet, calm sister with warm brown eyes.

On the other hand, the lake was cold, sterile and volatile, with eyes of icy blue. Melora knew all too well how dark the depths of the lake were and that its waters needed to be approached with utmost respect.

A couple of other plover nesting projects had been attempted over the years, but neither were effective. One site had not been maintained, and the beach became overrun with an invasive bushy plant called spotted knapweed. The other failed when the water level rose and washed away sand brought in to enlarge the beach and create a small island.

Melora secretly suspected another reason for the failure was that the plovers didn't know the sites were being prepared for them. In her heart, she hoped the drum ceremony would make it clear the birds were to come to this spot. The pounding drums seemed a heartbeat of the world welcoming the plovers home.

The chants of the drummers rose again, and she could imagine their entreaties flying through the air, carried to the little birds winging their way north on their spring migration. The Ojibway people had once lived on Minnesota Point, and it seemed fitting they be the ones to welcome the birds back.

In perfect unison, the drummers stopped. The crowd, surprised by the silence, took a moment before they began to clap. While several local dignitaries, including the mayor, made short speeches about the project and how they hoped it would restore plovers to the area, Melora scanned the crowd to see if the audience's attention was waning. A small gasp escaped her lips as she spied someone she hadn't seen in over ten years. With a mixture of anticipation and curiosity, Melora quickly made her way to a Native American woman standing at the edge of the gathering.

Seeing Melora approach, the woman smiled and opened her arms. Melora returned her embrace, stepped back and whispered, "Georgina, what are you doing here?"

"I heard through the tribal grapevine that you were involved in this." Georgina gestured with her graying head to the surrounding crowd. "I had to come see if you attract one endangered species as well as you steal another."

Melora sputtered, then laughed. "I never thought of it that way." She drew Georgina farther away from the crowd. "That was a long time ago, you know. How did you find out?"

A knowing smile crossed Georgina's face. "A boat goes missing, wolves vanish, you vanish. It wasn't hard to figure out. Good job, by the way."

In college in the mid-1980s, Melora had worked on Isle Royale as a waitress at a resort. The remote island was a national park in Lake Superior near the Minnesota-Canada border. It was known for its moose and wolf population, which scientists had studied for forty years. When Melora worked there, the wolves were mysteriously dying out. Scientists later discovered it was due to a combination of inbreeding and exposure to a deadly virus carried by a dog someone had brought to the island illegally.

Melora had become involved in a secret effort to save one of the island's remaining packs by taking them to the mainland by boat. Georgina had helped her find the pack's den under the light of a full moon when Melora had been looking for her then-boyfriend Drew, who had also been involved in rescuing the wolves. Although her hike with Georgina had not led her to her boyfriend or the pack, Melora had found them on her own shortly afterwards and they made a harrowing escape from the island. She had not seen Georgina since that night.

The crowd started clapping again. Melora knew Trevor would be looking for her since she was his ride back to the office. She desperately wanted to continue the conversation with Georgina. "Are you staying in town for a while?"

Georgina nodded.

"How can I reach you?"

Georgina took paper and a pen from her purse. She wrote a phone number on the paper and handed it to Melora. "I'm staying with my cousin Shelly for a few days. Call me soon and we can have lunch."

Melora squeezed Georgina's arm briefly before she turned to make her way back to Trevor. He was talking to Stewart Starkweather, the mayor of Duluth, a tall, thin and boyish-looking man in good standing with the citizens. The two men stopped talking as she approached.

"Thanks for your help with the ceremony, Stewart," Melora said. "It meant a lot to have you here."

"I was happy to do it," he said. "I was just telling Trevor here that we should train the city lifeguards to recognize plovers, since they're out on the beach all day. Although the birds might not nest where people swim, at least the lifeguards could tell you if any plovers passed through."

Trevor looked at Melora with a sparkle in his eyes at this suggestion.

"That's a great idea," Melora said. "Who should I call to set up a training session?"

"I'll make sure they call you," the mayor said. "This is a wonderful project for our city, and I want to support it in any way possible."

"Thanks so much." Melora shook his hand. "I'll be sure to keep you updated on our progress."

The mayor moved away to talk to others in the dispersing crowd. Melora turned with Trevor and started walking down the beach the half-mile back to the car. The nesting site was on an isolated end of the point, far from the crowds and activity that the plovers disliked.

"Sure can't hurt to have the mayor on our side," Trevor said.

Melora smiled. "I'm glad you thought to make him part of the ceremony. That was a great move, too."

They continued walking to the car in silence, drinking in the view of the bright blue waters of Lake Superior and the stately white pines that lined the land. They were her favorite kind of tree—so tall and straight, with feathery clumps of needles that looked like green peacocks sitting on the end of each branch.

When they neared the runway to the small airport that paralleled the beach, a heavyset man shuffled toward them. He wore flip flops, jeans, and a Hawaiian shirt. A small dog pulled on the leash the man held.

Melora usually liked dogs—she had one of her own—but this one did not like her. It started yapping as ferociously as only a seven-pound terrier could. The man stopped. "What's all the hubbub?" With his head, he gestured down the beach where Melora and Trevor had just come.

"There was a ceremony to dedicate nesting habitat for shorebirds," Melora said, struggling to be heard over the barking.

The man snorted. "Shorebirds? Who gives a crap about shorebirds?" He jerked the dog's leash and continued down the beach, mumbling, "Buncha nature whackos."

Melora and Trevor looked at each other, too stunned to say anything. After a moment they continued walking to the parking lot. Trevor shrugged and rubbed the bump on his nose. "There goes another soldier in humankind's war on nature."

Melora laughed, then quickly grew serious. "I wish I had a good answer for people like him, though—about why plovers are important."

"Yeah, people seem to relate only to animals that benefit them in some way," Trevor said. "If they can't eat them, wear them or have them as a pet, animals are worthless."

"Never mind that plovers are endangered because humans messed up the environment," Melora added. "You and I know they are important, but what quick reply can we say to people like that guy?"

"Even if we said something profound, it wouldn't change his mind," Trevor said.

"Yeah, but it would make me feel better." Melora chuckled. "That should be our assignment for the next week—to come up with an "elevator phrase" about WHY PLOVERS ARE IMPORTANT. I mean, you can have all the speeches you want like we did today, but it comes down to responding to that question with a short and simple answer. Why are we spending a quarter million dollars from the Fish and Wildlife Service over the next five years to restore these birds here? The fact that the service and our organization want them here isn't enough."

"An elevator phrase . . . I like that," Trevor said. "That's an explanation that's short enough to describe during an elevator ride with your local congressperson or something, right?"

"Yep," said Melora, "something that gets the point across fast and accurately. It's harder to do than you'd think."

Trevor stuck out his hand to Melora. "You're on Melora. Let's think up a good reply for guys like Hawaiian Shirt Man."

Melora reached over and shook his hand, surprised at its warmth. This was soon replaced by nervousness from the tingling she felt as his hand slid from hers. Since her divorce, Melora had been flitting from one man to another, often dating more than one at a time. It was easier not to commit her heart to any one man. She'd had enough of that for a while. Because Melora worked with Trevor, it would be hard to flit away from him since she saw him every day. Still, his dedication to his work, his good attitude and the way he filled out his jeans so nicely all appealed to her.

The only thing she didn't like was how easily he changed his mind about work-related things. They would agree to a strategy one day, only to have Trevor rethink it the next. Sometimes his ideas had merit. Other times, she wondered if he wasn't just changing his mind for the pleasure of changing his mind.

Once they reached the grass-lined trail to the boardwalk, the pair veered off the beach. The boardwalk led them to the parking lot. They hopped into Melora's used Honda Prelude. The drive back to their office would take them past cozy beach bungalows built in the early years, and more modern mansions built as the affluent coveted the uniqueness of Park Point living. At the other end of the point was Duluth's famous Aerial Lift Bridge, a lacework of metal that crossed the Duluth Ship Canal. The bridge's roadway lifted and lowered to allow the ore boats and sailboats that plied Lake Superior to pass, then cars along the roadway.

The city, which operated the bridge, was experimenting with a regular schedule for the span lifting, since it cut off traffic for several minutes each time. The experience was known to locals as being "bridged." The current schedule was for a lift every half hour unless there were no boats waiting. If they weren't already endowed with great patience, people living or working on the point had to develop it. More than residents in the rest of the city, they were at the mercy of the bridge and the weather. Those who were impatient didn't last long.

Trevor interrupted Melora's reverie. "Melora, I know we work together and everything, but I really like you. We make a good team. Would you want to go out with me sometime?"

Melora's hands tightened on the steering wheel. She concentrated on keeping the car between the lines of the roadway as she considered her answer. A combination of fear, happiness and hesitancy rushed through her. Finally, she glanced at him. "Are you sure that's a good idea? I mean, I know we didn't sign anything swearing we would *not* date our coworkers, but it's one of those unspoken things, you know?"

"I know," Trevor said. "But it could make work more fun. Spice things up a little." Trevor's grin crinkled the corners of his eyes.

"It could also make it a living hell." Melora concentrated on the road again. "What do we do if things go bad?"

"Things bad? With me? Not a chance." Trevor chuckled. "Besides, I'm in good standing with my former girlfriends. Parting well is one of my specialties, as long as nobody does anything unforgiveable."

"Oh, Trevor." Melora did like the way his grin gave way to dimples. "Let me think about it for a few days. I like you, but there's more to consider."

Trevor shrugged. "All right. I can handle that. But I think we could have a lot of fun together . . . I hope you'll see that."

They were at the bridge now, which was down, thankfully. Melora didn't know how she would handle sitting in the car with Trevor if the span was up and they had to wait for it to lower. She checked his expression to ensure it matched his words. Trevor didn't look too crestfallen. And she noticed the electricity she had felt from his hand now seemed to emanate from the side of his body closest to hers.

Melora was grateful their office was just a few blocks past the bridge and she could get out and put some distance between herself and Trevor. It was all she could do to slow down and drive over the bridge at the required fifteen miles per hour. The roadway hummed under the Prelude's tires like metal corduroy. The low sound stopped abruptly as they reached asphalt on the other side. This part of the city was known as Canal Park, an area where the land narrowed and formed the original beginning of Park Point before the ship canal was cut through it.

Melora parked her car in the lot across from their office building. Parking was free for now, but come May fifteenth, the tourist season started, and she would have to pay unless she discovered another spot.

As they walked across the street, Trevor looked toward the harbor. "Hey, there's a new boat behind the convention center," he said.

Anxious to get back to the office and all the messages probably waiting for her, Melora kept walking, just glancing over her shoulder. She barely registered the large navy-blue-and-white vessel before a building blocked her view of it.

Their office was in the DeWitt-Seitz Building, the tallest in the neighborhood. Inside, the brick structure featured thick white pine timbers, the kind not found any more now that the old growth pines were all cut. It began service as a furniture warehouse and was most recently a mattress factory. Now it housed upscale tourist shops selling artwork, cookware, clothing, and candy. June, Melora's best friend, and her husband, Steve, owned a restaurant in the back where Melora often ate. It was called the Duluth Portage Café, after Sieur Du Lhut, a French explorer who visited the area in the late sixteen hundreds and was the city's namesake.

She and Trevor walked up the outer steps together. Opening the building door, Melora inhaled. She loved the pungent smell emanating from the smoked fish operation in the basement. The odor wafted up the stairs and soaked into the wooden floors and walls. Even though her job with The Nature Conservancy didn't pay well, Melora often thought it was well worth it just to work in this historic, good-smelling place.

Their office was on the third floor, just above the shops, along with other environmental groups like the Minnesota Environmental Partnership and the St. Louis River Alliance.

"Race you up the stairs," Trevor said, and he started climbing at a brisk pace.

"What, you didn't get enough exercise on the beach this morning? Give me a break!" But Melora kept up with him.

They reached the top, breathing heavily. "And it's a tie!" Trevor announced like he was calling a horse race. They didn't have much time to catch their breath before they reached the office door. They burst in, startling Seth Anderson, their administrative assistant.

"Whoa!" Seth held up his hands in mock surrender. "Didn't anyone tell you running in the halls here is forbidden? You might knock over a tourist!" He chortled. "So how did the ceremony go?"

"Great," Melora said. "The mayor was there, plus the newspaper and all the TV stations. The dedication went off without a hitch."

"Glad to hear it." Seth pushed his wire-rimmed glasses higher on his nose and scratched his graying mustache. "Any plovers show up?"

"I wish," Trevor said. "That would have been perfect, but you know they wouldn't like all the people and the noise."

"True," said Seth. "It took us five years to attract them to Long Island in the Apostles. You guys need to be patient. It could take a while." Seth was a former National Park Service biologist who had quickly become bored during his retirement. He had told Melora and Trevor many times how he loved that this job helped him stay involved in the environmental community.

A phone call interrupted Seth. He answered it and began taking a message. Melora and Trevor walked toward their respective offices.

Although Melora's office held no photos of significant others or children, it was festooned with knick-knacks accumulated during her various careers: a collection of shield-shaped green pins from her Forest Service public affairs job, wooden lighthouses and plastic aquarium animals from her Sea Grant writing gig, a replica of the tallest building in Minneapolis from her stint as a big-city editor. She sat behind her desk and fired up her computer.

A moment later, Seth called out to Melora, "Peg called earlier. She wants to know how the ceremony went. Give her a call as soon as you can, okay?"

"You got it," Melora said. Peg Severs was their boss, who was stationed in Minneapolis at the state headquarters of The Nature Conservancy. Melora looked forward to talking with her. However, before she could dial the number, she heard the front office door open and someone start talking to Seth.

A low male voice was asking for her. Melora started to shiver at the sound and watched in detached fascination as the hairs rose on the back of her arm that was reaching for the phone. She could barely make herself look up as a figure came to stand in front of her office doorway.

"Hello, Melora."

Melora felt the Earth's axis tip as she slowly looked up to see the still-powerful build and Neanderthal good looks of her Isle Royale love, Drew.

Chapter Two

MELORA TOOK THE MOMENT she needed before speaking. "Hello, Drew. It's been a long time. What brings you here?" She rose from the desk and made her way toward him.

"The *State of Michigan.*" At what she was sure must have been her quizzical look, he added, "Didn't you see it docked in the harbor?"

Understanding dawned on her as she gave Drew a hug. While their bodies were pressed together she had a chance to marvel at how well they still fit. She didn't have to reach too high or crouch low. Everything felt so right. Then there was his breath against the back of her neck. She held the hug a moment longer than necessary. Or maybe Drew was holding the hug. Maybe both of them were. Who cared when it felt this good?

Melora backed away. The pained expression on Drew's face gave her pause. She noted the years had not changed him much. His hair was still thick and brown. A few more lines had perhaps gathered around his mouth. She asked, "How long is the ship staying?"

"Two days," came his strangled reply. Melora guessed the hug must have felt as good to him as it had to her.

"Well . . ." She looked at the mess on her desk. "I have a million things to do, but I think we should go for a walk. Let me get my purse."

Drew nodded and took a step back, clearing the doorway.

Melora led the way out of the office. "I'll be back in about twenty-something," she said to Seth, who was looking at her with a slight grin on his square face. She wasn't sure she liked that smirk. She respected Seth—

he was like a rock behind that desk, her calm in a storm. But rocks didn't have knowing grins.

She purposefully did not look at Trevor. She didn't want to see what emotions might be playing across his face.

They walked down the flights of stairs in awkward silence. At the bottom, Melora led the way out the front door. "Let's go to the Lakewalk, it's just across the street."

Drew gave a short nod.

They went down the steps and crossed Canal Park Drive. On the other side, a statue of a young Native American girl greeted them. Melora recalled how her airedale, Spencer, barked at it the first time he saw the figure. He seemed to think it was a real girl and couldn't understand why she wasn't moving.

They passed through an opening between two of the hotels that lined the lakeshore, and were greeted by the wide blue expanse of Lake Superior.

Melora noticed the day was turning unseasonably warm. She turned away from the crowded ship canal and led Drew down the boardwalk that passed the hotels and eventually stretched to the east end of the city. They walked a few moments before Drew said, "It wasn't just the ship that brought me here, I hope you know. It was you."

Melora ducked her head and looked away from him. She was never good at this direct, heart-on-your-sleeve stuff. Plus she found it surprising. They had exchanged a few letters over the years. Last she had heard five months ago, Drew was still married. His wife, Lana, did not consider Melora a threat, so they were able to correspond openly. But Melora was always careful about what she wrote.

She gathered courage to look at him, and he continued, "Sorry for interrupting you at work, but I couldn't stay away. Things with Lana are over."

Melora stopped walking. She never thought she would hear those words—never had the slightest hope that Drew would be free again.

Drew stopped, too, and looked intently at Melora. "She got bored and took up with some other guy. I'm still teaching at the Maritime

Academy and they needed me to help with this cruise. I jumped at the chance."

"Drew, I'm so sorry." Melora hugged him, oblivious to the passersby.

When they parted, Drew slid his hands along her arms. He still touched one of them when he said, "So here I am. The ship's here until Friday, and then we sail back to Michigan. I've got most afternoons and evenings off. I was hoping we could spend some time together."

A little thrill went through Melora, but she tried not to show it. She wasn't sure if it was wise. Her natural calm took over and she started walking. Drew let go of her arm.

"Yes, I should be able to free up some time. Maybe not the afternoons because I work, but we'll see how things go. How much time do you have now?"

"Only a few more minutes, but then I get off at two," Drew said.

"Want to do a late lunch then? I know some good places to eat nearby."

"Yes, that should work."

They continued walking, passing a large rectangular stone structure that stood about fifty feet offshore. "What is that?" Drew asked. "It looks old—abandoned."

"Uncle Harvey's Mausoleum, also known as the cribs," Melora said. "It used to be a storage building for sand and gravel."

"And who is Uncle Harvey?" Drew asked.

Melora stopped and looked at a sign that explained about the building. "It says he was Harvey Whitney of the Whitney Brothers of Superior. Ships would unload their gravel in the building."

"How did they get it to shore then?"

"See that round thing sticking out of the water?" Melora pointed to a smaller structure between the building and the shore. "That's the base of a conveyor belt that brought the gravel to shore, where trucks would haul it away. That way, the ships didn't have to go into the harbor, which was pretty busy back then. The builders thought it would be more efficient. But when the city didn't build the promised breakwater, use of the building stopped. It was too tricky for the boats to dock when they were at the mercy of the wind and waves."

"And that's a sturdy structure," Drew said. "I suppose it wasn't worth the effort to take it down."

"Yes, so it stands as a testament to Harvey's failed idea. But it makes for interesting speculation. Everyone always wants to know what it is." Melora looked at her watch. "Well, I guess we should be getting back . . ."

Drew turned from the building and looked at Melora. "Yes, I suppose so. You know, you haven't changed a bit since the Rock," he said, using the nickname they had developed for Isle Royale in their infrequent letters.

He reached up and briefly touched her hair. "Your hair is shorter, but your eyes, they're the same: midnight blue."

Melora couldn't help ducking her head again, blushing. She started walking back toward the hotels and Drew followed. She took a quick look over at him, and he was smiling at her—warm, genuine and loving. She smiled back tentatively and tried to shake the feeling of failure that the mausoleum imparted. She hoped it wasn't a harbinger of the outcome of Drew's trip to see her.

Melora wanted to break the mood that had come over her. "It's so good to see you, Drew. Sorry I'm not more upbeat, but you took me by surprise. I'd forgotten you even knew where I worked, it's been a while since we wrote."

Melora looked down at her feet and then back at Drew. "But I'm glad you came. You know I've missed you." She didn't want to mention the times she went back to Isle Royale over the years just to feel closer to him. Or the times she camped in Michigan's Upper Peninsula where he used to live, hoping to catch a glimpse of him in the forest. Or the times his name escaped her lips just before she fell asleep.

She had come to realize that getting over him just wasn't possible, although she had brought her life to a point where she had a semblance of satisfaction. Not happiness, but not despair, either.

Drew smiled at her and his chocolate-colored eyes brightened. "I've missed you, too, Melora. We have a lot to talk about."

By now, they were crossing the street to Melora's office building. In front of the structure, they embraced again. "So I'll see you at two. But you don't need to come to my office . . . let's meet just inside these doors and then we'll decide where to eat."

"All right," Drew said. "Until then."

Melora could feel his eyes on her back as she walked up the outside stairs. She wondered how she was going to get any work done in the next few hours. And she had to call Peg back. How could she hold a coherent conversation with her boss now?

* * *

THE SCREEN DOOR SLAMMED behind Demetri as he skipped out of the house into the backyard. A high wooden fence with a gate surrounded the grass and kept the beach sand from overrunning it. A swing set stood in one corner and a small grove of cedars stood in the other. A clutter of toys lay in between.

Demetri headed for the cedars, ducking into a natural tunnel formed by the branches. He settled, cross-legged, in the middle of the grove. The scent of the crushed needles under him filled his senses. He hoped his mama wouldn't look for him for a long time. He needed to be alone to do his "thing." This was not something he could explain. It just was. And it certainly wasn't something he could tell his mama about. She already worried about him and all the other things too much.

He closed his eyes and it was if he could feel the earth turning ever so slowly beneath him. The faint scratching of animals scurrying through the bushes in his backyard mixed with the sound of lake waves lapping the beach. Gulls called overhead. A warm, quiet breeze coming through the branches told him it wouldn't rain, not until the night. The plants, they were all right with this. They were just waking up from the long winter. A soft and steady rain had fallen the night before yesterday, so going another day without would not hurt them. It was all right for the plants to wake up slowly.

Demetri breathed in and out unhurriedly. Something woke him this morning—something he'd never heard before. It had sounded like drumming along with a faint chanting. Now he tried to listen and see if it was still going on. No. Nothing like that. Just the dishes clattering from his mama cleaning up after their lunch. She was listening to the radio—classical music, like she played in the orchestra.

Eyes still closed, Demetri smiled. He loved going to her practices and performances—lying down on the floor with his coloring books as the vibrations seeped through him, or sitting in the wings during concert nights watching his mama's long brown hair sway as she played her viola. But more often than not he spent time in Room Number Seven, the backstage practice room for the violas. Even though the room was bare—it was made up of muddy-yellow cement block walls—it felt like a home away from home for Demetri. One wall had a row of mirrors with lights around them and a counter in front. He liked to sit there and make faces in the mirrors while the viola players practiced—keeping at it until he cracked someone up.

What song author was playing on the radio? Brahms, maybe. His mama called the song authors "composers." But that was too complicated. Demetri liked the idea of them as song authors, just like book authors.

Brahms was a little too sleepy for him. Demetri enjoyed the soaring of Ravel or the energy of Mozart better. Before her practice, his mama always explained who all the song authors were so he could pick out their sounds. He was getting good at recognizing them now even when she got in a rush and forgot to tell him. And he also heard her explain about the song authors to the viola students she sometimes taught in their home.

So the drumming was gone. He wondered what it meant and if he'd ever hear it again. He'd have to try to find it if it started.

How were the animals today? He kept his eyes closed and turned his head slowly back and forth. The animals around him were all okay. No shrills of hurt or pangs of hunger reached him. All was well and the circle was whole.

Demetri opened his eyes, pushing back a lock of his blond hair. He picked at the ground, started clearing away the cedar needles down to dirt.

At lunch his mama had talked about preschool. She wanted to send him there. He'd make friends, she said. He'd have lots of fun and snacks. He wasn't so sure about that, and started digging a line in the cool dirt with his finger.

How could he do his "thing" in preschool? The neighbor kids already thought he was weird. He didn't have any playmates. Demetri couldn't see how preschool would be any different. He'd much rather stay at home with his mama or go to her practices.

During their talk, he'd pouted. "Haven't I been good?" he asked. "I want to stay home with you!" Once he realized there was no changing her mind, he'd run out the back door. How could Mama not see that preschool would be bad?

He wished his daddy were here. But the lake had taken his daddy before he was born. He'd heard the story: it was a pretty day but the wind was blowing and the waves were high. Two teenage neighborhood sisters got caught in a strong current, and they were frightened. His daddy called the fire trucks and then went into the lake to save the sisters. He got one girl back to shore, but when he went to get the second, she was so scared she climbed on top of him and pushed him underwater. Then she kicked him accidentally and he got stunned. When the firemen came, they rescued the girl but it was too late for his dad.

The sisters and their family moved away, but his mama stayed on the beach because it reminded her of daddy. His daddy had come from Russia where people loved the woods and the animals. And he had grown up by a big lake. Mama had told him that. Would his daddy send him away to preschool? No, his daddy would rescue him like he did those girls. And Demetri wouldn't be so stupid as to kick him.

Demetri sighed. The groove he was working into the dirt was getting deeper. Soil stuck under his fingernail and was beginning to hurt. He quickly looked around and noticed a nearby cedar branch was turning brown. He'd better stop.

He closed his eyes and relaxed, breathing slowly. When he opened his eyes, the branch was green again.

* * *

Melora steeled herself for the interrogation she knew was coming once she opened the office door. She relaxed her features, resisting the urge to plaster a smile on her face. Seth would see through that in a minute.

"So *who* was that?" Seth boomed as she walked through the door.

"Just an old friend from my Isle Royale days." Melora fought the urge to walk as quickly as she could to her office. She could see Trevor looking at her from beyond Seth's desk. "He's visiting for a couple of days, so we're going to do lunch."

Seth gave a noncommittal grunt. Trevor's questioning gaze lingered on her but she continued to her desk.

She really did try to get some work done. She called Peg and had a pleasant conversation as usual. Peg had some good ideas for the plover project, which Melora intended to put into practice as soon as she could. But mostly, all she did was stare at her computer screen and remember. And once she was done remembering, she began to wonder. And after the wondering came the terror.

Shortly after she and Drew became involved on Isle Royale, Black Wolf, the alpha male of a nearby wolf pack, turned Drew into a werewolf. Not a bloodthirsty, ravenous werewolf like in the movies, more like a regular wolf, or a shape shifter.

The wolves were desperate to escape the island. Turning Drew into a werewolf was the only way they knew to get a human to help them. They targeted Drew because he was a boat pilot. The wolves wanted to get their pack off the island by boat and start new lives on the mainland. Once Drew was a werewolf, the alpha could communicate with him.

As if having her boyfriend turned into a werewolf weren't bad enough, the female alpha wolf, Mate, compounded the situation by mistakenly making Lana, a waitress who had a crush on Drew, into a werewolf, too.

Melora, Drew, and Lana stole a tour boat to get the wolves safety to the Michigan mainland, despite being caught in a waterspout. Eventually, Drew made the painful decision to stay as a wolf and help the pack. And so did Lana. Where did that leave Melora, a human among wolves? Out in the cold.

Melora had no desire to be a werewolf. In the end, it wasn't even a possibility. Although it broke her heart, she had returned to life as a college student and made her way the best she could without Drew.

She knew that Mate and Black Wolf died after about four years. This broke the supernatural connection, making it almost impossible for Dew and Lana to become werewolves again. The couple moved from the forests of the Upper Peninsula to Traverse City, lower in Michigan on the coast. Melora started getting letters from Drew after that—about six years ago, when he had found her through her parents who had still been alive and residing in Duluth then. They didn't exchange letters often—maybe once or twice a year. And now here he was.

They had been apart for so long. Was this finally their chance to be together? If it was, would it work? How could she trust him after he had left her for Lana and the wolves? And what about Trevor?

And if things did work out with Drew, how could she allow herself to be at the mercy of a man again after the disappointment that had been her marriage? That sort of exclusivity and dependence scared her more than anything.

Melora was glad Seth and Trevor could not see into her office and notice what a basket case she was, staring off into space. Usually, the three of them called out comments to each other and bantered back and forth. Today the office was quiet. When Seth and Trevor left for lunch, Melora relaxed and tried to collect herself, but her thoughts were still scattered once her co-workers returned.

She did have enough presence of mind to decide that eating lunch at her friends' café would be a bad idea. June and Steve knew all about Melora and Drew's history. In fact, they had helped them escape the island. There would be no hiding from their curious stares and inevitable questions. She wasn't ready for that. She decided they would eat in the basement café that served her favorite West African peanut soup.

Finally, it was two o'clock. Melora gave Seth a "Going to lunch," explanation on her way out the door.

Her heart caught as she saw Drew waiting for her—Drew of the broad shoulders, narrow hips, and muscular arms. She greeted him and directed him toward the basement. The low-ceilinged café took up most of the area except for the building's mailroom and the fish smoking operation.

Melora was delighted that her favorite alcove was open—a cozy space surrounded by vines, a bench and table for two. They'd have some semblance of privacy there. They got their food at the counter and Melora led the way to the alcove.

She sat down, looked at her soup and then at Drew across from her. Her stomach immediately tied itself into a knot. She sipped her water and let Drew start the talking.

"You know that once the alphas died, Lana and I could not be wolves again."

His comment reminded Melora how direct he could be sometimes. She nodded behind her water glass.

"We stayed for a time with the pack, making sure they would be all right. Besides those still with the pack, our wolf pups are scattered across the U.P. Some of them have their own pups now."

Although some of this had been shared in letters, the two had never had the opportunity to talk about things face-to-face. Melora had always wondered about Drew and Lana's wolf pups—just what kind of babies did werewolves have? She interrupted him. "So, your pups—they looked like wolves, and they *were* actual wolves, right?"

"They were wolves through and through, except that some had Lana's green eyes." Drew took a sip of his water.

"And that's because the pups . . . happened when you guys were in wolf form, right?"

Drew's reply was matter-of-fact. "Yes, that's right."

Melora couldn't help herself. "Do you miss them? I mean, do you feel about them the way you feel about your human babies?"

"It's different, yet similar." Drew paused. "I miss them, but I worry a lot less about them than I do about my kids. I feel like the wolves are more capable of surviving in some ways. They are in a good place. Although there are a few conflicts between packs, the population is healthy in the U.P. and there's no hunting season."

Drew took a bite of his sandwich and chewed slowly. "We felt like we had accomplished our goal. We saved our Isle Royale pack. After Mate and Black Wolf died, we could have become werewolves again with help of the alphas of the other packs, but we didn't want to. And then Lana got pregnant with our first human baby." Drew sighed. "We decided it was time to go live among people again."

The knot in Melora's stomach tightened.

"Before she was due, we moved to Traverse City. Lana wanted to have the baby in a hospital. We have two boys separated by two years, Jason and Tony." Drew's voice lowered, "They are six and four right now." He took another bite of his sandwich.

"It must be hard to be away from them," Melora said.

Drew finished chewing. "Oh, yes. And when I'm there, I only get to see them every other weekend. It's not enough."

Melora took a tentative sip of the nutty curry soup, hoping it would help the knot. Nope. "So what happened with Lana?"

"When we moved to the city things were all right at first," Drew gazed through the street-level window above them. "But later on, it was like she lost her purpose. She missed the hunt, she missed leading the pack. We started arguing about silly things, and then more serious things. Before long, she had an affair."

His gaze returned to Melora. "Our family was broken and there was no putting it back together. I had to let her go. I stayed as long as I did for the children. But there I was, alone. Missing you. And you were five hundred miles away." He paused and spoke more softly. "You never said goodbye, you know."

The statement lingered between them.

Melora recalled her flight from the pack and from Drew one cold October night when they were away hunting. She looked deeply into his eyes. "I regret that. I know it was the coward's way out, but it would have too painful otherwise."

Drew gave a little nod. "I knew you couldn't stay. . . I did worry about you, though. More than once I thought about leaving and trying to find you."

Melora felt herself tearing up. She had to change the topic or she would soon be crying into her soup. "Do you have any regrets?" she asked.

He responded as though anticipating the question. "I regret not thinking harder about changing you into a werewolf. You and I probably would have had a better chance once we were back in the human world. But I didn't think that far ahead. I didn't know it would be like this . . ." He gestured a helpless hand in the air.

Melora didn't know what to do with this admission. She lowered her gaze from Drew's stricken expression to the table. Looking at the table top didn't hurt as much.

Drew continued, his voice soft. "You may think this is funny, but the wolves taught me how to be a better human being."

Melora glanced back up at him.

"The relationship that Black Wolf and Mate had . . . it was so strong and honest. It made me realize what Lana and I had was nowhere near what it could be. It made me miss you all the more." Drew stopped and took a large breath. "So what I'd like to know is . . . do we have a chance? Do you think there's any way we could be together?"

Melora felt herself tearing up again. She blinked and wiped away the moisture from the outer edge of one eye. Although her heart was saying, *Yes! Yes!* her brain was telling her otherwise.

"I don't know, Drew. It's been a long time. I hate to sound cliché, but a lot has happened." She tried to take another sip of her soup and gave up. She put down her spoon. "You know about my divorce from my letters, right?"

Drew nodded.

"We were together for five years, but it turned out Charlie didn't want children." Melora sighed and shook her head. At thirty-two, she knew her time was running short. "You know, it would have all been so much more efficient if we had figured that out before we got married. I would have loved to have had children, but now I'm glad we didn't. I guess that's what I get for marrying someone seven years younger than me. And it didn't help that his personality totally changed from an outdoors guy to a computer geek.

"When I was working as an editor in St. Paul, and commuting back and forth, things came to a head. Charlie told me to choose my job or him. Well, of course, I chose him. Our problems went away for a few weeks, but eventually, they resurfaced. Something would happen—we'd have a disagreement or a difference of opinion—and then he'd withdraw and I'd get sad. Then he would withdraw more and I'd get even sadder. There was no way to meet in the middle. We just kept repeating the same stupid pattern no matter how hard we tried. Even counseling didn't help."

Melora left out the part that when she'd get sad, she'd escape into thoughts of Drew. Now wasn't the time to gush about that. She picked her spoon back up and pushed around the peanuts and chunks of sweet potato in her soup. "I took a big pay cut but don't regret coming back here full time. I missed the lake and the way of life around here. I'm starting to appreciate the community and get more involved in it. It's weird. I grew up here, but I never really felt part of it until I decided to stay here. All that time I wasted.

"I don't know what I would have done if I hadn't gotten a dog after the divorce. Spencer kept me sane and on a schedule of sorts during my off hours. Otherwise, I probably would have wasted away in bed or in front of the TV."

"What kind of dog is he?"

"An airedale," Melora said. "He's three years old. I got him from the pound. They figured he'd been running loose in the woods for a couple of months. Nobody could catch him."

"How'd they finally do it?" Drew asked.

"He was eating a dead deer."

Drew paused a moment before replying, "Well, it sounds like Spencer and I have some things in common."

Melora smiled but then got serious and put down her spoon as Drew reached across the table and took her hand. "It sounds like you've had a rough go of it, too." He paused again. "Melora, I'm just going to cut to the chase. Are you free now or are you involved with someone?"

"No, I'm not really involved with anyone." Her voice was soft. "Listen, your visit is kind of freaking me out." She took her hand out of Drew's. "So you're sure you're not going to turn into a werewolf again and run away into the forest?"

Drew's chuckle was low as he leaned back in his chair. "No, Melora. You don't have to worry about that."

"Have you heard anything about how the wolves on The Rock are doing?"

"Last I heard they had another population crash," Drew said. "Their numbers grew to about fifty, but now there are only about twenty. The moose are doing well, though, so that should help. I see reports in the newspaper, plus sometimes I get to talk to guys at the academy who worked out there. I really hope the wolves can survive, but still, I'm glad our pack got off the island."

"It's good to know we did what we could. At least our pack survived." A thought dawned on Melora. "You know who else is in town?" She didn't wait for Drew's response. "Georgina."

Drew nodded in recognition.

Melora continued. "She came to the plover site ceremony this morning. I'm not sure how long she's around, but it was good to see her."

Drew asked what a plover was and Melora described her project to him. With the discussion topic on work issues, her stomach relaxed and she was able to eat most of her soup. "I was planning on going home after work to eat supper and let my dog out, and then visit the site. I need to meet with our new plover monitors and go over a few things with them. They're college students, so they can't meet during the day. Want to come home with me after work and meet Spencer?"

"I can think of nothing I'd rather do." Drew's warm smile cracked open Melora's heart.

Chapter Three

DEMETRI HAD EATEN SUPPER and was playing with his plastic farm animals on the kitchen floor when he heard the drumming again. This time, the sound wasn't coming from outside. He ran into the living room and stood in front of the television. From her place on the couch, his mama looked at him with raised eyebrows.

The news story described how the drums were part of a ceremony to dedicate the beach just past the airport as a nesting place for some little shorebirds. The picture went from the drummers to a separate shot of a cute bird with an orange beak, orange legs and a black band of feathers around its neck. Demetri could not remember seeing any birds like that before.

"Mama, do you know those birds?"

His mama smiled at him. "No sweetheart, they're new to me."

"Are the drums still on the beach?"

"I don't think so." She cocked her head as if listening. "They just brought them in special for the ceremony."

"I want to go see the birds, Mama. Can we go?"

"Maybe tomorrow after preschool we can look for them." She turned her attention back to the news, which was already showing another story.

Demetri twisted around and looked at his mama. "Mama, I don't like preschool. I don't want to go!"

Her gaze was focused on him again. "Sweetheart," she said in that patient way of hers, "it's only for part of the day so you can get used to it a little bit at a time. When we come home, then we can play."

Anger at being separated from his mama welled from deep within him, and a fear so large he couldn't give voice to it. It was just wrong, wrong, wrong, and he would have none of it. "No, Mama, no. I won't go!"

Demetri raced back into the kitchen. As he grabbed his favorite farm horse off the floor and ran out the back door, the red flower on the kitchen windowsill withered.

He did not head for the grove of cedars. Instead, he ran to the gate that led to the beach. He opened it as quickly as he could and crossed through it. Demetri heard his mama calling for him, but he did not look back. He was going to find those little birds.

After a while, running through the sand on the beach tired his legs, and he slowed to a walk. He looked back and could not see his mama. A small wave of triumph surged through him. He'd never done anything like this before. He put the horse in his pants pocket. It was a mustang with a tan body and black mane, its legs frozen in a running position. It looked fast, just like him.

Demetri knew where the airport was. It was just past the recreation center beach. His house was the last one by the beach house, so he'd walked this stretch many times, just never alone. The weather was still good. He'd be all right for a while. And when he got tired, he'd just go back home.

He passed a family having a picnic. Their scruffy dog came out to sniff him. Big dogs sometimes scared Demetri, but this dog was small. His fur was white and tan. Demetri crouched. The dog put his front paws on his knees and licked Demetri on the face. He giggled.

"Wow, he must really like you," the woman picnicker said. "He never does that to anyone!"

The little dog looked at Demetri with bright eyes. He was panting. Demetri petted his head. "Good boy," he whispered to the dog.

"Are you all by yourself?" the woman asked.

"No. I live down there," he said, pointing. "I'm just walking."

"Well, you be sure to stay away from the water, okay?"

"Yes. I will." Demetri looked down the beach to ensure he still wasn't being followed and then continued on his way. The dog trailed him until its owners called it back.

He passed people lying in the sand or throwing Frisbees and footballs. The lake was still too cold for swimming. A breeze ruffled the water, causing a patch of sparkles. The diamond fish were swimming again.

Although the gentle wind kept him from getting too hot, Demetri was starting to get thirsty. He looked back toward his house again, a bit disappointed that his mama wasn't coming. He kept walking until he saw the big pines that lined the beach beyond the airport. They always looked like they had been there forever. Like nothing could change them.

The crowds had thinned. Demetri scanned the beach in front of him and saw what looked like a sign. He thought he'd seen a sign like that in the news story. He continued toward it. When he got close enough, he saw a drawing of a bird that looked just like the one on TV. There were words on the sign, but he didn't know how to read those yet.

A large log had washed up on the beach just beyond the sign. Demetri sat on it, surveying the area. He didn't see any drums or people. No little birds either, just the gulls wheeling overhead.

This was a good spot, a peaceful spot. Demetri took the horse out of his pocket and began to play with it on the log.

* * *

THIS TIME, MELORA WAS able to think more coherently when she returned to work. She was accomplishing what needed to be done, although her flow was interrupted several times with thoughts of Drew's question: *Do we have a chance?* She wished she had answered it with more enthusiasm. Quietly, she damned her practical and cautious nature.

How much of a chance did they have with all that they had been through? She couldn't just forget Drew's past choices. They had shaped the path of her life like nothing else had. And now here was another turning point.

Okay, so maybe she had cause to be cautious. She wished life weren't so complicated.

It was four o'clock, the time that early-to-rise and early-to-work Seth went home. As usual, he touched base with Trevor and Melora before he left. "Take it easy, kid," he said to her. "See you tomorrow. Good luck with the plover interns tonight . . . among other things."

Melora decided to ignore the implication behind his words. "You take care, too, Seth," was her breezy reply. Eventually, Trevor came into her office with a question about the next step in the public relations campaign for the plover project. He sat in the chair beside her desk as they discussed it. Once that was done, Melora started turning back to her computer when Trevor asked, "So, did you decide about my question yet?"

Trevor's question! Melora had been so busy thinking about Drew's question, it had totally eclipsed Trevor's. Trevor had only asked her to go out with him this morning, but already it felt like days ago.

"Give me a few days to think it over, okay?" Melora didn't like the overwhelmed and pleading note to her voice. She was overwhelmed—but in a good way. Two men wanting her—that was refreshing. "My friend is visiting now, which was not expected, by the way, so I'll be busy for a couple of days."

"All right," Trevor said, raising his hands in mock surrender. "I can handle that." He got up to leave. "Just don't forget, okay?"

"I won't."

"I can be patient. I know how to do patience. But you know me, I change my mind a lot."

"Well, I certainly hope you won't change your mind about something as important as this," Melora said.

Trevor's mischievous grin softened. "Okay, I won't. Not for a few days, at least. Hey, I'm going sailing tonight—first sail of the season. If you went out with me, *we* could be going sailing . . ." The phrase lingered in the air as he walked back to his office.

Damn, he knew Melora's weakness for sailing. She had wanted to learn ever since she returned to Duluth full time, and they had discussed it several times. Trevor had his own boat and he regularly participated in local yacht club races. It didn't help that his sailboat happened to be named *Pilgrim Soul,* after one of Melora's favorite poems by Yeats.

"That's just cruel," she protested.

"Methinks it's cruel to make me wait like this," Trevor taunted from his office.

Melora let out an exaggerated sigh. Trevor laughed.

The lines to the Yeats poem, "When You Are Old," appeared in her head unbidden: How many loved your moments of glad grace / And loved your beauty with love false or true / But one man loved the pilgrim soul in you / And loved the sorrows of your changing face . . .

She sighed again, this time for real and to herself. She finished what work she could, and then it was time to meet Drew. Melora walked down the stairs and found him waiting for her. On the drive home, he regaled her with tales of his recent voyage—most involving the mishaps of inexperienced sailors learning the ways of a ship.

The route to her house took them straight up one of the steepest roads in town. Melora stopped her Honda in front of a duplex nestled among others perched on Duluth's hillside. The house was a tired, dirty white with brown trim. She had chosen it because the rent was reasonable and the view couldn't be beat. Even the car's parking spot offered a commanding vista of the harbor and Lake Superior.

They crossed the small yard, and Melora showed Drew into the entryway. "I'm upstairs," she said. They walked up a narrow stairway and were greeted by the sound of furious scratching on the other side of the door. As Melora withdrew her key from the lock, a large blur of tan-and-black fur came charging through the doorway. The dog circled Melora as she tried to work her way into the kitchen from the landing and pet him at the same time. As Drew walked in behind her, the dog stopped his enthusiastic wriggling and stood on the tile, nose in the air, sniffing him.

Melora turned to face Drew. "This is Spencer. Spencer, this is Drew."

Spencer positioned himself directly between Drew and Melora as if he were protecting her. Drew reached forward to offer the dog his hand to smell. Spencer turned his nose, having none of it.

"Whoa, talk about the cold shoulder." Drew withdrew his hand.

"Spencer!" Melora petted the dog and looked into his round brown eyes. "He's usually friendlier."

"Well, I'm not your usual person, Melora. I don't blame him." Drew cautiously walked around Spencer's haunches and sat in a chair by the kitchen table. "He kind of looks like a Doberman with wool instead of fur."

"Doesn't he?" Melora said. "His nickname is the Dober-lamb."

"I like that." Drew grinned. "Very fitting."

Spencer positioned himself again between Melora and Drew and tentatively approached Drew, who stuck out his hand again. "C'mon boy, it's all right."

His words were soft, and Melora watched as Spencer sniffed Drew's hand. The dog sat and looked at Drew, cocking his head.

"He's probably never smelled a former werewolf before," Drew chuckled.

"Do you think it's made you smell different?" Melora knelt and petted Spencer along his back.

"It wouldn't be the first time a dog has reacted this way to me. Some dogs run for cover, others growl. At least he isn't doing that." Drew leaned back in the chair and regarded Spencer. "He knows something's up. Give him time and he'll get used to me."

"All right." Melora joined Drew at the kitchen table. "I'd give you a tour of the place, but maybe that's not a good idea right now."

"True." Drew looked around the small kitchen, which opened into a living room with large windows. "Nice place you got here from what I can tell."

"Yeah, I chose it for the view." Melora nodded toward the windows. "At night you can see the city lights, and in the morning, sunrises. I love watching the boats come and go under the lift bridge. You can even see my office building."

"Cool." Drew shifted in his chair. "I don't recall—how long have you lived here?"

"Since my divorce—about three years."

With the attention off him, Spencer relaxed and started panting from his recent exertions. He stood near the table, within arm's reach of Melora.

"Let's get up and walk around. I think it's safe now." Melora laughed as she rose from the table. Spencer followed right behind her into the living room.

Drew came and stood in front of the picture windows, gazing at the city and harbor below. "Quite the panorama. How do you ever get anything done?"

"It's hard sometimes." Melora turned and sat on a couch that faced the windows. "I hardly ever watch TV, either. The view is better."

Drew sat beside her. Spencer lay in front of her on the floor. They spent time catching up on what had happened to friends they had on Isle Royale, and then it was time to walk Spencer and make supper. During their walk, the sun shone on big puffy clouds gathering on the horizon. The breeze was fresh, carrying the scent of clean water from the lake up the hill.

As Drew helped her make the walnut and dried cranberry salad, Melora marveled at how easy it felt to be with him. And sexy. Their bodies brushed against each other in the quest to reach and cut and arrange—their movements in slow harmony. While the attraction with Trevor had been nervy and electric, the feeling with Drew was hot, thick and slow—like molten lava.

Melora was glad she hadn't shown Drew where her bedroom was yet. They didn't have much time until they needed to leave for the plover site. Cautious nature aside, she found herself wanting plenty of time for him to thoroughly explore her bedroom. She didn't want to waste this opportunity for them to be together.

Drew asked her where another knife was, and Melora blushed as she told him. Her mind was on the bedroom.

He picked up on it. "What? Is there something embarrassing in the knife drawer?"

Her response was strangled. "No. Everything's fine. Just fine."

The moment passed as quickly as it had come over her. Melora added some leftover chicken to the salad and the preparation was done. They ate and decided to leave Spencer at home when they went to the plover site. Melora would have preferred to bring him along, but she didn't want him to scare away any birds that might be scoping the site.

Melora had arranged to meet the three plover interns at the beach parking lot. The interns were already there when Melora and Drew arrived. Melora introduced Drew to Jacob, Cody and Natalie, students from the University of Minnesota, Duluth. As the group walked to the site, the interns described their majors to Drew. Most were studying biology.

When they arrived, Melora went over their duties. Most of their work would be done in the mornings and evenings because that's when piping plovers were most likely to be active. The monitors were responsible for watching for the birds, posting signs and roping off the section of the beach so people and dogs wouldn't scare any that landed there.

Public relations was a big part of the job, so at least one of them would have to explain to beach users why they couldn't pass the ropes. Melora had already developed a flier for the interns to hand out in the parking lot to people who were headed toward the plover site. She took copies of it from her purse and went over it with them.

The monitors were also responsible for coordinating volunteers who would watch the site when the monitors were in classes. Both the monitors and the volunteers would keep detailed records of when and where plovers were spotted, and what types of behaviors they were exhibiting.

If any plovers nested, the monitors would build a rectangular enclosure to keep people and predators away. The exclosure was made from wire attached to a wooden frame that the plovers could enter and exit, but the openings were too small for cats and skunks. Seth had assured Melora that the exclosures didn't bother the plovers, as long as they were placed over the nest when the plovers weren't sitting on it.

Lastly, Melora took three pairs of small binoculars out of her purse. "You'll need these." She handed them to the interns. "We've got some GPS units on order also, so that you can take coordinates if"—she caught herself—"*when* you spot them. I know it's a lot to digest, but if you think of any more questions by tomorrow, Trevor can answer them when he meets you in the morning."

Orientation over, the monitors departed. Melora and Drew decided to stay a while to watch for plovers. They sat on the back edge of the beach where the grass started growing. They had observed for maybe five minutes when a small boy emerged from behind the large log that lay at the edge of the plover site.

Melora did a double-take. She and Drew arose and walked toward the boy.

When they were a few feet away, Melora was the first to speak. "Well, hello there." She bent over—hands on her thighs, to get a better look at the boy and to make herself more his height.

"Hello," he said.

"My name's Melora. What's your name?"

"Demetri."

He had the prettiest blue eyes and blond hair. "Nice to meet you, Demetri." Melora pointed to Drew. "This is my friend Drew."

"Yes," Demetri said. "He's the different one. The wolf one."

Melora looked at Demetri with her eyebrows raised. Drew shrugged and nodded.

The boy continued, looking at Melora. "Are you the one who brought the drummers here?"

Melora was confused for a second, then realized he was referring to this morning's ceremony. "Why, yes, I did. Did you hear them?"

"They woke me up." The boy rubbed his eyes. "It worked though."

"What worked?"

"The drums. The birds heard it. They will come here." He clambered up on the log and sat on it, his legs dangling.

Again, Melora looked at Drew, who just shrugged. She wanted to ask the boy how he knew this, but with all the surprising statements he was uttering, she didn't even know where to begin. Instead, when she reached the log, she asked, "Is it all right if we sit with you?"

33

"Yeah, sure," Demetri moved over slightly to make room.

"Wow," she said. "You seem to know a lot of stuff. Can you tell me where your parents are?"

"My mama's back home . . . I think." The boy scratched his cheek and looked down the beach.

Drew joined them on the log. He sat on the opposite side of the boy from Melora.

"How about your dad?" Melora asked.

"I don't have a dad. The lake took him."

"Oh . . . I'm so sorry to hear that." Melora gave Drew a quick but significant look over the boy's head. She knew that neither of them would press the boy for more of an explanation about his dad. They already knew what the lake could do.

"So you're out here all alone?"

"No." Demetri motioned to the lake and the land. "The plants and animals are here. How could I be alone?"

"Well, you got me on that one!" Melora laughed.

Drew chimed in. "You said your mom's at home. Do you live nearby?"

"My house is down the beach." Demetri pointed the way. "Last one before the beach house."

"Oh!" Melora looked over the boy's head at Drew in relief. "Would you like us to walk you back?"

Demetri looked from Melora to Drew and back. "Sure. Mama's probably getting worried."

"I'll bet she is," Drew said. "We're done here, right, Melora?"

"Yes. Let's get our nature boy home."

They walked down the beach with the boy still between them. As if it were the most natural thing in the world, Demetri reached for Melora's hand. She clasped his in hers, smiling over at Drew.

In the distance, they heard sirens. Melora wondered if they were for the boy. As they neared the trail to the parking lot, Melora asked Drew, "Should we take the car?"

He shook his head and Melora nodded hers in agreement. It wasn't much farther to the boy's home. Although Melora felt urgency to return Demetri to his mother, she suspected it would be less threatening for him just to walk home. Plus, they were less likely to be mistaken as kidnappers.

Along the way, Demetri looked up at Melora. "Did you ever go to preschool?" he asked.

"Ah . . . no. I don't think they had it when I was little." She paused. "Do you go to one?"

"No, but my mama wants me to. I don't want to go."

"I see," Melora said. "I hear you learn lots of good stuff there. Important stuff."

Demetri shook his head.

"Maybe it wouldn't be so bad?" Melora rubbed the back of his hand with her thumb.

Apparently, this was the end of that topic of conversation, because Demetri just kept walking. After a few moments, he asked if they had any water.

"No water," said Drew. "But if you're tired, I could give you a piggyback ride the rest of the way."

Demetri regarded Drew. "Sure," he finally said.

Drew knelt down, and the boy clambered upon his back. Drew cinched Demetri's legs around his waist. "Ready?"

"Yep." Demetri giggled as Drew took off at a trot and Melora followed. Beach-goers smiled as they passed. Soon they reached a Tudor-style white house with tan timber frameworks on the outside. The backyard wooden privacy fence was high and had a gate in it.

"This is it," Demetri said simply. Drew helped him off his back and Demetri opened the gate.

The backyard was empty except for a swing set and a scattering of toys. "C'mon." Demetri motioned them in as he walked toward the house.

Chapter Four

DEMETRI LED THE BIRD LADY and the wolf man into his house through the back door. Nobody was in the kitchen, but as they approached the living room, he could hear a commotion: lots of voices, the squawk of radios, car doors slamming.

He stopped at the entryway. People he didn't know were milling about. His mama sat on the careworn couch, clutching a tissue, her face hidden behind the curtain of her brown hair. Through the front windows, he could see several black-and-white police cars parked in the driveway.

Demetri looked back at Melora and Drew, who seemed as shocked as he was.

He turned back toward the room and said, "Hello, Mama." When nobody reacted, he tried again, louder. "Hello, Mama!"

His mama dropped the tissue. Her face quickly changed from sad to happy, and she shot off the couch. "Demetri!"

She knelt down and hugged him way tighter than usual. Then his mama broke the hug and looked him up and down. "Where did you go? I was so worried!"

Before Demetri could answer her, Mama noticed Drew and Melora. "Did you find him? Did you bring my Demetri back to me?"

Drew and Melora could only nod. Mama hugged him again. "Thank you, thank you!"

By now, the rest of the room had silenced and the searchers were watching the scene play out.

"I took a walk on the beach, Mama. I was okay."

"Demetri, don't you ever do that again! That is *not* a good thing to do, no matter how upset you are."

She rose and shook Melora's and Drew's hands. "I'm Samantha. Thank you so much! Where did you find him?"

"Just past the airport," Melora said. "He was at the site we're preserving for shorebird nesting."

A light went on behind his mama's eyes. "Of course. Why didn't I think to look there?"

They were interrupted by a policeman. "Ma'am, is this your son?"

"Yes, yes it is." Her voice was shaky.

Demetri wanted to take a step back away from the man, but his mama held onto his shoulders.

The officer knelt down and looked at Demetri. "You okay, son?"

Demetri nodded. "Just thirsty."

Mama went to get him a glass of water. Demetri was glad when the policeman decided to talk to Melora and Drew instead. It gave him time to look around the room again at all the people, who were now readying to leave. He couldn't believe they were all here because of him.

His mama brought the water and he gulped it down, enjoying its coolness. Demetri wondered how long Drew and Melora would stay. He liked them. Maybe they could be his friends. His mama was talking to them.

After a few moments she came over to him. "Demetri, is it okay if Melora and Drew come visit you? They're thinking of stopping by tomorrow evening."

A flowery fragrance wafted into the room. Demetri smiled wide. "Yes, Mama."

She went back and talked to them again. They nodded and came over to him.

"See you tomorrow, Demetri." Melora ruffled his hair. "Stick around home, you hear? We'll talk more about this preschool stuff."

"Give me five." Drew held out his palm. Demetri slapped it with his.

* * *

O<small>N THE DRIVE HOME,</small> Melora stopped to buy some wine for the evening. When they got to her house, Spencer greeted them enthusiastically, any trace of his former coolness toward Drew was gone.

Drew and Melora sat on the couch, drinking wine and watching the evening shadows lengthen over the harbor. Lightning played across the thickening clouds in the distance over Wisconsin, creating quiet snakes of brilliance.

"How do you think Demetri knew I was a wolf man?" Drew swirled his wine and took a sniff.

"I have no idea," Melora said. "He knew stuff no four-year-old should, if you ask me. Kinda spooky. And then there was that thing he said about the plovers, that they would come to nest."

"I feel sorry for his mom," Drew said. "That kid's going to give her a run for her money. I suspect it won't get any easier for her."

"Still, he's a neat kid. I wouldn't mind having a child like that, even if he made me prematurely gray." Melora took a sip of her wine.

Her hand was next to Drew's on the couch and he took it in his own. "Want to get started on that? The children part I mean, not the gray part . . . I could help."

"Drew!" Melora broke his hold and playfully punched him in the thigh. She knew what was about to happen between them was as inevitable as the approaching storm. It couldn't *not* happen. That would be an insult to the cosmos. But she couldn't let him get away with such flippancy.

"Sorry," he said. "My seduction skills are a little primitive."

Drew's face turned serious as he put down his wine on the side table. This time, he took Melora's hand in both of his, rubbing it as he looked into her eyes. With his voice soft and strained, he began. "Melora, even though we saved the wolves, even though I was finally part of something—the pack—staying with them wasn't worth it without you. I realized that much too late."

Tears sprang into Melora's eyes and she looked down.

"I didn't choose Lana over you. She just came along with the wolves . . . there's been so much wasted time, so many excuses." Drew paused. "That stops now. I apologize for hurting you. I want to be with you, whatever it takes, however long it takes. I won't waste any more time without you."

Melora looked back up at him, her eyes brimming. "I've missed you so much," she said. A tear escaped and slid down her cheek. Drew reached up and wiped it with his thumb, his hand cupping her face. Melora put her wine glass on the coffee table. She leaned forward and their lips met.

Their kiss felt like coming home on Christmas morning. Like hot chocolate on a snowy evening. Like tulips in spring. Like jumping into a pile of fall leaves. It began soft and slow, becoming harder and more urgent.

Drew's hands moved from her face down her body, hugging her to him. Melora responded in kind. He felt so good, so fit and solid—all man.

After a while, they broke to breathe. Spencer whined from his post next to the couch.

"It's okay, Spencer," Melora breathed. "Lay down."

"Good idea." Drew leaned over her. Melora laughed and scooched her legs underneath him. They lay on the couch, Melora on her back, Drew on his side, his back against the back of the couch.

"Sorry, Spencer's not used to people coming here and accosting me," Melora said.

"Oh no, not accost." Drew stroked her cheek again. "Just love."

And they kissed again. Drew's hand moved from her face to her neck, to the tops of her breasts. "Oh, my god, you are soft," he said.

Melora arched her back in pleasure and then rolled onto her side, facing him, so her free hand could roam his body. It rested on his butt, kneading the muscles there, roamed up his back, and then was drawn back to his butt. She lifted her leg and laid it atop his, bringing him closer to her.

Dimly, she noticed the sound of thunder. The room darkened as the storm drew near.

Drew put his hand under the back of her shirt and slowly unfastened the clasp of her bra, still kissing her. Then he brought his hand around to her front, caressing her breasts. He broke contact with her mouth long enough to groan.

Behind her, Melora could feel Spencer sit up. She knew he must be looking at them, worried.

"We'd better go to my bedroom for some privacy," she breathed. "Spencer's just not used to this. He might think you're hurting me."

"All right." Drew removed his arm from her so Melora could rise. She did, in time to see a sheet of rain approach outside. "Rain's coming," she whispered, and bent down to pet Spencer.

Drew stood by her side and took her hand. He started pulling her toward the living room closet door. "This way?"

Melora giggled, pulling him in a slightly different direction. "No, this way."

When they reached the doorway to her bedroom, Melora needed to feel Drew again. She leaned against the wall. The sound of rain hitting the front windows echoed through the house. Drew leaned up against her and began kissing her. Melora wrapped a leg around the back of his thighs and brought him nearer. That worked for a time, but she needed more. She put her arms around Drew's shoulders and hoisted herself up, both legs encircling his hips. Drew clasped her hips and pressed her against the wall. Melora closed her eyes and let the delicious sensations take her.

After a while, Drew said, "These jeans are in the way." He eased Melora down to the floor. She opened her eyes to see Spencer sitting a few feet away, watching them again.

"We still have an audience," she whispered.

Drew turned and saw the dog. He knelt down. "It's okay, Spencer. I won't hurt your lady."

Spencer came close and let Drew pet his head. Lightning flashed. "Is he afraid of thunder?"

"No," Melora said. "He does all right with that. He'll be okay out here."

They went into her bedroom and closed the door.

Standing by the bed, Drew worked on Melora's belt buckle. She started on his. He finished first. "You win," she said.

Drew started kissing her again, pulling down her zipper. She had to break the kiss briefly to finish his buckle and zipper. Their kissing resumed, interrupted by laughter as they tried to get each other's pants off at the same time. With one leg now free, Melora resorted to using it to push Drew's pants down the rest of the way until they pooled around his ankles. He stepped out of them, still kissing her. Long deep kisses. Her knees were turning to gelatin in a way only he could evoke.

Melora backed away and pulled her top over her head with Drew's help. She shrugged out of the loose bra and lay down on the bed. Drew took off his shirt and lay beside her. Their hands roamed each other, seeking. Melora felt like she was trying to memorize his form through touch. It had been so long since they had been together like this. Who knew when it would come again?

Tentatively, Melora touched Drew through his underwear, growing bolder with his sounds of pleasure. Drew started massaging her and soon their underwear was off.

Melora gave a little cry of protest as Drew left the bed. He said. "Just a second."

She watched as he took his wallet out of his pants pocket and produced a condom package. "Carry one around for emergencies, do you?"

"Oh no, only special occasions." Drew opened the package. "And this is definitely a special occasion. I was just joking about the children part. You don't want to start that right now, do you?"

"Well, my clock is ticking, but no, not just yet."

Drew stood and put the condom on. "Lay back."

Melora complied and Drew lay between her legs. As he entered her, a bright flash of lightning came through the bedroom window, followed quickly by thunder. In the back of her mind, Melora noted the storm was right on top of them. But it was Drew's movements above her that made her lose all powers of speech and thought.

* * *

Thursday, April 13

JUNE POURED MELORA a cup of coffee, but her gaze focused on Drew. They were in the Duluth Portage Café in Melora's office building, having lunch. June and Steve had been Melora's dear friends ever since she met them on Isle Royale. She was thankful their friendship had lasted through the years and that she ended up working in the same building as their café.

That morning, Melora had turned off her alarm and fallen back asleep. Once she woke an hour later, a mad dash ensued to get her to work and Drew to his boat. Melora would have rather lazed around, enjoying the delicious afterglow and replays of events in her mind. She supposed there would be plenty of time for that once Drew left for Michigan tomorrow.

Melora only had time for the briefest phone conversation with June to warn her about Drew's presence—and now, here they were, feeling the full brunt of best-friend scrutiny.

"So how long are you here for? . . . How are your kids? . . . how's Lana?" Drew answered each of June's questions in turn, giving a condensed version of his situation.

"And are you guys having fun so far?" June turned to Melora.

Melora blushed. "I guess you could say that. Actually, we met the neatest little kid yesterday at the plover site—blond hair, blue eyes, *adorable*. He lives on the point. We're going back to visit him this evening."

Melora told June how they met Demetri. "We're going to help his mom figure out how to convince him preschool isn't evil. Got any ideas?"

June looked up at the ceiling, her long black hair swaying. She thought for a moment. "Ah ha!" Her arm came up, finger pointed up. "Have you tried bribery? That always worked on me."

Melora laughed. "Bribery. Not so bad." She turned to Drew. "What do you think we could bribe him with?"

"His mom already said he wasn't buying the snack angle," Drew said.

"True." Melora rubbed the sides of her head with her hands. She stopped quickly. "How about a pet? He seems to like animals—"

Drew sat back and regarded her. "You mean promise him a pet if he goes to preschool? That just might work."

"So we just need to find out what kind of pet he wants," Melora said.

"You'd better talk to his mom first," June said. "She might not want the responsibility."

"True," Melora said. "But it's a decent idea. If it doesn't work, we can try something else."

Even though she owned the place, June took their orders and went to tell the cook. Then Steve came out. He shook hands with Drew.

"June told me you'd be coming. Good to see you. It's been a while!"

"Yes, it has," Drew said. "It feels good to be here, though. I'm glad I got the chance."

"So you ship out tomorrow then, eh?" Steve asked.

Drew glanced at Melora. "Yes. It's too soon, but I need to finish training the crew. That's a million-dollar ship, and I'd hate to see where it might end up without me."

Steve laughed. "Well, I'd better get back in the kitchen. Nice to see you again." He gave Drew a little salute and left their table.

After the waiter came and gave them some water, Melora said, "I wish I could take the rest of the day off and spend more time with you, but I just started this job and hardly have any vacation days, plus there's so much to do with my projects."

Drew put his arm on the table, taking her hand in his. "It's no problem, Melora. My visit was unannounced. I don't expect you to miss work for me."

"If I had known, I would have. If there's a next time . . . I will."

Drew looked deep into her eyes. "There *will* be a next time Melora, I promise. I'll figure out a way to make it happen."

"I would like that. Very much."

Chapter Five

AFTER LUNCH, DEMETRI CLAMBERED into the cedar grove. He sat cross-legged and closed his eyes. The grass, winter brown but with spikes of green beginning to show, whispered. The plants were doing well from last night's rain. But he sensed it would be a while before rain came again.

A flock of cedar waxwings flew above his house and carried his vision with them. He was able to stay with the birds as they flew over house roofs lining the beach on Park Point to the busy streets and tall buildings of downtown Duluth—farther than ever before. Once they were downtown, they flew past his dentist's office—a brick high rise with a long fire escape down the outside—and then past the low, wide grocery store. After that, the birds continued, but he could no longer follow. He could see them in the distance, but it was as if he had run a long way and could not go any farther.

He hovered, scanning the downtown area. The types of animals and plants here were different than those near his home. There were more bugs and rats, pigeons and sparrows—city creatures. He had seen them when his mama took him downtown, but it was different seeing them on his own—somehow new, and a little scary.

His attention was drawn to one of the tall buildings. He could feel an animal suffering there. He focused his vision and saw a small sparrow lying in a scrap of grass on the ground below a window pane. The smudgy patch on the upper part of its white chest heaved as the bird tried to catch its breath. Its eyes were glazed and its beak was part way open.

Demetri had heard the kids in his neighborhood call it a trash bird. He didn't like the idea of some animals not being worth anything. All he knew was that this bird was alone and suffering. Although life and death were one to him, suffering deserved his attention.

Demetri noticed a black-and-white cat not far away under a bush that grew from a crack next to the building. The cat could end the bird's suffering in a moment, unless it decided to play with it. He knew how cruel cats could be after watching the ones in his neighborhood. And this cat looked well-fed and cared for—its fur had a healthy shine. He knew the cat didn't really need to eat the bird to survive.

Demetri focused on the bird again. Life was still strong in it. The bird just needed time to get its wits back from hitting the window. The cat's tail twitched. Time was not with the bird. Eyes still closed, Demetri rubbed his hands together until they tingled with warmth. Gradually, his hands parted, shaping an imaginary ball between them that grew larger as he gently juggled it.

When the ball was as wide as his body, Demetri pushed it inside his chest and drew it up and out of the top of his head, arms spread wide, head thrown back. He could feel the energy spreading through the cedars and down their trunks. The energy followed their roots and pooled in the soil. Demetri opened his eyes and pointed in the direction he wanted the energy to go, which was toward the little bird downtown. He could feel a dull heat underneath his legs as the energy shot off in that direction.

Demetri closed his eyes again and brought his hands back to rest in his lap. He looked down upon the bird in time to see the grass surrounding it transform into a circle of bright green. Several small sparks left the tips of the grass blades nearest the bird and entered its chest. Immediately, the heaving of its chest relaxed and the bird's beak closed. With clear eyes, the bird jumped to its feet and flew onto the window ledge, just as the cat pounced.

* * *

"JACOB'S ON THE LINE!" Seth called out to Melora. She picked up the phone.

"Hey, Jacob, how did this morning's monitoring go?" She could hear the chatter of a busy college hallway in the background.

"Sorry, this was as soon as I could call." Jacob sounded out of breath. "We saw a plover on the site!"

Excitement scrambled through Melora's chest. "Awesome! Did you get an ID?"

"It was a male. From the leg bands, it looks like a bird from the Apostles."

"All right. Are you able to go back out this evening?"

"No, I've got a test tomorrow, but Cody and Natalie will be there."

"Okay. I'll try and go out, too, and get some pictures in case it comes back." She hoped the bird would stay.

"If I get enough studying done I'll be back there in the morning."

Jacob's breathing seemed to return to normal, but Melora felt like hers was revving up. "All right. Good luck on that test. Thanks for the news." She said goodbye and hung up.

Trevor called out from his office, "Did Jacob find a bird?"

Melora rose and walked quickly over to him. "Yeah, a male, most likely from the Apostles. I'm going to the site this evening. Want to come?"

"Heck, yeah!" Trevor's smile was wide. "I'm not going to let you have all the fun seeing a plover first. Hey, I've had some thoughts about that question."

For a moment, Melora thought Trevor was referring to the dating question. She furrowed her brow, and her sense of excitement dimmed.

Trevor noticed her consternation. "No, not that question, the elevator-phrase question."

"Ohhhh." Melora couldn't help but sneak a quick look at Seth to see if he was sensing any undercurrents. His quest to stick mailing labels on a stack of envelopes continued without interruption.

"What did you come up with?" Melora asked.

"Well, plovers are important because 'A' they are cute, and 'B' they help control beetles and flies, which is good for people who use the beach." He beamed at her. "Isn't that good?"

"B is getting there. It relates the problem to people and what they like to do. But cute? Come on."

"Hey, it worked for pandas . . . I think," Trevor protested, his voice trailing.

"What do you think about the argument that when we protect plovers and their habitat, we protect other beach birds as well, like terns, nighthawks and owls?"

Trevor paused. "Weeeell, like that guy we saw on the beach, if people don't care about plovers, they won't care about those other birds, either."

Melora had to admit he had a point. "Damnable logic. So true. Let's think about that B option some more. Let it simmer for a while."

"Okay." Trevor turned his attention to his computer.

"Trevor."

He looked back up at Melora.

She sat in the chair near Trevor's desk. "A little boy was at the plover site last evening."

"What was he doing there?" Trevor cocked an eyebrow.

"Running away from home." A trace of laughter crept into her voice.

Trevor laughed. "Did you find out where he lived?"

"Yeah, he lives on the point, the last house before the beach house on the lake side. My friend, Drew, and I took him home. Of course, his mom was frantic and the cops were looking for him. But he seems to know a lot about local plants and animals. I'd love to ask him our question about plovers."

"Neat idea," Trevor said. "Kids say the darnedest things sometimes. Out of the mouths of babes—"

Melora interrupted his platitudes. "His name's Demetri. Drew and I are going to his house before we visit the site tonight, but maybe we can bring him out there to meet you."

Trevor's eyes narrowed. "I'd like that. The monitors are going to be there at seven. I could do their briefing and maybe we could meet afterwards."

"Sounds good," Melora said. "It's just going to be Cody and Natalie this evening. See you at the site."

* * *

A STIFF APRIL WIND off the lake whipped Melora's hair as she and Drew got out of her car in front of Demetri's house. Samantha met them at the door.

"Hello, we've been waiting for you." Samantha was wearing a peasant blouse, a long cotton skirt and beach sandals. Her brown hair tangled around her shoulders.

Demetri peeked out from behind her skirt. "Hello," he said, smiling up at them as his mother smoothed his hair with her hand.

They walked into the living room, which held a smattering of plastic cowboy and Indian figurines on the floor.

Drew knelt to inspect them. "Hey, Demetri, these are cool!"

Demetri began showing him which ones were his favorites. "The cowboys are fun, but I usually pretend I'm an Indian," the boy said.

"Oh, why's that?" Drew asked.

Demetri studied Drew for a moment and took up an Indian figurine in his hand. "They know more about animals than the cowboys do," he said softly.

Samantha interrupted, "Would you like any tea or coffee?"

Melora looked at Drew. "Tea would be nice." Drew nodded.

Melora followed Samantha into the kitchen and sat at the table. As Samantha took teacups from the cupboard, she asked, "Say, have you had any luck changing Demetri's mind about preschool?"

"No." She sounded dejected. "I haven't wanted to bring it up. I'm afraid he'll run away again."

Samantha moved over to the stove where a teapot stood on a burner. She took it to the sink and started filling it, looking at Melora and talking over the sound of the water. "I think it would be so good for him—to be around other kids, I mean. Even though there's lots of people on the beach, we're so isolated here. He needs to be around children his own age. For some reason, the neighborhood kids don't play with him. And I need time to do errands and things."

Melora didn't know how the preschool system worked, so she asked, "Will starting in the spring be sort of disruptive? I mean . . . haven't the other kids been there since the fall?"

A frown had crossed Samantha's forehead, but then it eased. "Oh, no. It's not like a regular school. It's more like a daycare where they prepare the children for kindergarten."

"I see." Then Melora leaned forward, elbows on the table. "Do you think making the experience a positive one would help make Demetri want to go?"

"What do you mean?"

"Well, my friends and I were talking"—Melora chuckled—"what do you think about bribery? Do bribes work on him?"

Samantha put the teapot on the stove and turned on the gas burner. "I've never really had a problem like this before—something that he just does not want to do. But I guess for less serious things bribes work—better than threats. Anyway, I'm not a threat sort of person." She sat at the table with Melora.

"I hope we're not overstepping our bounds, but Drew and I were wondering if offering him a pet might work," Melora said.

Samantha sat back a little in her chair. The edges of her blue eyes crinkled as she began to smile. "That might work. He does like animals. I've been thinking that maybe a pet might be good for him."

"Maybe we can try out the idea on him. What kind of pet do you think he would like?"

"Perhaps a cat," Samantha said. "Cats are easier to take care of than a dog. But I'd be okay with a dog, too, if that's what he wanted. Maybe a small one . . ."

"All right then." Melora slapped the table lightly with her palm. "We'll try it and see. Who do you think should bring it up?"

"Maybe one of you. It might seem cooler that way." Samantha rose to attend to the teapot, which had started to whistle.

Once the tea was ready, they went back into the living room where Demetri and Drew were sprawled on the floor, in the middle of an imaginary gun fight with the cowboy figures.

"Sorry to interrupt boys, but tea is ready." Samantha set the tea tray on the coffee table.

Demetri quickly got up and came over. "Do I get some, Mama?"

"Yes, I made the raspberry kind you like."

"Goody." Demetri took his cup and started adding sugar from the bowl on the tray.

"Demetri," Samantha cautioned, "you need to let our guests serve themselves first. It's not polite otherwise."

"Sorry, Mama." Demetri took a step back as Melora and Drew reached for their cups.

"My, what the gentleman you are," Melora observed. "I'm impressed."

The four of them drank their tea for a while, talking about the weather and speculating how the spring might be—standard conversational fare for Duluth. Samantha invited Melora and Drew to her next concert in a week, but Drew had to decline, since he would be gone then.

"Maybe Demetri could be my date," Melora teased, "if it's not past his bedtime."

"Cool!" Demetri looked at his mother hopefully. "Can I go with Melora?"

Samantha looked at Drew. "Only if Drew wouldn't be too jealous."

"Dude, you have my blessing." Drew ruffled Demetri's hair. "I'd rather have you go with her than some schmuck. You can protect her for me."

Demetri smiled.

"Hey, Demetri." Melora put down her teacup. "I was talking to your mom about preschool."

Demetri's smile vanished. He took a sip of his tea, avoiding her eyes.

"What do you think about this—if you go to preschool, you'll get to have a pet?"

Demetri looked at Melora but she couldn't tell what he was thinking. He asked, "Like a dog or cat?"

"Yes," she said. "We were thinking of a cat, but maybe a dog, if you'd like that better."

Demetri gave a little shake of his head. "Cats are mean," he said.

"All right, a dog then," Samantha said.

Demetri stood very still, then shook his head again. "Pets are nice, but they don't like it in houses. They want to be outside. I don't think a pet is a good idea."

Melora sat back, disappointed. She looked from Drew to Samantha. She sensed both knew better than to argue with Demetri where animals were concerned.

Drew set down his teacup and picked up two Indian figures. He placed them on the table, facing each other. "What do you think about this, Demetri?"

Demetri watched the figures in Drew's hands.

"How about instead of worrying about yourself and how everyone will treat you, what if when you go to preschool, you pick out someone who you would like to help and have as your friend?"

Drew brought the two figures together until their hands were touching. "Maybe there's somebody in that preschool who needs you as their friend. They're just waiting for you."

Demetri looked up at Drew. "Somebody's waiting there for me?"

"I think so. Maybe more than one person." Drew gathered two other figures and brought them together with the original ones. "Everyone else in preschool misses their mom, too, you know. That's why all the kids need to be friends with each other and help each other until they see their moms again at the end of the day."

"What if I don't choose the right person?" Demetri looked at all the figures on the table.

Melora understood his fear. "You might not, at first. But you just keep trying with a different kid until you find the one who needs a friend."

"Oh." Demetri took a sip of his tea. "What if I don't find anyone who wants to be friends?"

Drew took over again. "You know what? I think there is someone there for you. You just need to try, and I'm *sure* it will work out."

"All right," Demetri said.

Samantha gave a little smile.

"But if I don't find my friend, I'm not staying."

Chapter Six

MELORA, DREW, SAMANTHA, and Demitri walked down the beach, dressed in fleece and windbreakers against the bite of the east wind off the lake. It would be weeks before Lake Superior warmed up to its summer temperature. Melora could feel every foot of frigid water the air had passed over during in its three-hundred-and-fifty-mile journey. When they arrived at the plover site, Trevor was waiting.

Melora introduced everybody. When she got to Drew and Trevor, there was a long pause before Trevor shook Drew's hand. Drew seemed not to notice.

"Good to meet you," Trevor said.

However, when she introduced Samantha to Trevor, Melora noted a small spark of interest in Trevor's blue eyes. She swallowed the hint of jealousy that rose in her. She was here with Drew, after all. She shouldn't be greedy where Trevor was concerned.

The group slowly continued down the beach, scanning for plovers. Trevor explained the goals of the plover project to Samantha. Demetri skittered closer to the shoreline, throwing sticks into the water and running from the waves that threatened to wet his shoes.

After a moment, Melora looked at Drew and nodded toward Demetri. The two went to join him on the shore. They ended up having a competition to see who could throw a stick the farthest into the water. Of course, Demetri won every time.

Melora stopped her stick throwing for a moment and kneeled by Demetri. "What do you think of plovers, Demetri? Do you think they're important?"

Demetri twirled his stick in his hands. He looked at Melora and asked in a matter-of-fact tone, "Plovers live on the beach, right?" When Melora told him he was right, he continued. "It's the only place they live, right? They don't live anywhere else?"

"True. They don't live in the forests, only on the beach."

"And they used to live on this beach, but they don't now?"

"Yes," Melora said.

"Okay. I got 'nother question then."

Melora looked at him, wondering what he would say next. "Go ahead."

In almost a whisper, Demetri asked, "Do you believe in ghosts?"

Melora gave a little laugh. "Ghosts? What do they have to do with plovers?"

Demetri stopped playing with his stick. He used it to point to the expanse of beach behind them. "Plovers are like the ghosts of the beach."

Melora felt her mirth change to a shiver.

Drew took one look at her and then joined the conversation. "How's that, Demetri?"

Demetri continued in a matter-of-fact voice. "The plovers used to live here, but now they don't. They wanted to come back, but they couldn't because the beach was dying. Their ghosts are still here. They're waiting and watching for when the beach gets better. And now it *is* getting better, so the ghost plovers will tell the real plovers it's okay to come back."

Demetri turned his attention back to the water. "And what makes things good for the plovers, makes things good for us, too."

Drew stared over Demetri's head into Melora's eyes. His eyebrows were raised.

Demetri wasn't done yet, though. As Trevor and Samantha walked over and joined them, he said, "And the drums helped tell the ghost plovers it was okay. They heard them, so they're telling the real plovers."

"Wow, you've got a good imagination, kid," Trevor said.

Demetri looked over at him and stamped his foot in the sand. "I'm not 'magining!"

"Whoa!" Trevor raised his hands in mock surrender.

Samantha went to Demetri and steered him away from the adults, her hands on his shoulders. Soon mother and son were digging in the sand with sticks.

"I don't know if we could use that theory as an elevator message." Melora looked out over the lake. "But I like it."

"You could use it," Drew interjected. "He was basically saying that what's good for plovers is good for people. Clean, quiet beaches help everyone."

"I suppose," Trevor said. "But I don't think the ghost thing would go over well."

"You don't have to mention them," Drew said.

The tension building between the two snapped Melora out of the weirdness she'd been feeling over Demetri's observations. To deflect an argument, she addressed Trevor. "Didn't I say the kid had some neat ideas?"

"That you did," he conceded.

Melora looked at her watch. "Shoot, I better get home. Spencer needs letting out."

The group walked back together. When they got to the parking lot, Trevor offered them a ride to Samantha's house. They all took him up on it, crowding into his Jeep Liberty. Once at Samantha's, Drew said his good-byes to Demetri, Samantha, and Trevor. Then he and Melora headed back to Melora's house. As they were leaving, Melora heard Samantha invite Trevor inside.

Conflicting feelings rattled around inside her as she drove. On the one hand, she was thinking, *Hey, what about my decision to date you or not?* On the other hand, she was fairly certain she was not going to be able to date anyone else after Drew's visit. They had such a connection, she didn't know how she could see anyone else. She should not begrudge Trevor. But still . . . what if Drew left and never returned?

She shook it off and turned in her car seat to Drew. "You're good with kids."

"Comes from having my own, I guess."

"So what do you think about the ghost thing?"

Drew paused for a moment. "We don't know everything. Maybe Demetri is in tune with things most people aren't, and that's why he has a hard time making friends. If you would've asked me a few years back if I believed in werewolves, I would've said, 'hell no!' Nature works in mysterious ways. Keep an open mind."

"True," she said.

When they arrived at Melora's, Spencer wriggled around her, eager for his walk. As they took him around the neighborhood, crepuscular rays of the sun shone on sections of the City of Superior and the lake below, like God playing with a spotlight. When they went back inside, they broke out the wine, watching the world from the couch. Spencer lay nearby.

Melora poured a glass of pinot grigio and handed it to Drew. She poured one for herself and savored its fruity sweetness. "I can't believe you're leaving tomorrow," she said.

"I need to be on board at seven. We leave just before noon, so we won't have much time in the morning." Drew raised the glass to his lips.

"Are you sure I can't convince you to jump ship?"

"Who would teach the cadets then?"

"Ah, yes, that could be a problem, but not a very large one . . ."

"Oh, Melora, don't tempt me. Leaving you is going to be hard enough as it is." He paused. "Like I said before, I'll come back. I'll figure something out."

Melora put her wine on the coffee table. "You better!" She straddled his lap and took the glass from his hand, holding it out to the side. Her thighs were deliciously stiff from the night before. Drew looked at her with raised eyebrows, and she kissed him.

It still felt like coming home. Tears welled in her eyes and she had to stop for a moment. She took his wine glass and put it down on the table as an excuse to turn her head and cover her changing emotions. How could she survive his leaving?

When she turned back to him, she gave a slight smile at his questioning look. She hoped her smile appeared more mischievous than she felt. She dared not talk about what she was feeling or she would start blubbering all over him. That was not how she wanted him to remember their last night. Instead, she cradled his face with both her hands, moving her hips against him. Drew sighed and she kissed him again. For balance, she put her hands on the back of the couch on either side of his head.

Drew's hands roamed up her back and underneath her shirt, caressing and massaging. Through his jeans, she could feel the hardness of him. She ground into it and then lightened up, teasing.

Drew growled into their kiss.

Once he quieted, Melora could hear the rustle of Spencer sitting up. She broke her kiss with Drew to say, "It's okay, Spencer." Her voice was breathless.

Drew found her bra hooks. He undid them and brought his hands around to the front of her chest, pushing her bra out of the way underneath the fabric. When he found her nipples, a small gasp escaped her lips. His hands held, circled, teased. Now she kept her hips firmly locked to his, questing for her own enjoyment. She arched her back to give him better access, but this caused her shirt to tighten. He withdrew his hands and started working on her shirt buttons.

Melora watched his slow progress, then she started unbuttoning his shirt. She only made it half-way by the time he had her shirt open and started sliding it and her bra from her shoulders.

"No fair," she protested.

Drew chuckled and leaned forward, taking one of her breasts in his mouth, caressing the other with his hand. Eventually, he switched sides. All Melora could do was close her eyes and enjoy, her hips rocking slowly. Her legs tired and she reluctantly got off his lap, but not before doing away with the rest of his shirt.

They both sat there a moment, catching their breaths. Spencer sat under the windowsill, watching them, his head cocked. Melora handed Drew his wine and took a sip of her own.

"I think it's time for the bedroom again," Drew said.

"I think you're right," Melora replied. "Spencer, sorry, but you get to stay out here again."

At the sound of his name, the dog's floppy ears pricked forward. He rose to his feet as Drew and Melora left the couch. They brought their wine with them. Drew held out his hand to Melora and they walked into the bedroom and closed the door.

Inside, Melora lit candles scattered around the room. When she was done, she joined Drew, who stood waiting by the dresser, watching her every move. They kissed.

After a while, Drew broke the kiss. "Do you realize that last night was the first time we've been together in a bed since that time on Isle Royale in your room in the employee dorm?"

The images played through Melora's mind: both of them hot and sweaty from their canoe trip, showering together to "conserve water," Drew showing her the erotic art of eating oranges in the shower, then both of them collapsing onto her bed only to be discovered by her roommate, MaryAnn. After they had escaped the island, they had lived and slept in the forest.

Melora gave a little chuckle, recalling the surprised and outraged look on her MaryAnn's face. "Oh, yes. I remember it well." She caressed Drew's hair. His hands found their way down her back and into her jeans pockets. His chest was warm against hers.

He pulled her closer and took his hands out of her pockets. He raised them to her face and began caressing her hair. "Melora," he whispered.

The tenderness of his gesture made her breath catch in her throat. *I am not going to cry. Don't let yourself cry.* She opened her eyes and could see the silhouettes of their bodies in the dresser mirror. She wondered if they would ever be together like this again, and it made it even harder not to cry. She needed to do something or she was going to lose it.

Drew must have sensed her dilemma. "Just enjoy it . . . don't worry about tomorrow. That will take care of itself."

Melora closed her eyes and nodded, kissing him again.

This time, there was no laughter as they shed the rest of their clothes. Drew reveled in her nakedness, touching every part of her as they stood. He lowered her gently to the bed. Melora lay on her back and Drew lay on his side next to her. He traced lines down her chest and belly with his fingers, making her shiver.

"Ach, you're cold." He covered her partially with the comforter. Melora felt paralyzed with the sensations coursing through her. Drew brought his hand slowly down between her legs. As he caressed her, he caught her sighs with his mouth.

Soon, the tension was unbearable. "Drew," she whispered. "Please."

He withdrew his hand and got off the bed. He put on a condom and then returned, helping Melora roll on her side so that she faced him. She lifted her upper leg so that it rested over his hip, bringing them close. Drew slid into her.

Melora looked into his eyes, biting her bottom lip. Drew moved in and out, making her back arch a little farther with every thrust. It wasn't long before the wave of passion they were riding crested. Drew shuddered and Melora moaned. They rested in each other's arms, spent; their wine forgotten on the dresser.

Chapter Seven

Friday, April 14

MELORA STOOD BEFORE the dusty windowpane, watching as Drew's ship slowly left its berth behind the convention center. She had escaped to the eighth floor of her office building so she could watch the departure alone among the boxes and clutter of the storage area. Conflicting emotions coursed through her: gladness that Drew was back in her life, sadness that she would be without him for a time, and fear that he wouldn't return.

When she had dropped him off at the ship this morning, Drew had promised yet again to return. She appreciated his resolve, but she also knew things could happen. She flashed back to the time on Isle Royale when he had left her on a hike to join in the search for Lana. She had lost him then—lost him to the wolves and then to Lana. Things were never the same after that.

She sent up a little prayer that he would come back to her, whole and unchanged, his love for her intact.

Although she needed to be solitary for now, when she arrived at her office earlier that morning, she knew she would need people around her to see her through what was bound to be an emotionally trying day. So she had called the number Georgina had written on the slip of paper. They were going to have lunch at the Portage Café in a few hours.

The *State of Michigan* pivoted in the harbor and headed toward the lift bridge and ship canal. Melora pressed a hand to the windowpane, as if she could reach through it and hold the ship—stop it from leaving. She could faintly hear the ring of the lift bridge warning bells. The span was rising, almost to the top. The ship seemed to pause a few moments, then it continued its forward motion, gliding under the span, on its way to the open lake.

The ship slipped from view.

So that's it. Drew's gone. Melora sat down on a box in a ray of dusty sunshine. She needed time to collect herself before going back to the office.

Trevor was in the field. Seth had known the minute she stepped in the door that morning something was wrong. She had explained her friend was leaving, and said no more. Seth hadn't tried to engage her in conversation or the regular light-hearted banter. She had been thankful.

But she'd have to go back there sometime. Although they hadn't seen any plover activity on the site last night, perhaps the morning monitors had something to report. Then there were the other projects she was working on . . .

Melora sat brooding for a few minutes. Eventually, she stood, dusting off her pants. She pulled on the bottom of her shirt to straighten it, and walked out of the room.

* * *

DEMETRI SCANNED THE LARGE ROOM of the preschool, looking for his friend. His mama had just left, and the teacher hadn't come to bring him to his place at one of the tables yet. The children were all busy, their heads bent over coloring books, crayons in hand.

Just then, a girl with long red hair and red spots all over her face looked up at him. Demetri had seen freckles before, but never so many or ones this bright.

The girl smiled at him.

The teacher, Ms. Monroe, appeared by his side. "Let's find your place, Demetri."

"How about there?" Demetri pointed to the red-haired girl.

"All right," Ms. Monroe said, taking his hand. "Let's see if we can make room for you by Christine."

Upon seeing the teacher, the girl dropped her gaze to her coloring.

Ms. Monroe introduced them to each other and gave Demetri the same Easter coloring book the other children around the table had. Then she walked off to a different table to break up an argument two boys were having over a crayon.

Demetri grabbed a purple crayon from the pile in the middle of the table and opened the coloring book, searching for a picture.

He found one he liked of a small bunny and started coloring. He looked over to see what Christine was working on.

"What's that?" He pointed to her picture.

"It's a big Easter egg." Christine held it up so he could see better. "See, this is how the Easter bunny made the egg pretty." She pointed to the squiggles and circles she had colored on the egg.

"Do you think my picture is the Easter bunny?" Demetri pushed his picture closer to her.

"No." She spoke with certainty. "That's one of the Easter bunny's babies."

"Oh." Demetri was a bit deflated at this news.

"But it's a very cute baby." Christine smiled at him.

"What are those things on your face?" he asked.

Christine turned away, her cheeks reddening.

"Don't feel bad," Demetri said. "They're cool. They look like you could make patterns with them, like people do with stars in the sky."

She glanced back at him, then resumed coloring. "They're just freckles. They're not catchy."

"I'm not afraid of freckles," he said. "That would be *dumb*."

"Lotsa kids are," Christine said softly. "They call me measle-face."

Demetri tried to make his voice brave. "Well, that's just stupid." Then he said louder, to the kids around him, "*I'm* not afraid of freckles." The other children at their table looked up at him, then back to their coloring.

Christine and Demetri colored in companionable silence.

* * *

GEORGINA WAS WAITING for Melora when she arrived at the Duluth Portage Café. Melora sat in the booth, breathless from her hurried trip down the stairs of her office building.

Melora beamed at Georgina, despite the heaviness of her heart. "I've looked forward to talking with you again so much!"

Georgina reached across the table and gave Melora's hand a little squeeze. "I've looked forward to seeing you, too."

"How long are you in Duluth?" Melora asked.

"I'm staying through tomorrow with my cousin in a hotel. Shelly lives in Hawaii, but likes to come back here in the spring sometimes. They don't really get spring in Hawaii."

"I guess I never thought about that," Melora said.

"It's either wet summer or dry summer," Georgina explained. "Shelly misses spring. It was her favorite time of year here."

"How did she get from here to Hawaii?"

A faint look of exasperation crossed Georgina's usually placid features. "She met a surfer *dude*—is that what they're called?"

Melora chuckled and nodded.

"She met this *dude* when he was surfing on Lake Superior in Grand Marais. They struck up a friendship. Before you know it, she's moving to Hawaii with him. She's been there seven years now."

"Surfing on Lake Superior?" Melora furrowed her brow. "I've heard of that, but I've never seen anyone do it."

"Oh, yes." Georgina's dark eyes took on a soft glow. "There's this whole subculture of people who follow the waves wherever they're high across the world. These people come from money. They have free spirits and love adventure. Shelly got caught by one."

"How long since you last saw her?" Melora picked up her menu and began scanning it.

"Two years. She likes Hawaii, but she misses her family here, too." Georgina also scanned her menu. When the waiter approached their table, they ordered.

While they were waiting for their food, Melora asked Georgina how her husband was doing and if he still piloted the boat from Grand Portage to Isle Royale. Her questions caused a slow smile to cross Georgina's face, giving Melora a pang of envy. Georgina's relationship with her husband was obviously still solid.

"He's still captain of the *Voyageur*," Georgina said, "although he's training in a replacement. This summer will be his last running six-hour trips to the island three times a week."

"Why's that?" Melora asked.

"He loves it, but it's just getting to be too much. And we haven't had a summer vacation in years." Georgina shrugged. "It's just time. How has your life been since we last saw each other?"

Melora took a drink of water before answering. "Well, I was married for five years. Divorced now. I worked in St. Paul for a while as an editor. Did the commuting thing. Decided to come back here. That's when I got my job with The Nature Conservancy."

Melora didn't want to mention anything about Drew because she was sure she'd get emotional.

But after the waiter brought Melora some tea and Georgina a Coke, Georgina looked her in the eye. "So what happened to your island boyfriend—the one who was with the wolves?"

Melora chose her words carefully, knowing that anyone who overheard the conversation might think she was crazy. "Drew stayed with the pack once we got off the island. I ended up coming back here. Then, once things were . . . settled with the pack, he moved to Traverse City with Lana." She said the last few words softly.

"So you're not together then?" Georgina frowned. "That makes me sad. I imagined you would have been."

"Well . . . we just might be." Melora smiled.

Georgina took a sip of her Coke. "Your smile doesn't reach your eyes."

Melora gave a sad chuckle. "Drew was just in Duluth. I saw him the same day we met at the plover ceremony. He told me he's divorced now. We spent a few days together. But he had to leave—this morning, in fact."

"But he is coming back, yes?" The glow returned to Georgina's eyes.

"That's the plan." Melora clasped her hands together on the table and began slowly rubbing one thumb against the other. "But who knows . . ."

Georgina put her hand over Melora's to still her agitation.

"You've got to believe it will happen." Georgina looked at her deeply. "I can tell there's a strong connection between you. I'm sure he'll do everything he can to return."

Melora could feel tears welling. "I hope so," she said faintly, turning as the waiter brought their food.

They ate in silence for a while, which allowed Melora to collect herself. She scanned the café for June, but didn't see her. Perhaps this was her friend's day off.

Georgina was first to break the silence. She took a bite of a French fry and pointed at Melora with the remainder. "I find it interesting you're involved with plovers now."

Melora was chewing her whitefish sandwich, so she just gave Georgina a quizzical look.

"We've lost any stories about plovers around here—they've been gone for so long—but my cousin was saying they have plovers in Hawaii."

Melora had done some research while writing the grant for the plover project. She remembered Hawaii had the Pacific golden plover, which migrated from Siberia and Alaska each winter.

"The golden plover," Melora offered. "I know a little about it."

Georgina took another bite of her fry. "Do you know its story?"

Melora shook her head.

"Shelly told me that, in Hawaii, the plover is thought of as selfish. Not many birds there migrate, which might be the reason for it. Golden plovers come to the island, eat until they're fat, and then fly away."

"I suppose that could seem selfish—the bird takes from the island and doesn't give anything back," Melora said.

"Yes," said Georgina. "The Hawaiians aren't used to that. They never get to see the birds nest or have babies. It's like their life is split. The birds eat in Hawaii and have a family in Alaska. The Hawaiians say the plover's heart is in Alaska and its head is in Hawaii, and it won't be happy until its heart and head are linked."

The story made Melora remember how—for the longest time, even growing up in Duluth, she had not allowed herself to feel a part of the community. Later, she had been so absorbed by the breakup of her marriage that she hadn't put much effort into becoming involved. She started feeling more connected when she decided to stop her commute. Even the tumult of her divorce hadn't interfered with that. And now this project was giving her even deeper roots to the land and the people who lived here. She pictured Demetri, smiling behind his mother's skirts.

Melora cocked her head. "Huh, I can relate to that—with doing my own 'migrating' thing to St. Paul and all."

"That's what animals are good at—teaching us different things," Georgina said. "The plover teaches how to be happy."

Their waiter came by to check on their food. Without looking at him, Melora told him it was great, and he left.

Georgina finished chewing a bite of her cheeseburger. "Did you ever come across the Hawaiian name for the golden plover?"

Melora shook her head.

"The Hawaiian name for the bird is 'kolea.' It is based on the call the plover makes in flight, but it also reflects the bird's challenge." Georgina lowered her voice. "*Kolea* means to drag to orgasm."

A laugh sputtered from Melora's lips and she covered her mouth. Nearby diners glanced over at her. Melora caught herself and whispered, "What does an orgasm have to do with anything?" She thought for a moment and then grinned. "Do birds even have orgasms?"

Georgina smiled and continued her explanation in even, soft tones. "It's hard to have an orgasm if your head and heart aren't linked, isn't it?"

Melora thought of all the problems she and Charlie had near the end of their relationship—both in and out of bed. "Yes, I guess," she said.

"Apparently, the Hawaiians think that's a problem with their plover," Georgina said. "They say it's good at sex, but to be happy, the plover needs to learn to be satisfied wherever it lives, whatever the circumstances. It needs to stop being selfish and it needs to cry other bird's names rather than its own. Only then will the plover find its soul mate." She sat back and looked at Melora expectantly.

Melora shook her head in wonderment. "It's going to take me a while to get my head around that one."

Georgina smiled again. "So do you think you're working with the right type of animal?"

Melora smiled. "It would seem so."

Chapter Eight

GEORGINA AND MELORA continued eating, each lost in her own thoughts.

"You know," Melora said after a while, "there is someone who has another theory about the plovers."

Interest sparked in Georgina's eyes. "Who is this?"

Melora described how she and Drew had discovered Demetri behind a log at the plover site, and how when they had taken him back to the site later, he seemed to know things no four-year-old should.

"He said that plovers are like ghosts of the beach. The ghosts of the plovers that used to live here before heard the drum ceremony. And because the beach is healthier now, the plover ghosts have told the living plovers it's okay to come back to Park Point again. When we asked him to tell us the reason why plovers are important, he said what makes things good for plovers, makes things good for people, too."

Georgina sat back. "He sounds like a wise little boy. Where does he live?"

"Right there on the beach. His mother plays in the Duluth symphony, but his father's dead."

Georgina's brow knit together. "I'd very much like to meet him, but I have to return home soon, and Shelly and I have plans until then. Are you going to stay in touch with Demetri?"

"Yes." Melora smirked. "He and I have a date next week to go to the symphony to hear his mother play—she plays the viola."

"That's good," Georgina said. A pained expression flickered across her face. "I suspect he'll need some good friends. It's especially difficult when one is so young and so different."

Melora nodded. "His mom's trying to get him to go to preschool so he has more friends. Apparently, the neighborhood kids won't have anything to do with him. After some resistance on his part, we helped convince him to go. Today's his first day. I'll have to call his mom later and see how it went."

Out of the corner of her eye, Melora saw someone striding through the restaurant doorway. It was Seth. He scanned the tables and walked over to them.

"Excuse me," he said, with a little bow to Georgina. His eyes were glowing as he turned to Melora. "Natalie just called from her lunch break at school. It looks like a pair of plovers is getting ready to nest on the site!"

"Oh, my gosh, incredible!" Melora turned to Georgina, looking to her for approval to leave. "I've got to go, Georgina. Can you forgive me? I need to go check it out."

Georgina just laughed. "Of course. Go to your birds! I do hope they nest."

Melora gave Georgina enough cash to cover both of their lunches. Before she left, she hugged her. "Enjoy the rest of the time with your cousin. Sorry I had to cut things short."

"No problem," Georgina assured her. "Thanks for lunch."

"Keep in touch, all right?" Melora commanded as much as asked. "Let's do this again before eleven more years pass." She took out a business card from her wallet and gave it to Georgina. "Keep in touch!"

"You go girl," Georgina chuckled.

Melora and Seth left for the office.

* * *

DEMETRI SAT ON THE COUCH, playing with his Etch-A-Sketch. He was trying to draw a bunny like the one he colored in preschool, but it was too hard. He kept having to draw over lines he already made so that the bunny didn't look weird. To get to the other side of the body to draw a new leg, he'd have make the drawing thingee go over the bunny's back so that a bunch of extra lines didn't run all over the gray powder screen.

Finally, he sighed and shook the Etch-A-Sketch by its bright red frame, erasing his efforts. Maybe an Easter egg would be easier.

Demetri heard a knock at the back door. His mama was already in the kitchen, cleaning up from supper, and she answered it. When the sound of Melora's voice followed, he threw the Etch-A-Sketch down on the couch and ran into the kitchen.

"Well, hi there, Demetri!" Melora knelt and opened her arms. Demetri ran into them and gave her a big hug. "I was going to call, but decided to stop by since I was in the neighborhood. I've got some big news for you guys." She stood up and they all went over to sit at the kitchen table.

"What is it?" Demetri asked.

"My, what round eyes you have." Melora grinned at him.

"Don't keep us in suspense," his mama said.

Melora leaned forward and whispered dramatically, "It's just like you said, Demetri. The plovers are nesting!"

Demetri clapped and clapped. His mama smiled.

"I want to see them. Can we go now?" he asked.

"Not right now," Melora said. "We have to let them alone for a while so that we don't scare them away."

Demetri did not like that answer. Melora explained, "The plovers need to feel this is a safe place, so we need to stay away until they lay their eggs."

He looked at his mama with his best begging face. "But, Maaaama, I want to see them!"

"No, sweetie, we have to listen to Melora. You wouldn't want the birds getting scared, would you?"

"But I'm not scary!"

His mama laughed. "Not to me, you aren't, but to a little bird, you might be."

Demetri was about to continue arguing, but then he had an idea. There was another way he could visit the birds rather than walking there. He sat back and looked around the kitchen. "Do we have any cookies, Mama?"

His mama looked at Melora, confused. With a little shrug, she said, "Ah . . . yes we do. Just a minute." She got up and rummaged through one of the cupboards.

"I wish you could see the plovers, though," Melora said. "They're so cute. They're small and they have orange legs that move so fast!" She ran her fingers across the kitchen table. "It's like they run on toothpicks."

Demetri smiled and took a bite of the chocolate chip cookie his mama handed him. She put the package on the table so Melora could have one, too.

"How do you know if they're nesting if there's no eggs?" he asked.

"Good question!" Melora said between bites. "We can tell because the male plover lies on his stomach in the sand and kicks his legs backwards. That's how he builds a nest. But he usually does a lot of these scrapes, as they're called, so we wait until the plovers start laying eggs before we protect their nest."

"How can you tell which is the boy and which is the girl plover?" Demetri asked.

"From their behavior," Melora said. "The male is the only one that does the scraping. And also—have you ever seen people with an eyebrow that goes all the way across their forehead?" She held her finger up across her nose and between her eyebrows.

Demetri giggled. "Yeah. It looks funny."

"Well, the male plovers have a unibrow like that, but the females have two separate brows. Of course, they aren't eyebrows, they're just dark feathers. But they look like eyebrows."

His mama asked a good question, too. "How do you protect their nests?"

"Well, when they start laying eggs, we build an exclosure. It's about four feet by three feet with a wooden frame and wire." Melora stretched her arms out, showing them the shape. "We put it over the nest when the birds are off searching for food, so we don't scare them."

The enclosure sounded like a cage, and that worried Demetri. "But how can the birds get back on the nest if there's a cage on it?"

"The openings in the wire are just the right size for the birds," Melora explained, "but they're too small for other animals like raccoons and cats. Those kinds of animals like to eat plover eggs."

Demetri looked to his mama. He couldn't help it, he had to ask, "Are you sure we can't go see the birds, Mama?"

"No, sweetie," she said. "You heard what Melora said. We have to wait until they lay their eggs."

He looked to Melora. "How long does that take?"

"These birds are nesting pretty early. It might take a couple of weeks."

"Oh," he said. That was a long time.

Melora ruffled his hair. "Now it's my turn to ask you some questions." "What?"

"How was preschool today. Did you meet some nice kids?"

Demetri smiled. "I found a friend, just like Drew said."

Demetri thought Melora looked sad for a moment, but then she asked, "What's your friend's name?"

"Christine. She has freckles, but I'm not afraid of them."

Melora and his mama exchanged a look he couldn't read.

"He's scheduled to go back next week," Samantha explained. "Two— maybe three times a week. We'll see how it goes."

"Well, good for you, Demetri!" Melora put out her hand for a high five, which he returned. "I think it's cool you were so brave."

Demetri shrugged and took another bite of his cookie.

His mama cleared her throat quietly. "So, your co-worker Trevor seems very nice."

Demetri noticed that Melora shot her a quick glance. "Yes. He's very devoted to the work of the Conservancy," Melora said. "Did you have a nice visit with him last evening?"

"Oh, yes," his mama said, a little red coming to her cheeks. "He told us all about his work and his sailboat."

"His sailboat sounds like fun," Demetri said. "Can we go on it sometime?"

"Maybe," his Mama said. "It's up to Trevor to invite us."

"It's a little bit cold yet to go sailing," Melora said. "Maybe he'll invite you when it gets warmer."

"I hope so." Demetri fished out another cookie from the bag.

"And Drew left this morning on his boat?" his mama asked.

Melora paused a moment before answering. "Yes. It was very good to see him again." Then softer, "It had been a long time."

"He's coming back, right?" Demetri asked.

"Yes. That's the plan," Melora said.

"Well, you must let us know when he returns. We'll have you over for supper."

"Yeah, he plays good cowboys and Indians," Demetri said.

*　*　*

A WARM FEELING ENVELOPED MELORA as she drove toward home from Samantha's. Memories of the events of the past few days swirled inside her. She was so glad that Demetri's first day of preschool had gone well and that he found a friend. She remembered what Georgina had said about Demetri: *I suspect he will need some good friends. It is especially difficult when one is so young and so different.* She supposed that was true, and she had a feeling Georgina might know more about Demetri than they'd had time to discuss.

Melora liked Demetri's interest in the birds. She would have to find some way to make his wait to see the birds more bearable. She remembered from her own childhood how long a few weeks could be when she wanted to do something. Even now, waiting to hear from Drew was bad enough.

And Demetri had been right about the birds coming back to nest. She had never expected such a quick response from the plovers. When she had seen them this afternoon, excitement had coursed through her like few times before in her life. The male and female birds had been running around on the beach as fast as their little orange legs would take them. They scurried to and fro in unison, looking for bugs to eat. Every once in a while, they peeped to each other. Sometimes, their sand-colored feathers made it hard for her to see them.

If the pair bred, it would be the first documented nesting in twenty-five years. Something she was doing would make a difference in the world—in the environment. Melora smiled as she drove. There were so many problems that needed tackling—mercury polluting the lakes, zebra mussels invading the harbor, changes in the climate. Just this afternoon on her drive to the point she heard a plea by the United Nations on the radio. Measures to limit the increase of global temperatures that nations had agreed to in 1992 were deemed inadequate. Temperatures were rising too fast. More needed to be done to limit greenhouse gas emissions from fossil fuels—coal and natural gas.

In the face of such seemingly insurmountable issues, it heartened Melora to think she could have a direct effect on restoring an animal long gone from her city.

Even though Demetri was so young, sometimes when he spoke, Melora felt she was listening to ancient and mysterious wisdom. It had given her the shivers when he said plovers were like the ghosts of the beach. *The ghosts were waiting and watching for the beach to get better.*

And Drew's response: *Nature works in mysterious ways. Keep an open mind.* She felt if her mind got much more open, her brain would fall out of her skull.

And then there was her discussion with Georgina about how the birds were connected to happiness, sex, and a sense of community. Those were a lot of disparate things to bring together in one little bird. But it was just what she needed to hear right now.

As she neared the Lift Bridge, she could see several cars stopped in a line. "Bridge must be up," she muttered.

She braked and cut the engine. On the other side of the bridge, the sun was setting over the hill the rest of the city was built upon. The air was still. A low fog was beginning to form and creep over the road. As she sat there, it drifted over the lower half of the bridge.

Melora's thoughts turned to Samantha. She wondered how hard it was to care for Demetri by herself and pursue her career with the symphony. She seemed so brave—like it wasn't a burden at all. Melora supposed that when a person was doing what she loved, everyday tasks did not seem like a burden.

Melora could see why Trevor was drawn to Samantha. Melora was perhaps a teensy bit jealous of her because of this and because Samantha had a child the sort that Melora wished she could have. But Samantha was so good-hearted and kind that Melora couldn't begrudge her anything.

She sighed. She couldn't believe Drew had left just this morning. A familiar loneliness quickly encroached upon her warm feelings. She knew it would be several days before she heard from him. The phones on the boat were just for emergencies, and although she thought loneliness could be considered an emergency, that was probably a hard sell to the other guys on the boat who were also separated from loved ones.

Loved ones. She hoped she was a loved one of Drew's. Was he her soul mate? Were her head and heart finally linked? It felt like the potential was there, if the fates would allow it.

Lights were coming on across the hillside above the fog. The foghorn sounded its mournful cry.

Chapter Nine

Sunday, April 16

EVEN THOUGH DEMETRI WANTED to see the plovers, his mama kept him too busy accompanying her to symphony practices to do his *thing* for a few days. But on that late Sunday afternoon nothing much was going on. He put on his jacket and went to the grove. He sat cross-legged and closed his eyes.

This time, he did not direct his sight toward downtown. He directed it opposite, down the beach and toward the plovers. It was a pretty spring day. The sky was sunny and blue. The tree tops were fuzzy with buds and the grass was growing greener. A few gulls passed, soaring on white wings. He followed them past the recreation area and the airport. Soon, he could see the log that marked the boundary of the plover site.

He stopped, hovering over the area, looking for the birds. After several minutes he found them, tan little things running on the beach with their orange legs. They ran next to each other along the edge of the water in spurts, stopping and then starting again.

Demetri drew nearer and saw one plover snatch a small insect from the sand. He looked to see if the bird had a unibrow or not, but it was too hard to tell with all the stopping and starting. The birds looked funny and he was so excited to see them, he felt a giggle break loose from him where he sat under the trees.

After a while, the plovers slowed and stood together. They were facing the water. A slight breeze ruffled their feathers. Demetri turned in a circle and scanned the rest of the beach. He saw a young man with binoculars sitting on a dune behind the beach. Demetri had heard Melora talking with his mama about her plover helpers. This must be one of them.

Besides the man, Demetri saw only gulls and insects. He moved inland and turned around, sensing in all directions. He was on his way back to the plovers when he saw a fox trotting toward them through the dunes. When the fox saw the birds, it crouched between some clumps of grass.

Demetri didn't want anything to hurt the plovers. He rushed to the beach. The birds stood where he had left them. They didn't see the fox because they were facing the water. The breeze was blowing the wrong direction to bring its smell to them.

The fox stood and trotted toward the plovers again. When it was out of the grass, it began to run.

Demetri quickly looked at the man, who was standing up now, but the man was too far away to do anything.

Back under the cedar branches, Demetri formed an invisible ball with his hands as fast as he could. He wanted to shield the birds. This time he pushed the ball inside his chest and then down through his body, underground and toward the plovers. The fox was close to the birds now, maybe fifteen feet, and they still didn't see it. Demetri joined his hands and brought them up to his forehead. He locked his arms together in a semi-circle.

The fox was almost upon the plovers when it yipped and was thrown backward. Blue-and-white sparks sizzled through something that looked like half of a clear bubble, then disappeared. Startled, one of the plovers broke into flight. The other ran down the beach, dragging its wing and calling.

The fox got up and ran back a few feet. It sat down and shook its head, staring at the spot where it had seen the bubble.

The flying plover circled overhead, calling in distress. The other plover stopped where it was, but held out its wing as if it were broken.

Demetri let out the breath he'd been holding and lowered his arms. He waited to see what the fox would do. It stood and looked at the plover on the beach. Then the fox turned and trotted back into the grass. The man stood with his face scrunched in perplexity.

Demetri smiled. He flew over to the plover in the sky. He didn't know if he could talk to it. He'd never tried.

"Little bird, little bird, it's okay. Go back to your friend on the beach."

But the plover just kept up its calling and circling flight.

Demetri came closer to the bird until he could feel the flapping of its wings, as if the plover were inside him. He tried to feel calm and to share that feeling with the bird. It seemed to work. The plover called less often.

Demetri wondered if he could help direct the bird somehow. He looked down at the other plover on the beach and slowly started to move toward it. The flying plover was going with him!

He kept his slow downward path until he could tell that the plover was going to rejoin its friend. Demetri parted from it and at once missed the fluttering feeling that had been inside him. Soon, the plover landed and stood near its mate whose wing was tucked back in place.

Demetri watched the pair for a while as they resumed scurrying for insects along the waterline. He hoped the run-in with the fox wouldn't scare them away. He wanted them to have eggs so he could see their babies when they hatched. That would be so cool!

It looked like the birds were calming down, but he wanted them to know this was a good place where they should stay. He zoomed down and hovered over them. The pair was close together, trotting in unison. Demetri encircled them like he had done to the bird in the air. He tried to send them feelings of home and safety. Melora and the other plover people would watch out for them. And if they couldn't help, he would be there. The birds would be all right. This was their place.

The plovers stopped walking. He could feel their hearts beating so fast. But he sensed they were calm. The fox would not make them leave. Demetri hovered for a few moments more and then slowly rose.

He soared around the site for a while, making sure no other animals were around that could hurt the birds. He noticed that the man had sat down and put the binoculars up to his eyes again.

Demetri decided to go to the very end of the point where the breakwater was. He wanted to check to make sure the plants were doing okay. A few of the bushes he had seen on the way were starting to get dry, but he knew rain would come tomorrow. They would be all right then.

As he started zooming away, he thought he caught sight of two gray, ghostly bird shapes by the plover pair. His heart smiled.

* * *

THAT SUNDAY AFTERNOON, Melora was hoping for a call from Drew, so except for Spencer's afternoon walk, she stayed close to home. But she didn't want to sit around brooding. The smell of barbecue ribs wafted from her crock pot, and her bathroom and floors sparkled.

In the evening, she started vacuuming, but soon got distracted by the view from her living room window. She sat on the couch, Spencer by her side, watching the lowering sun play across the lake, casting deep blue and purple cloud shadows.

On the table next to the couch her phone rang. A thrill shot through her as she reached to answer it. She was afraid to speak, afraid it wouldn't be him. She waited for the caller to talk.

"Hello, Melorahh." Drew's low and distinct voice came through the line.

She couldn't help the smile that spread across her face. "Hello, Drew," she replied.

A short silence passed while the two of them got used to talking with each other again.

"How have things been with you?" Drew asked.

"Plovers are nesting at the site, Demetri found a friend at preschool, and I had a great talk with Georgina."

"Wow. That's a lot to happen in just two days. That's good to hear."

Melora filled him in on the details. Sharing her day-to-day life with Drew felt so good. She had missed having someone she could confide in.

She had made it through the plover story and Demetri's story when she came to a stall describing her meeting with Georgina. "I'm not sure how to describe what Georgina and I talked about. Why don't you tell me what you've been doing? Then maybe I'll figure out what to say."

"My trip back was good," Drew said. "No bad weather. I've got my boys today. I enjoy seeing them."

"That's good to hear. Did you get to do anything special with them?"

"I took them roller skating. We've got an indoor rink here."

"That must have been fun."

"Yeah, it was a riot to see them trying to skate. It was their first time, so I had to help them. We fell down a couple of times, in a big pile. You should've seen it."

"I wish I could have." Melora's voice trailed off.

"But about work . . . I found out that in about two weeks I can take a couple weeks off."

". . . And visit me?" Melora tried to downplay the excitement creeping into her voice.

"Yes, and visit you." Drew chuckled.

"All right! That'd be great." Spencer sat up. Melora clutched the phone between her neck and shoulder to free her hands so she could hug him.

"I'm looking forward to it already," he added, and paused. "So tell me about Georgina . . ."

"I still don't understand it all myself," Melora confessed. "Georgina said that plovers have been gone from around here for so long that her people have lost their stories about them, but her cousin knows a myth about the Hawaiian plover, and Georgina told it to me."

"So what is this story?" Drew asked.

"In Hawaii, the plover is one of only a few birds that migrate. It comes to Hawaii in the winter to hang out and eat. Its summer home is Alaska and Siberia, so it flies away there to raise its family. That's caused the Hawaiians to think of it as a selfish bird because it just uses the island for food.

"The Hawaiian name for the plover is 'kolea.' That's the call the bird makes, but in Hawaiian it means . . ." Melora paused. She felt a blush rush to her cheeks. "Let's just say, it has sexual connotations."

Drew gave an amused snort. Spencer looked at her from under his bushy doggy eyebrows.

"And just what are these . . . sexual connotations?" Drew asked.

"The Hawaiians say the plover is good at sex, but that its happiness can't last unless its head and heart are linked," Melora said. "To be happy, the plover needs to learn to be satisfied wherever it lives. It needs to stop being selfish. Georgina said it needs to cry other bird's names rather than its own. Only then will the plover find its soul mate."

A moment passed before Drew responded. "I suppose that thinking about others first is good advice for anyone, including birds."

Melora giggled. "I agree. And it was what I needed to hear right now."

"How so?"

"It seems to fit where I'm at." She paused. "I feel like I've been way too focused on my own problems—the breakup with Charlie, and the commute to St. Paul. Even though I grew up here, I never really invested myself in this place . . . in this community. But it was like, when I decided to come back here to live and stop commuting—that's when I started caring about this city and the people in it."

"So I suppose this means I won't be carting you off to live with me in Traverse City any time soon?"

The idea of leaving Duluth clutched at Melora's heart. She knew she wouldn't want to leave her work here, especially the plover project, when it showed so much promise. But this was Drew—what would she be willing to sacrifice for him?

It was too early to know at this point. And his tone confused her. "I can't tell if you're joking or serious," Melora said.

"I'm not sure myself."

They were quiet again.

"I suppose that's something we'll have to deal with eventually," Melora said. "But it does seem like I'm working with the right animal."

Drew's reply was soft. "I would say so."

"Anyway," Melora said, "I'm so excited you can come visit in two weeks!" She stroked Spencer with her free hand. "I've been missing you."

"I've been missing you, too." Drew's voice was low and a bit choked.

Melora didn't want to prolong the long-distance agony, so she added, "Until then, call me. Evenings are best."

"I will," said Drew. "Good night, Melora."

"Good night."

Melora hung up the phone and looked out the window. The sun had set and a purple-blue darkness lay across the water. Hearing Drew's voice made her feel like she was watching his ship leave the harbor all over again. She felt happy, sad, and afraid all at the same time. Each emotion jostled with the others inside her, but in the end, she was left with happiness that he was back in her life, and she battled the fear that something—anything—could happen to him, making it impossible for him to return. There were so many things: car accidents, illness, a work emergency . . .

Melora sighed. There was nothing she could do about those things. What would happen, would happen. She just had to be strong and have faith that fate would be with them.

As if sensing her fear, Spencer jumped up on the couch beside her and pressed his body against hers. She gave the dog a hug.

Chapter Ten

Thursday, April 20

AS PEOPLE FILED INTO the auditorium, Demetri looked at Melora, seated next to him. She looked so pretty. Her dress was black, the same color as his mama's concert dress, with see-through black sleeves and a V-neck covered with the same see-through material. Her necklace was silver with a big shiny stone in the middle. He wondered if it was really a diamond.

Mama had told him Trevor would be at the concert, too. But Trevor wasn't sitting with them since he had bought his ticket only a few days ago. Demetri wasn't so sure about Trevor, but Mama seemed to like him. They had all met in the lobby before the concert. Then his mama had gone backstage, and the rest of them went to their seats.

Melora turned to Demetri and grinned. "Your mother looks so nice," she said. "I see from the program she's a soloist in the first song."

His mama had told him all about "her" song. Demetri couldn't wait to tell Melora what he knew. "It's called Trauer . . . musik." He sounded out the unfamiliar word. "It was written when the King of England died a loooong time ago. The song author only had a day to finish it before the funeral. That's why it's kind of short."

"Is that so?" said Melora.

"Mama says the music is sort of sad since it was made for a funeral. But she gets to play the most important parts in it." Demetri did not want to tell Melora that Mama said she played the song in memory of his father. That was too sad to talk about.

"I can't wait to hear her." Melora looked to the stage where the orchestra was seated. "I didn't realize she was first chair."

"Yeah. She plays the hardest music." Demetri sat back and tried to smile and make the sad feelings that were coming disappear. He was wearing his fancy black suit coat and pants with a white shirt, and blue tie that his mama said matched his eyes. Since he had a date for this concert, he sat on the main floor instead of in the wings like usual. The main floor had fuzzy dark purple seats that he always thought of as a cross between a plum and a peach. His legs couldn't reach the floor and, feeling better, he swung them a little, just because he could.

All the players were on stage except for his mama and the conductor. Demetri studied the backdrop behind the players. The nice stage manager lady once told him it was made up of a lot of fours, just like how old he was: there were four different sections that each took four people to move into place before the performances. It had four colors of wood strips on it—blonde, tan, red, and a dark brown—that made sort of a design, plus the middle of the center sections had a rectangle of wavy gray stuff that looked like polished metal until you got up close and could see that it was really foam. The stage manager called it acoustic material. It was supposed to make the orchestra sound nicer.

In a few minutes, the lights dimmed and Paul, the conductor came out. People clapped, and Demetri and Melora joined in. Then his mama walked on stage until she was standing next to the conductor. Her black dress wasn't as long as Melora's. It only reached her knees and kind of fluffed out at the bottom. He liked the sparkly beads covering it. She was wearing the number two pair of three pairs of black shoes she used for concerts. Mama had explained to him once that the first pair, which had flat soles, was for comfort, in case she had to stand for a long time. The number two pair had high heels and was pretty, but the heels weren't so high that she was uncomfortable in case she had to stand for a while. The

84

number three pair was high and sparkly and was for concerts when she sat most of the time.

Paul stood on a low riser that had a music stand on the front of it and brass railing on the back. Paul always tried to tickle Demetri's belly when he came to practices. Demetri liked that. And Paul always corrected Demetri when he said the word "song."

"They aren't *songs*," Paul would say, "they're *pieces*," and then he'd reach for Demetri's belly again. Demetri would giggle and ask the question he always asked: "What's the difference?"

Paul would answer the way he always did: "Songs are what people sing. Orchestras play pieces of music."

Paul raised his arms. His mama raised her viola. He always thought the squiggly openings on either side of the strings of the viola looked like moustaches. The music started.

The notes she played with her horsehair bow were slow. Demetri could imagine a coffin being carried into a church to the tune. The sounds from her viola were like sad singing, but gradually, the music sped up. The rest of the orchestra echoed what his mama played until the music slowed again and she played alone, notes that were thick and dark, like chocolate.

After a while there was a pause. Then his mama and the orchestra started playing a tune that sounded almost lively. Yet there was still a sadness and seriousness to it. It reminded Demetri of his time under the cedars. He felt different there than when he played with other kids or even when he played by himself at home. Whenever he returned from his flying, as he liked to think of it, his shoulders felt heavy—not because he'd been flapping his arms around or anything, but as if what he did was very important.

Demetri didn't know if any other kids flew like he did. He had tried talking to one of the neighbor kids about it once and he just looked at Demetri funny, like he was crazy. After that, Demetri decided maybe it wasn't such a good thing to talk about.

He even tried to stop flying, but he just couldn't. Something seemed to push him to do it at least a couple times a week. If he didn't fly, he would start feeling anxious and scared, and a pressure would slowly build in his chest like he would burst.

Demetri had kept it a secret, even from his mama. He didn't think she'd understand and it'd worry her. He didn't even understand it. But he did know he was able to fly farther and farther each time. He wondered how far he would be able to go some day—across Lake Superior, even to the ocean? The idea scared him and excited him at the same time.

His flying wasn't something anyone else talked about, even on TV. He didn't think what he was doing was wrong, he just didn't want anyone else to look at him like that kid had.

Demetri wondered if he could tell Christine about it. He'd been to preschool a few more times and they were still friends. Their moms were even talking about getting them together for play dates. Maybe he could tell Christine. But it seemed like they needed to play more together first. And there was no time to fly during preschool, or good spot to do it.

The music slowed, and his mama's playing sounded like the sun rising; the notes echoed up to the high ceiling of the auditorium. It made him want to throw his head back and spread his arms wide like he did sometimes under the cedars. Before he knew it, the piece was ending.

After the final chord, His mama held her viola in place a moment, letting the notes echo through the auditorium. Then she slowly lowered it to the applause of the audience. Paul even turned to her and clapped, which made the audience clap even louder. A few people started to stand up.

Demetri knew this was called a standing ovation. He had done it before. He stood up on his chair seat, and Melora stood up quickly and put out a hand to steady him. He clapped along with the audience. His mama turned to him and beamed.

* * *

MELORA SCANNED the intermission crowd to see if there was anyone she knew. Demetri stood next to her in the walnut-paneled lobby of the auditorium, holding her hand. He was so darned cute in his suit, it just about killed her. And his knowledge of music and the song Samantha played impressed her. But she knew she shouldn't be surprised. He was so unusual for his age. And Samantha had done a dazzling job. Melora knew the crowds in Duluth were easily pleased at times, giving standing ovations for the slightest bit of excellence, but Samantha's ovation had definitely been warranted. Her playing had run chills up and down Melora's arms, which slowly abated as the symphony continued through its program.

It had been years since Melora listened to a symphony. She had been struck by how natural and organic the music was. She found herself thinking about how the instruments were all human-powered—not one electrical impulse among them. Maybe that was why it was so easy to get transported by the music—to find oneself thinking about vast outdoor landscapes when the music played.

Seeing how proud Demetri was of his mother gave Melora bittersweet pangs—happiness for the obvious strength of Demetri's and Samantha's relationship, and sadness as she wondered whether she would ever have her own child and that sort of closeness.

She could tell from how Drew talked about them, that he loved his boys, Jason and Tony. Besides the question of where she and Drew would be together, she supposed the boys would be an issue. Who would they live with? Would Lana want to keep them for herself? Melora hoped not, she suspected Drew could not live with that. And then there was the question about whether she was ready to be involved with the boys.

Melora shook her head as if to clear it. These were all questions ahead of their time—nothing she could answer tonight. Soon, she noticed a black head of hair that could only be Trevor's, as he made his way steadily toward them.

When he got there, Trevor bent down and put his hands on either side of Demetri, giving him a playful shake. "What's happening, big guy?"

Demetri giggled.

"Your mom plays a mean violin!" Trevor stood and turned his attention to Melora. She was about to correct him, but got distracted by his black slacks and dark-purple dress shirt—quite a change from his work clothes of jeans and T-shirts. She wondered if her appearance was just as much of a shock to him.

Demetri corrected Trevor for her. "It's called a viola."

Trevor's gaze cut back to Demetri. "Sorry, dude. Your mom plays a mean *viola*. Standing ovation and everything."

Trevor looked back to Melora with raised eyebrows. "Nice dress."

Melora found herself blushing and looking at the floor. "Thanks." Her gaze slid over to Demetri. "I wanted to look nice for my date."

Demetri just smiled and held onto her hand even tighter.

Melora noticed a bar set up across the lobby. "Are you thirsty Demetri?"

"Yes, please," he said.

"Let's go see if they have anything you can drink." Melora started leading him through the crowd. She turned back to Trevor. "You want anything?"

"Sure," Trevor said. He followed as they approached the bar. Melora ordered Demetri a Sprite.

"Here, let me get that." Trevor reached into his pocket for his wallet. He asked Melora what she would like, and ordered the glass of wine she requested. He ordered a Coke.

As the trio milled back into the crowd, Demetri pointed to a boy a few yards away. "That's Sam. His mom plays the viola, too." He looked up at Melora. "Can I go see him?"

The boy looked a few years older, but Melora couldn't see the harm in it. "Sure," she said, and Demetri snaked his way through the crowd and began talking with the boy.

Trevor cleared his throat. "Speaking of dates . . ." He paused. "We still have to resolve *our* dating question."

Melora wished she could be anywhere but here, in front of Trevor, who was expecting an answer. *Now.* She took a sip of wine.

"Trevor . . ." she started, but found she couldn't look him in the eye. Her gaze flickered away from his and then returned. "I don't think it's a good idea. I appreciate your patience with this and everything, but I'm interested in someone else."

"Is it Drew?" he asked.

"Yes," she said, surprised she could hold his gaze after this admission.

Trevor shrugged and sipped his Coke. "That's all right. I'm kind of interested in Samantha, myself."

"I noticed," Melora said wryly. She lowered her voice, "That surprises me, since she's a package deal and everything." That wasn't a phrase Melora liked or would normally say, but she wanted to keep the mood light, and she had spent enough time with Trevor over the years to know it would resonate with him.

Trevor chuckled. "I know," he said. "But she plays a mean *viola!*"

Melora laughed.

"Hey, have you talked to Jacob lately?" Trevor asked.

"No," Melora said.

"He said a fox tried to attack the plovers the other day."

Melora frowned. "Are they okay?"

"The fox was almost on them when it was like this force field went up and stopped it mid-pounce. Jacob said it was the weirdest thing."

"That *is* weird." Melora found herself looking over to Demetri, who was jostling around with Sam in play. "What did he mean by force field?"

"I don't know," Trevor said. "He said it was something shiny—like an electrical bubble—and it kept the fox from completing its jump. After the fox ran into it, it turned and walked away."

"That doesn't make any sense. Maybe the fox got startled and braked on its own. Maybe it was just a trick of the light."

"Beats me," Trevor said. "Jacob is a serious guy. He wouldn't make it up. Wish I could've seen it. Jacob said the plovers were alarmed, but the fox didn't scare them off. They're still using the site."

"Well, whatever it was, it sounds like a close call." Melora's gaze returned to Trevor. "We'll have to keep our eyes open . . . for foxes *and* force fields." Just then, Melora noticed the crowd parting. Mayor Starkweather walked up to them.

"Hello, you two." The lanky man opened his arms and patted them on their shoulders. "Just who I hoped to see."

"To what do we owe this honor?" Melora tried to keep her comment playful, even though she was excited the mayor had sought them out.

The mayor took a moment to scan the nearby crowd. He leaned in toward Melora and Trevor. "I received some disturbing news yesterday that has to do with Sky Harbor Airport."

Melora felt her breath catch. The plover site wasn't far from the airport.

"Apparently, the Federal Aviation Administration wants all those big pines cut down at the end of the runway. They say the trees are unsafe."

"But that would disrupt the birds." Melora's voice started to rise. She lightly touched the mayor's arm, and then said more softly, "A pair is starting to nest on the site, have you heard?"

The mayor looked into her eyes, and after a moment, smiled. "Bravo! I suppose that will complicate things. You see, the FAA wants the trees cut right away, or they will cancel Sky Harbor's airport license, *and* the airport will have to pay money back that the FAA has spent to bring the airport up to code."

"Right away?" Melora felt like a parrot repeating the mayor's words, but she couldn't help it. She glanced at the wine glass in her hand. If she ever needed a drink, it was now, but she suspected it would be tasteless.

"Surely there must be some way to delay the cutting," Trevor said. "Does the FAA even know about the plover project?"

"I'm unclear on that point," said the mayor. "But I'm willing to help mediate in any way needed."

Melora regained her composure. "We appreciate that, Stewart. Sounds like we'll need all the clout we can get. This is a critical time for the birds. A disturbance right now could ruin everything, not to mention wasting a quarter million in government grants. And there are hundreds of old growth pines past the airport. I would think the public outcry at cutting would be huge." Melora looked the mayor steadily in the eye.

"I would think so," said Stewart.

"Could you arrange a meeting for us with the airport and FAA people?" Trevor asked.

"Sounds like a good idea," Stewart said.

"Soon, if possible," Melora added.

Just then, the lobby lights blinked three times, signaling the end of intermission. Melora scanned the room for Demetri. He and the other boy had wandered off, but not too far. "Sorry, Stewart, I need to go find my date," she said.

"Date, eh?" He looked from Melora to Trevor.

Melora gave a little laugh and pointed in the general direction of Demetri. "He's playing over there with one of his friends. He's only four."

Now it was the mayor's turn to laugh. "No problem. I'll be in touch."

"Great. Thanks!" Melora handed Trevor her half-full wine glass. "Would you mind taking care of this, please?" He nodded and she turned. As she made her way through the crowd toward Demetri, her stomach churned. First she had been stressed out by her conversation with Trevor, then she'd learned about the fox attack on the plovers and the mysterious force field, and now it looked like she had the FAA to contend with. She desperately hoped the second half of the symphony would soothe her, but suspected even the power of organic music wasn't going to be enough.

Chapter Eleven

Friday, April 28

IN A LITTLE OVER A WEEK Melora found herself about to enter a room at the Sky Harbor Airport. Inside, she and Trevor would meet with Mayor Starkweather; Mark, the airport manager; Karen, the Park Point Neighborhood Association's environmental committee chairperson; and Bob, with the Federal Aviation Administration in Minneapolis.

In most instances, a week might seem like a long time to wait for a meeting. But when dealing with the government, Melora knew this was nothing short of a miracle. The speed was due to Mayor Starkweather's close ties with Minnesota's federal representatives, who pressured the FAA to arrange the meeting quickly.

Except for the mayor and Trevor, Melora had not met the others. She shuffled the papers in her hand—handouts about the plover project. As she and Trevor waited outside the conference room for the mayor to arrive, Melora surveyed the small airport's lobby. It was decorated in a style she immediately dubbed as "cabin yard sale." It featured pine-paneling, including the low walls that surrounded the lobby. Cheaply framed photos of seaplanes and other small private planes were scattered across the walls along with cast-off "art" like one could find in a yard sale. *Maybe the pictures came from the pilots' homes,* she mused. A small round table in the lobby was ringed with chairs of differing types and heights.

She and Trevor had discussed entering the conference room with the mayor in a show of solidarity. In a matter of such importance, their boss, Peg, would normally attend, but she had a conflict in the form of a dedication ceremony for a new land preserve.

That morning, Melora had awaken earlier than usual, breathing hard and sweating from a nightmare. Most unsettling, unlike in some bad dreams, she had not been an observer, but had been part of the experience. The setting was the beach. She was a plover, sitting on a nest in the sand. She could feel the warm bulges of her eggs beneath her and the latent heat of the smooth stones that lined the nest. She watched as the nearby lake washed the shore with cold waves.

The sound of the surf lulled her, and she fluffed her feathers to keep the eggs warm. Although she was alone, she knew her mate would return shortly from his hunt for beetles. But soon, a different sound intruded: a mechanical buzz that grew louder.

She looked down the beach. A monster was coming.

The beast was black and square. Smoke billowed from its behind and its head was set atop its middle. On rounded legs, it approached fast—the noise growing louder and louder. Melora wanted to protect her eggs. She knew that sometimes this did not mean staying on the nest. Sometimes it meant luring a monster away—putting herself in harm's way instead.

The thing was coming right toward her. Melora leapt off the nest, leaving the three brown-speckled eggs open to the sky. She called, "Peep-lo! Peep-lo!" and ran, dragging her left wing behind her as if it were broken. The monster kept coming. Heart hammering, she called louder and veered back toward the nest. She must make the monster see her and leave the nest alone!

But the monster did not relent or change course. In a last effort to distract it, Melora veered away from the nest again. The monster passed. When Melora saw the shattered remains of her eggs, she awoke, gasping.

Of course, Melora knew the "monster" was an all-terrain vehicle, but she had been so inside the mind of the bird, she hadn't realized it until after she awoke.

She shook her head to clear the memory and thought instead of the coaching that both Peg and Seth, with their long experience with government bureaucracies, had given Trevor and her in the past few days. Entering the room with the mayor had been one of their tips, and they had talked with him beforehand about it. Another had been to class-up their normal office wear. Melora wasn't dressed as fancy as she had been for the symphony, but she sported tan dress slacks and a white blouse. Trevor wore black dress pants and a light blue long-sleeved shirt.

Trevor caught her gaze and murmured, "This dressing up stuff better not become a habit. It's not what I signed up for with this job."

"You and me both." Melora smiled, glad for the touch of levity.

Just then Mayor Starkweather walked through the building door. "Ah, a greeting committee. Nice to see you." Then he gestured to the open door of the meeting room. "Shall we?"

With the mayor in the lead, the trio walked into the room. Two men sat next to each other on one side of a long rectangular table in the Spartan room. The one who looked like an auburn-haired Red Baron said his name was Mark and that he managed the airport. He wore tan khaki pants and a white cotton shirt, open at the collar. Although she couldn't see his feet under the table, Melora suspected he wore some sort of outdoorsy leather boots. All he needed was a scarf and some aviator goggles to make his character complete.

During the requisite handshakes, the man sitting next to Mark introduced himself as Bob. He had wavy dark-brown hair and wore a white shirt with a navy-blue and red-striped tie. Several files and a stack of papers lay on the table next to him. Melora could have been swayed by his square-jawed good looks, but his complexion appeared as though he hadn't been outdoors in at least a decade. She chuckled inwardly, glad to get him out of whatever sort of government jail he'd been in, at least for a little while.

Any mirth died inside Melora when she shook Bob's hand. It was ice cold and clammy. A chill shot through her as she briefly met his serious gaze. What was with this guy? Her "peace radar," an ability she had noticed when she was younger that allowed her to judge the character of people she met and tell if they were at peace with themselves and truthful, or otherwise, chose this moment to sound an alert in her head.

As the three seated themselves across from Mark and Bob, Melora tucked the hand Bob had touched beneath the outside of her thigh, as much to warm it up as to wipe off any traces of him. Although her peace radar didn't work so well with those she was closest to, it was sure working now.

That just left the environmental committee rep to arrive, which she did in short stead. Karen was a thin woman with long black hair and glasses. Those seated around the table half rose to shake her hand, which Melora noted with relief felt nothing like Bob's.

Once Karen sat next to Mark, Stewart began. "I'd like to thank everyone for gathering on such short notice." The mayor's gaze traveled around the table to each person, and he nodded several times. "I wanted to let you know I appreciate that. But the short timeframe was warranted due to several circumstances. The FAA"—the mayor nodded at Bob—"is under a deadline to address the tree issue at the airport. And the piping plover project"—he nodded at Melora and Trevor—"has just begun and would be impacted by any cutting. I'd like to see if there's some way we can come to an agreement about the timing of activities so that needs are met for both projects without harm coming to the pilots or to the birds."

The mayor took a deep breath. "Bob, why don't you start by explaining what the safety issue is for the airport."

Bob took the stack of papers and began passing out one that looked like a map of the airport and runway. He pushed his gold-rimmed designer glasses higher up on his nose. "Safety rules have changed recently for airports, and several weeks ago, we informed the Duluth Airport Authority that Sky Harbor is in violation of the rules because of the trees surrounding the southeastern side of the airport." Bob held up his copy of the map and pointed to the cloud-like blob drawn on it that featured the words "tall trees." He continued in a smooth, even tone, "Due to the runway design and prevailing winds, the location of the trees is the same location where airplanes approach the runway to land. For safety, a cone-shaped approach is required."

95

Apparently noticing the puzzled expressions of the others around the table, Mark chimed in. "That means a triangular area of clear land needs to be at the beginning of the runway. As you can see, over the lake, there's no problem. But here," he pointed to the blob of trees, "trees block the airspace that planes need for landing."

Bob cleared his throat. "Yes. We estimate that thirty-six planes use the airport per day, which is approximately thirteen thousand landings and takeoffs per year. The grove of trees in question measures twenty-six acres and contains approximately seven hundred trees. In order to ensure pilot safety, we would need to clear most—if not all—of it."

Melora noticed Karen squirm in her chair. Her fair skin became even paler. Melora could tell the woman wanted to say something, but was held back by meeting decorum. It seemed like Karen would wait her turn, but it was costing her.

Bob continued. "If something isn't done to address this safety hazard, we will have to close the airport. We can't have the liability of it operating under violation of safety rules. The airport authority has had our letter for several weeks and has not informed us of any activity on a decision. We've given them a deadline of May twenty-second to inform us how they plan to address this issue. If we don't hear a plan by then, as I said, we will need to revoke the airport's license."

"And take back all the funding they've given us over the years for improvements," Mark said.

"How much does that amount to?" asked the mayor.

Mark shrugged. "I don't know. We've been here a lot of years. It's probably in the neighborhood of hundreds of thousands of dollars." Lightening the mood, he added, "Not counting for inflation."

"Okay," said the mayor. "Sorry, but I don't want to get into a discussion about that just yet. I'd like to give everyone an opportunity to explain their position, then we can get into a conversation." He turned to Bob. "Do you have anything else you'd like to add?"

Bob tugged on his tie. "Yes. Since time is getting short, we've started the process of hiring a contractor to remove the trees because that can take a while through government channels. Other than that, that's it in a nutshell."

"Mark, let's hear from you."

Mark leaned back in his chair and clasped his hands across his stomach, looking relaxed for a man whose facility could be shut down in only a few weeks. "As I mentioned, this airport's been around for a long time. We were here before the airport up on the hill," he gestured in the general direction of the city's commercial international airport, which lay twelve miles away, near the small settlement of Hermantown.

"Like Bob said, we handle thousands of flights per year, mostly seaplanes. Next to Alaska, Minnesota has the largest contingent of seaplanes in the country." He paused a moment to let this fact sink in. "Now, I've been talking to our pilots. They don't want to see the trees cut, but they do want to operate safely. We haven't had any accidents yet because of the trees, but I suppose it's just a matter of time, and height, as the trees grow taller. And I suppose they are a hazard now, because they're especially hard to see at night."

"Anything else, Mark?" the mayor asked.

He shook his head.

"All right. Let's hear from Melora and Trevor."

As Trevor passed their handout around the table, Melora swallowed, took a deep breath to calm her nerves, and began speaking. "The piping plover is a shorebird that lives on ocean coasts and in the Great Lakes. They stopped nesting here about twenty-five years ago due to beach development and pollution and have been listed as an endangered species by the federal government." She snuck a look at Bob, hoping to see some glimmer in his eyes that showed he recognized she and Trevor were also working on behalf of the government. But his stare was impassive. Nothing.

She shook it off and continued. "These plovers are one of the most endangered shorebirds in the world. Their restoration is a high priority for the U.S. Fish and Wildlife Service. Our project is part of an effort that's going on across the Great Lakes to restore and maintain a population of the birds with the goal of establishing one hundred fifty breeding pairs so that they can be removed from the Endangered Species List."

"How many pairs are there now in the Great Lakes?" asked Stewart.

"Fewer than seventy," Melora said, "and they live mostly in Michigan. The closest population is on the south shore of Lake Superior in Wisconsin's Apostle Islands National Lakeshore. Although there aren't many birds, the population is on the upswing and much of the habitat in Michigan is filling. The birds are migrating west looking for new places to nest. We already know they come here during their migration. We hope to give them a reason to stay. The fish and wildlife service has given us a quarter-million dollars for a five-year project to attract plovers to Park Point. Perhaps you saw the coverage we recently received in the newspaper and on TV."

Melora picked up the fact sheet and pointed to the photo of the plover on the front. "As you can see, the bird looks similar to a killdeer. If you look at the map on the back, you'll see that the area we're concentrating on is just past the airport and parallel to the grove of trees." She paused while the group turned over the paper. "This spot was chosen as the best plover habitat after careful consideration and several field trips by a committee of wildlife managers who are advising us. The project involves controlling factors that disturb the birds, such as access to the area by humans and animals. If you've visited this spot lately, you'll notice we have signs posted that it's protected. People can still walk their dogs there, but they need to have them leashed. And we have a group of plover monitors working to inform the public, watch for the birds, and protect the nests."

Bob spoke up. "Is there any way you could move the project?"

"That could have been possible several months ago, but now we have a pair of plovers that have begun to nest on the site." Melora took time to smile. "This is very exciting for our group, but we've kept quiet about it because we don't want to start a stampede of birdwatchers to the area. The plovers are at a very sensitive time in their nesting period. Any disturbance now, for instance, tree cutting, could scare them away and ruin our efforts." She couldn't help but look at Bob as she said this. His face was still frustratingly blank. Either he had a very good poker face or he was dumb as a post . . . or as heartless as an ATV rider barreling down upon a nest of eggs.

"Anything else to add, Melora?" the mayor asked.

She turned to Trevor. "Trevor will finish up."

Trevor straightened and looked around the table calmly. "Putting the facts that the birds are endangered and it's our responsibility to restore them aside, why should we care about restoring them?" He looked expectantly at the group. "Because their survival and our survival are linked. The things that hurt plovers—water pollution, beach pollution, over development, and noise—hurt us, too. By making the environment better for the plovers, we make it better for ourselves. In short, what's good for plovers is good for people."

Melora looked around the table to see how their elevator message was received. Trevor had their attention—everyone's eyes were riveted on him, and there were a few nods. Not from Bob, though.

Trevor's voice turned to steel. "You cut those trees, and you're wasting not only a bunch of money, but you're setting back a project years in the making." His voice got quieter for emphasis. "This is the first time in twenty-five years these birds have tried to nest here . . . let's not screw that up."

The table was silent for a while. Melora thought Samantha was a very lucky woman. Then the mayor spoke. "Thank you, Trevor. I appreciate your passion. Let's hear from you, now, Karen."

Karen used a hand to smooth her lavender-checkered shirt and spoke quietly yet clearly. "The Park Point Community Club has long been interested in the old growth trees at the end of the point. Many of the trees are two hundred years old or older. The trees are a significant natural feature of our city. It's uncommon for an old-growth forest to be in an urban setting like this, let alone on one of the longest freshwater sandbars in the world. The forest is important habitat for many species of birds, in addition to the piping plover, and we know area environmental groups, as well as the Fond du Lac Chippewa Tribe, would be opposed to any cutting on those grounds.

"We had a discussion at our last meeting, and some of the options we were wondering about, other than cutting the trees, include whether it's possible to shift the airport runway harborward so that the trees are not an issue." She paused and looked around the table. "If needed, more land could be built using dredged material from the harbor for the runway. Another option would be to move the airport to another site, say the old U.S. Steel site in Morgan Park. Float planes could still land here on the water, but other planes that need a runway to land on could go there, or they could land at the regular airport. The Morgan Park land is a contaminated site, but it could be a good option for clean-up for an airport. In short, the club is committed to preserving the trees in any way possible. I am hoping we have the opportunity to discuss options to cutting at this meeting."

"Shifting the runway is an interesting idea," said Stewart. "Now that everyone's had their say, let's get into a discussion. Bob, what if we decided that shifting the runway was the best option. Would that address the FAA's safety concerns?"

Bob looked down at the map on the handout. "Yesssss, it could. But we'd have to know what the plans are by May twenty-second." He looked up from the map, meeting Stewart's gaze. "The project doesn't necessarily have to be completed by then, but as I mentioned, we would have to know what plans are in place to address the tree issue. I would think that shifting the runway would cost quite a bit and take some time."

"I suspect it would," said Stewart. "But it's probably cheaper than cleaning up a brownfield in Morgan Park or building a new airport. Mark, what do you think of the idea of using Sky Harbor as a seaplane base and having the other planes land at the international aiport?"

Mark cleared his throat. "Having a runway on land is a larger issue than just take-offs and landings. If that's all it was, sure, we could move to the airport up the hill. But there's a reason why pilots choose to land here instead. Some of it has to do with the close proximity to downtown and to the freeway, also the air traffic here is less congested. Another issue is plane storage. These are privately owned planes and people need a place to store them when they're not in use. At the international airport, all the storage space is taken, and there's a long waiting list when a hangar finally opens. If we switched to that airport, more storage facilities would have to be built. From my understanding, there's no more room for storage there or it would have happened already. Here, we have several private hangars and there's room for more, when needed." He shrugged. "So it's an issue of location and space."

Stewart turned to Melora. "What's the timing for the plovers—how long until noise and people aren't such an issue for them?"

"If the plovers that are here now are on a similar cycle to the ones in the Apostle Islands, they will lay their eggs later in May or early June. The chicks will be fledged and on their own by the end of July," Melora said.

"I can't image we would be set to go with any sort of runway construction before then." Stewart said, turning to Bob. "How about it, Bob? Is it enough for the FAA to get a letter from the airport authority saying that we plan to investigate shifting the runway? Will that meet the requirements?"

"Yes, as long as we got the letter in time," Bob said.

Trevor spoke up. "What's the deal with these rules anyway? It seems sort of arbitrary. The airport's been operating all this time without any problem. Is there any way to change the rules?" His line of questioning impressed Melora. Only Trevor would have the courage to think of changing the rules if they don't work.

Bob shot Trevor a sharp look. As he spoke, he looked past him, as though he were reading the words off the wall behind Trevor. "FAA guidelines can be changed with variances to accommodate existing land uses and community values."

"Well, there you have it," Trevor said. "That opens up a whole bunch of possibilities."

The mayor sat back, pondering this new development. Melora could feel the mood of the whole room shifting—lightening—except for Bob, who was a knot of tension.

Karen was the first to break the silence. "The Park Point community values the old growth trees," she said. "I think we could make a clear case for that." She turned to Mark. "But it does seem like something needs to be done to ensure that planes don't crash into the trees." She paused. "Would there be some way we could avoid the disruption and expense of shifting the runway, still keep the trees, yet make things safe for the pilots?"

Mark rubbed his hand through his beard, which was red like his hair, but shot-through with white. "Well, my main concern is that some pilot who's not used to this airport won't see the trees at night. My preference would be to put warning light poles near the trees at the beginning of the runway. Also, the runway is about five-hundred feet longer than it needs to be. We could shorten it so that it begins farther away from the trees. That way they're not such a factor in the approach path. From a risk perspective, I'd be more comfortable with a shorter runway than one so close to those trees."

"Those sound like measures we could take right away," Stewart said.

"Buying and installing the light poles wouldn't take much money," Mark said. "We've probably got enough in our maintenance budget for something like that. Shortening the runway would take some time—mainly to communicate with the pilots and update charts, et cetera, but yeah, we could start that any time."

"And activities like that shouldn't impact the plovers," Melora added.

"You would have to request an official waiver to the current rule from our district office in Minneapolis then," Bob said in clipped tones. "And although those things seem like a fine short-term solution, something still needs to be done to address the issue of the runway being too close to the tress."

"How about this," Stewart said. "Let's draft a letter proposing the light poles and shortening the runway, and say we plan to investigate alternatives for shifting the runway harborward as a long-term solution."

"Sounds like a plan to me," Melora said.

"All agreed?" asked the mayor.

Everyone around the table nodded, except Bob. "Remember, the letter needs to be to our district office by May twenty-second," he said. "Until we receive it, we will continue our efforts to procure a contractor to cut the trees."

Annoyance flowed through Melora. It seemed like the guy wanted those trees cut no matter what. She couldn't shake the feeling that despite his civilized, if somewhat bureaucratic appearance, Bob wanted to hurt the plovers. Was this man the monster from her dream?

"We'll do our best," said Stewart. The meeting adjourned.

Chapter Twelve

Saturday, April 29

THE MORNING DAWNED hot and humid. A warm breeze wafted across the land. Demetri and his mama pulled weeds from their flower garden in the front yard. "So warm for this time of year . . . unusual," his mama clucked. "And it's getting so dry. I'd better water the flowers today. Maybe that'll help them to finally grow more."

He had worked with his mama to plant things she called "bulbs" last fall, which she said would grow into pretty tulips, crocuses, and grape hyacinths in the spring. But so far, they had only just peeked above the ground. The trees were just beginning to grow leaves. The grass had been green for a few days, so maybe the flowers would come soon. He wished he had something pretty like flowers to show Christine when she came to play with him today. He sat back from his work and sighed. "When's Christine coming?"

"Pretty soon." Mama looked at her wristwatch. "Her mother wanted to run some errands on the way, so they should be here in about twenty minutes . . . if they don't get bridged."

The two of them bent to their work, with Demetri asking Mama every so often what was a weed and what was not. To him, all the plants were good. He had a hard time understanding why she wanted some plants and not all of them. ". . . Because they'll crowd out the pretty plants we want," she explained to him more than once.

Before he knew it, a navy-blue station wagon pulled into their driveway. Christine was so short, only her red hair cleared the dashboard. He rubbed his hands on the grass, then on his pants, and jumped up to meet them.

A tall woman in a white sundress got out of the car. Like Christine, she had red hair, but it was lighter, more like what people called strawberry blonde, which reminded Demetri of something good to eat. Christine opened the car door by herself and scampered over to stand beside her mother. As Demetri and his mama neared, the woman held out her hand to Mama. "Hello, I'm Bella. Thank you for inviting us over on this lovely day."

Mama shook her hand. Christine's gaze was shy.

"I'm so glad you could come," Mama said. "You know, it's warm enough the children could play on the beach. Why don't you come inside and the kids can change into their swimsuits. I'll make us some drinks. Do you like iced tea?"

"Yes, I could use some," Bella said. "Do you think the lake's warm enough for swimming?"

"Oh, no." His mama led the way into the house. "But at least the kids can play in the sand and wade. That should be fun, don't you think?"

"Sounds wonderful."

Once inside, Mama showed them where the bathroom was so Christine could change. Demetri ran to his bedroom to get his swim trunks on. Then he dug around in his closet for his beach toys, which he hadn't used since last summer. He found a pail, shovel, bulldozer, and then for good measure, he picked out a few plastic horses and put them in the pail. He figured Christine might like them better than the bulldozer.

The two of them had to wait in the kitchen before they could go to the beach. His mama did not let him on the beach by himself, especially since the day he ran away. Demetri put the toys in a pile by the back door and showed Christine all the cool stuff in his kitchen: the cookie jar in the shape of a giant mushroom, the red flower in the pot by the window, his drawings from preschool that hung on the refrigerator—this they talked about for a while because Christine had done similar drawings—and the small desk where his mama had a bunch of papers.

Finally, Mama prepared the iced tea. She carried it out on a tray and had him and Christine carry two folding chairs to the beach for the mothers. Then Demetri ran back into the kitchen for the pail with the toys.

When he got back to the beach, the mothers were sitting in the chairs, drinking their tea. Christine stood at the edge of the water in her pink two-piece suit, freckled face and all.

"Have you tried it yet?" Demetri stopped at the edge of the water.

"No." Christine brushed a strand of hair out of her face. "But I want to see if it's really too cold. I was waiting for you."

"You go in first." Demetri gave her freckled shoulder a light push.

"What's wrong—you chicken?" Christine taunted.

Imitating adults, Demetri said, matter-of-factly, "No. It's ladies first."

"Chicken!" Christine turned to him and stuck out her tongue, then ran a few steps into the water. She stopped abruptly. "That's cold!"

Demetri giggled and stepped into the water. "No swimming today! C'mon, let's play in the sand. I brought some toys."

The two ran out of the water and dropped into the sand near their mothers. Demetri chose the bulldozer and Christine took a horse. Demetri chased the horse with his dozer, keeping the bucket up so it wouldn't get slowed in the sand. As they played, he caught snatches of the talk the two women were having. Bella was describing Christine's daddy—saying how he was an electrician and a "good man." Mama talked about his daddy, Yuri, and about how, although he had been a construction worker from Russia, he had been in tune with the weather and the growing season of the plants in the forest, even though many of them were different here. He'd shown her where the blueberry bushes were at the end of the point and how to recognize the Juneberry trees that lined the trails. His mama liked to make jam from those. Yuri also taught her how to avoid the poison ivy that lurked just off trail, waiting to cause welts and itching in the unaware. His daddy knew all the mushrooms that were good to eat, although sometimes she couldn't bring herself to trust him on those meals, so she didn't eat them.

Demetri was glad Mama didn't talk about his daddy and the lake, especially since they were right beside it. Tiring of the game and the conversation, Demetri grabbed the pail. "Let's build a sand castle!" Christine picked up the shovel and they moved closer to the water where the sand was wet and good for building.

Christine shoveled the sand into the bucket and Demetri turned it over to create the start of a building. Once the building was a few storeys high, they found sticks and stones to decorate it. Then they decided to dig a moat. As Christine worked in the sand with the shovel and Demetri with his hands, a gull flew past, just skimming the top of the water. "Have you ever wished you could fly?" Demetri asked.

"Sure." Christine looked up from her task and watched the bird. "I have dreams about it sometimes. Plus my mom read me this book about a boy who grew wings on his back and could fly around like an angel! He kept it secret though, and only did it at night."

"Cool." Demetri stopped digging and sat back on his heels. Maybe Christine would understand, so he whispered, "What if I told you I can sort of fly?"

"What do you mean, sort of?" Christine stopped her digging.

"There's this *thing* I do that's like flying . . . only I don't go anywhere. But I can see *everything*."

"Everything—like what?" Christine was looking at him. Not with a look of fear like the neighbor boy had, but more one of plain curiosity.

"I can see my house and the beach and the trees and the lake." Demetri motioned to the landscape around them.

"Cool. Can you do it whenever you want?"

Demetri shrugged. "Yeah."

"Show me! Show me!"

Demetri glanced at the ladies and then back to Christine. He put a sandy finger to his lips, "Shhhh. You have to promise not to tell anyone."

"Promise!" Christine solemnly crossed her heart. "Hope to die if I tell."

"C'mon, I'll show you." Demetri got up and started walking to the backyard and Christine followed.

His mama paused from her drink tea. "Where are you kids headed?"

"We're going to play in the backyard." Demetri said.

"All right, but if you end up going into the house, let us know before-hand."

"Yes, Mama."

The two children went through the gate and into the small yard. Demetri led Christine over to the grove of cedars. "This is where I do it, so no one can see."

He ducked under the branches and Christine came behind him. He settled, cross-legged and Christine sat opposite him, mirroring his movements. "I've never showed anyone this. I think I can talk when I do it, but I've never tried. I laughed one time. I'll try to tell you what I'm seeing."

"Okay." Christine's look was still one of open curiosity.

"All right," Demetri said. "I just sit here and close my eyes and think about flying, and it . . . happens."

"How did you know you could do it?" she asked.

Demetri looked at her, dumbfounded. "I don't know. It just . . . happened." His gaze traveled up into the cedar branches and then back to her face. "It's like . . . how did you know you could eat? How did you know you could breathe? You just did, right?"

"I guess so." Christine's tone was serious.

"Okay, I'll show you. Still promise not to tell?"

Christine gave her head a big nod. "Yes. Promise."

Demetri closed his eyes and sat with his back straight and his arms relaxed. His thoughts went up through the cedars and into the sky. Soon, his vision followed.

He had been quiet for a while when Christine asked, "What do you see? What do you see?"

"My house and our moms . . . I feel like going toward the bridge to see how the plants are doing. They seem really dry."

He was quiet for a while again. "What do you see now?" Christine asked.

"Lots of houses and cars. People are in their backyards doing stuff . . . having cook-outs and raking the dead grass of winter off the lawn. There's lots of birds and squirrels. The animals seem like they're doing okay."

"What do you mean, they're doing okay?"

"I check on them—the animals. If one is hurt, I try to help it."

Awe crept into Christine's voice. "You can help animals? Like . . . what can you do?"

"I don't know." All this talking was distracting Demetri. "Like there was this bird once that ran into a window and I helped it wake up so a cat couldn't get it."

"Coooool." Christine said.

Demetri soared some more, getting the feeling that the plants were thirsty. Their need tugged at him, soft and insistent. "I feel like the plants need some rain. I want to see if I can do that."

"Do what?" Christine asked.

"Make it rain, silly!" Demetri was almost to the Aerial Lift Bridge. He decided to turn around and head home. "Mama said our garden needs rain. I'm coming back to my house."

Christine was silent for a while. "How do I know you're not making all this up?"

"Well, if I make it rain, you'll know." Back under the tree, Demetri felt his lips smile. It was dry. Although the grass was green, it was limp. If some rain didn't come soon, it would start turning brown. The trees were impatient to unfurl their leaves. Demetri decided to start the rain at his house and then see how far he could spread it. He had protected the bird from the cat. He had protected the plovers from the fox. He hadn't known he could do those things before they happened. He had just wanted it to happen and somehow knew how to make it so. He wasn't sure he could make it rain, but he felt inside that he could. Like it was something he was supposed to do. But how to start?

He was above his house now. He could see the brown shingles and the mothers sitting on the beach. Then it came to him: tears. Maybe if he cried, the rain would start. He told Christine, "I'm going to try and cry and see if that does it. Quick, what's the saddest thing you can think of?"

Christine stammered.

"Never mind," Demetri said. "I thought of something." What came to him was the Trauermusik. He thought of the first part of the song—the part that was slow and funeral-like. Then he thought of his dad sinking beneath the water's surface. He missed how his dad smelled—spicy like cloves—and the warmth of his strong arms around him. He would never feel that again. The music got louder in his mind and two tears squeezed out from between his eyelids and slid down his cheeks, one from each eye.

"It's working!" Christine said. He could hear her shifting under the tree. "You're crying!"

Demetri was concentrating so hard, her words seemed to come to him from far away. But he could hear her and he was glad to have someone to talk to while he flew, even though it was sort of distracting.

Like he felt the plover when he was flying, Demetri could feel wet prickles of a mist forming around him. His vision blurred as white clouds gathered above his house. Gradually, more and more clouds came. He kept playing the music in his mind and a few more tears escaped his eyes.

"I see clouds!" Christine's voice was a little closer this time, but it had shifted direction. She must be looking outside the grove.

"I *feel* clouds," Demetri said. "They're wet!" Soon the clouds covered his yard and a few of the yards on either side. Demetri lowered himself until he was underneath the clouds. Elsewhere, it was still sunny. The music stopped in his head and he thought, *Let it rain.*

And it did. The rain came, gentle and steady—the kind of rain his mama called a sunshower. Christine's voice was even farther away this time. She must be outside the grove.

"You did it!" She said. As he looked down, he could see her spinning around, her arms outstretched in the rain that fell through the sunshine.

In a moment, Bella came through the gate into the backyard. "Christine, you're getting wet!"

"It's okay, mother, I have my swim suit on!"

"Where's Demetri?" Bella asked.

Demetri's heart skipped a beat. He did not want to have to explain what he was doing—why he was sitting under the trees crying. Bella would have questions and maybe she wouldn't let Christine play with him anymore.

As if Christine sensed this too, she stopped twirling and stood in front of the opening to the grove, blocking it. "He's staying dry under the trees." By now Demetri's mama came, carrying the tea tray. Demetri hoped she wouldn't get worried, too, and start looking for him.

Christine faced her mother, her body shielding the entry. "I'll go under the trees, too, mother, if you want." Her voice shook a little.

"Yes, please do that," Bella said. "But if you start getting too wet, or if it starts to thunder, come inside."

"Okay!" Christine said, and she ducked into the trees. Demetri resumed breathing. Both of the women disappeared into the house.

The rain kept its gentle steady pace. The sun shone and Demetri could see a rainbow forming over the lake a few houses away. "Look, Christine—over there—it's a rainbow!"

Christine popped back out of the trees, giggled, and looked around. "I see it! How cool is that?!"

"Very cool." Demetri giggled, too.

* * *

MELORA LAY ON THE COUCH. The sun had set, leaving her house dark except for the small lamp on the side table. Spencer lay on the floor next to her. Drew was coming tonight—a day or two earlier than he originally planned. He said he didn't want to wait any longer to see her. And she wanted to see him.

Drew said he'd be driving, coming in around 7:00 p.m. It was now 10:00. A million possibilities had run through Melora's head during the last half hour she had lain there. Had Drew changed his mind and stayed home? Was he injured by the side of the highway? Maybe he hit a deer while driving across Michigan's Upper Peninsula. No, probably something came up at work that had made him late.

110

She wanted to wait up for him, but was too tired to do so after a full day of work and then puttering around the duplex in an effort to keep busy. She turned onto her side. How had she gotten so stuck on one man? Look what it was doing to her. Pathetic, that's what she was—mooning around, waiting for Drew to travel across the countryside to see her, at the mercy of his arrival. Part of her wanted to take off out the front door and just keep walking. Let him arrive to an empty house. See how Drew liked not knowing where she was or when she would come back.

But of course, she wouldn't do that. What they had was too intense, too strong, too overdue. She just had to be patient and see what happened. She sighed and turned over on her back, looking up at the darkened ceiling. Her mind drifted over the events of the past few days—the meeting with the FAA, the symphony concert. How she wished Drew had been with her during the concert. Granted, Demetri was a great date, but it just wasn't the same.

The drone of a motorcycle coming up the hill eased its way into her awareness. The noise grew louder and nearer until it sounded like it stopped in front of her house. That couldn't be Drew, could it? He hadn't said he'd be riding a motorcycle. Then again, he hadn't said he'd be in a car, either. Melora roused herself to get up and look out the window.

With the street light, she could see the bike was silver, black, and blue. The rider was dressed in black chaps and a dark jacket. He still had his helmet on. He took off his helmet, shaking out his dark, curling hair. It was Drew!

Melora turned and ran through her kitchen and down the stairs, Spencer barking at her heels. She unlocked the door and opened it, waiting for Drew on the threshold. Drew took the porch steps two at a time. When he got to the landing, Melora rushed into his arms.

"Hey, Melora," he whispered, his warm breath tangling in the hair around her ear.

Drew felt so solid, so real. "You made it!" Melora let her hands slide down his arms, feeling the hard muscles beneath the leather of his jacket.

"Sorry I'm so late. Got caught in a patch of bad weather going across the U.P—hail and lightning—had to stop twice."

"I was beginning to worry." Melora gave his arm a light punch. "You didn't tell me you were riding a motorcycle!"

"Oh, I forgot to mention that?" Drew gave her a sly smile. "Guess you'll have to hug me wherever we go now. I hope that's not too much of a hardship."

"Did I ever say I would ride on it with you?" Melora's eyebrows raised in mock indignation. "You're assuming an awful lot."

"Not assuming, just hoping," Drew said in his simple, honest way that always disarmed her. Spencer whined and wagged his tail. Drew leaned down to pet him behind the ears. The dog gave him a wide-mouthed, tongue-out doggy smile.

Melora walked backwards into the house, one arm tugging Drew. "Come inside."

Drew didn't need coaxing. He picked up the bag he had dropped on the porch and entered, closing the door behind him. They went up the stairs into the kitchen. Melora asked, "Are you hungry? Do you need anything?"

"Only you." He dropped his bag on the kitchen floor and stepped in close. Melora backed up until her hips touched the edge of the kitchen table. Drew took her in his arms and slowly kissed her. He tasted salty. The clean scent of night air clung to him. His lips felt soft, and the way they brushed hers sent a shot of adrenaline through her stomach and down her legs, which were starting to feel wobbly. The lingering tension of her worry began to drain away.

Spencer whined and pressed close to her, his head at her hip. She used one hand to pet and quiet him, and wrapped her other arm around Drew. As they kissed, her hand slowly made its way down his back until it rested on the smooth, cool leather of his chaps. She caressed him and pulled him closer. As they kept kissing, Melora felt faint—like there was no way she could ever stop or move from the spot. Her senses were overwhelming, and there was nothing she could do—or wanted to do—to stop them.

Spencer tried to distract her, however. He moved to her other side and nudged her leg. It took all her powers of concentration to switch hands and pet him. Her other hand explored Drew's chaps. She found the belt that held them over his jeans and a buckle in the front. She stopped petting Spencer long enough to unbuckle them.

Drew gave a low growl and hoisted Melora onto the table. Spencer's whining grew louder. Between breaths, Melora said, "That's enough, Spencer. It's okay . . ." Out of the corner of her eye, she noticed the dog sit down. Her hands found their way into Drew's hair, combing through the damp curls. Her legs wrapped around his hips and she pressed herself to him.

Drew pulled up the front of Melora's tank top and pushed up her bra with it. He caressed her breasts with both his hands and a whimper escaped her mouth. She wasn't going to be able to take much more of this without getting seriously naked. She wasn't sure if she wanted to get naked on the kitchen table. And shouldn't they be talking—catching up on what had been happening?

Drew stopped kissing her and moved his mouth to her breasts. Then again . . . maybe getting naked on the kitchen table wasn't such a bad idea . . . . talking could wait until later. Melora arched her back and took her top off while Drew worked on the clasp to her bra.

As Drew removed it, he paused to look into her eyes. "I missed you so much, babe." Melora melted just a bit more. All she could do was nod and reach out to him for another kiss. Drew's hands found their way down her back. Her jeans were just roomy enough for his hands to fit underneath them and he caressed her, pulling her even closer—urgent. Melora was all too aware of the hardness of him through his jeans and she started to work on his front button.

Before she knew it, Drew had slid her off the table and was walking, her legs still around his waist, to the bedroom. She started to worry about his chaps getting tangled in his legs, but they must have fit snugly enough to stay on because she, and Drew made it to the bedroom without incident. She watched Spencer trailing them. "It's okay, boy," she said. "Go to sleep." Drew closed the bedroom door.

Melora slid her legs down the sides of Drew's and regained her footing. She worked quickly to finish the job she had started on his jeans.

Drew helped by sliding both his jeans and chaps off. Then she worked on his jacket and shirt. Soon he stood bare-chested before her, in only his underwear. "Love those tighty-whities," she said, caressing him.

"And what kind are you wearing?" Drew asked between kisses. He made quick work of her jeans. "Hot pink lace. Very nice."

Melora slid Drew's underwear down, rubbing her body against his. She had to lean over to complete that last part of the task, and as her hair tousled around his erection, Drew moaned.

Melora gave a little laugh and then jumped onto the bed, lying on her stomach. She wanted to try something different this time. Drew joined her, the weight of his body pressing against her. "No fair," he said. "You still have your underwear on." He proceeded to gently outline the edges of her lace with his fingers, pausing here, probing there. "You are so damn soft," he said, his fingers still teasing. Melora squirmed. Soon, she couldn't help it, her back arched and her hips raised off the mattress, inviting him. She wanted him, now.

"You have the nicest—forgive me for saying this—but you have *the* nicest ass." He began slowly to push her underwear aside and move his fingers to the spot that attracted him the most. Melora gasped as one of his fingers found her slickness. Drew leisurely felt the inside of her and then began a slow, relentless in and out rhythm. Melora clutched one of her pillows and moaned into it. Her back kept arching, seeming of its own accord, until soon, she found herself on her knees with her elbows resting on the pillowcase.

Drew gently withdrew his hand and used it to peel down her underwear. She worked her legs until they were free of it. He got behind her and pressed himself to her. She felt his warmth and his hardness and his softness all at once. "Oh shit, almost forgot!" Drew jumped off the bed and dug around in his pants pocket. Back again, condom on, he rubbed himself between her legs. Melora arched her back and spread her legs wider. She turned her head and let out a sigh as she felt him enter her. He thrust forward and back a few times, then rocked sideways, shifting his weight from one leg to the other. Melora felt him lean on her back and then she shivered as his teeth grazed the back of her neck.

For a fleeting moment, she wondered if this was how wolves made love. If it was, she didn't mind it. She bucked up against him, encouraging him. He answered by cradling her breasts with his hands and moving in and out, increasing his tempo. Soon, all she could do was brace against the bed and give herself to him. Sounds of pleasure escaped her lips. They became louder as Drew straightened up and caressed her back with his hands, moving faster and faster. In some dim recess of her mind that recalled light and logic, Melora could hear Spencer howling outside the bedroom door, seemingly in answer to her cries. But that was soon eclipsed as the intensity of Drew's pace increased, until he stopped with a series of guttural cries of his own.

Spent, Melora rested with her arms in front of her, head resting on the pillow. Drew lay over her back, breathing hard. "Oh, my god, Melora," was all he said. She had no words available to reply. They lay there for a few minutes, breathing slowly. Then Drew eased back away from her.

As they lay together, face-to-face, the power of speech returned and Melora couldn't help but ask, "Is that how wolves do it?"

The question caused Drew to start, then he laughed. "I love how your mind works. Well—along with other parts of your anatomy. It's sort of the same," he said. "But we would get stuck together for a long time afterwards."

"A long time?" Melora asked. "How long is that?" A stab of jealousy regarding Lana spiked through her. She hated to think of them together, much less *stuck* together in the throes of passion.

"I don't know—sometimes a half-hour," Drew recalled. As if sensing her distress, he continued, "But this is much more comfortable," and he hugged her to him. "As wolves, all we could do was stand around until um . . . things subsided, while the pack milled about. It was sort of weird."

That placated Melora a bit. "Well . . . I'm glad you like this better," and she returned his hug. She paused for a moment, listening. "Spencer's stopped howling. Did you hear him?"

"Oh," Drew cocked an eyebrow. "I thought that was me!"

Chapter Thirteen

MELORA AND DREW LAY IN BED, listening to the sounds of the night coming through her open window. Above the dull roar of the freeway traffic at the bottom of the hill, they could just make out the trilling of spring peepers in some far-away pond. A ship approaching the lift bridge gave the distinctive three-whistle signal for the bridge to rise. A few moments later, the bridge answered in kind.

The two still faced each other, their eyes closed. From somewhere in the west end of the city, an ore train made a rhythmic rumble as it hauled taconite pellets to the docks along the harbor. The sound had a musical quality that reminded Melora of the symphony. She opened her eyes and saw that Drew's were open, too. He said, "So what have you been doing since our last phone call?"

Melora thought for a moment. "I had a good time with Demetri at the concert."

Drew looked at her with mock jealousy and then hugged her to him. "I'm glad," he said.

"Samantha played the most haunting piece of music, and little Demetri told me all about the song's background."

"I bet he did." Drew gave a low chuckle.

Melora couldn't help it, she let out a sigh.

"What's wrong?" Drew asked.

She explained the issue with the Sky Harbor Airport and the FAA to him.

Drew's heavy brow furrowed. "But won't cutting the trees scare away the plovers?"

"Yes." Melora rose up on one elbow. "But when we had our meeting, everyone there, except for the FAA guy, was against cutting the trees, especially now, when the plovers are starting to nest."

"Well, that's good," Drew said, "except for the FAA guy. What's his beef?"

Melora thought for a moment. "I really don't know. I got the feeling that he wanted to go ahead with the tree cutting just because that was their original plan. But we came up with an alternative. For the short-term, we're going to put up warning lights and shorten the runway. Then for the long-term, we're going to look at moving the runway closer to the harbor so that it's farther away from the trees."

"How can that be done?" asked Drew. "From the beach it didn't look like there's much room."

"They'd use the soil dredged from the bottom of the harbor."

"Won't that be kind of expensive?"

"Yeah, but maybe the FAA will pay for it." Melora snickered.

"It doesn't sound like you like the FAA much."

"The guy they sent was so intent on cutting the trees, and he gave me the creeps—he looked pretty normal but was all cold and clammy and bureaucratic." Melora shuddered involuntarily. Drew put a hand on her waist, which she found comforting. After a moment, she said, "Anyway, the mayor is taking the lead to draft a letter, asking for permission to do those other things rather than cutting the trees. We've got to get it to the FAA in three weeks or they'll go ahead with their plans to cut."

Melora lay back down and sighed again.

"Now what's wrong?" Drew asked. "I thought you guys had it all figured out."

"Well . . ." Melora turned on her back and looked at the ceiling. "It means I won't be able to take much time off from work while you're here. I was hoping I could take a day or two off, but . . ." she turned to look at Drew.

He hugged her to him again. "That's okay, babe. Any time I can spend with you will be wonderful. I don't expect you to drop everything just for me."

"But I would!" Melora hugged him back, then said more softly, "If I could. It's just I can't let them bother the birds."

"How are your birds doing?" Drew started running his hand along her ribs, kneading her muscles.

"The male scraped out a nest and it seems like the female might be sitting on some eggs, but we haven't been able to get a good look yet. We've built a nest exclosure, though—it's all ready to go for when we see the eggs." Drew's hand on her felt good.

"Why do you have to wait to put it on—why not just do it now?" Drew asked.

"Because the birds are still very skittish. We don't want to scare them away by placing the exclosure. But once they lay their eggs, they're a lot less likely to abandon the site. I promised Demetri I'd take him to see the birds then. If we're lucky, they'll do it while you're here and you can see them too!"

Drew smiled at her enthusiasm. "That would be great."

"Oh, and Samantha's invited us for dinner tomorrow night."

"I would like that." Drew moved his hand to her back and started massaging her.

"Trevor's going to be there, too. They're sort of an 'item.'"

"Ah huh," Drew said. "And how is Demetri taking this?"

"Well, it seems a bit awkward." Melora enjoyed what Drew's hand was doing and she was finding it harder to think of words to say. ". . . But I haven't seen them together much. It'll be interesting to see how things go at dinner."

Drew stopped his massage and they both lay back, quiet for a moment, listening to the chop of a helicopter making its approach to one of the hospitals downtown. "What's new in your world?" Melora asked.

Drew bent his elbows and put his hands behind his head. "Lana's got a new boyfriend." He said it with a sigh, as if the news made him tired, or it was hard for him to keep up with her many "friends."

"Oh. What's this one's story?" Melora turned to him.

"He's from Australia. His family has some business interests in Michigan, apparently, but he runs a sheep ranch in Australia. He's her latest new *thing,* so, of course, she wasn't interested in having the boys around. I got to see them more than usual while I was home, which was fine with me."

"I bet they miss you already," Melora said.

Drew let out another sigh. "Yeah, I just hope it doesn't come down to a big fight over them." He must have seen the questions in Melora's eyes because he continued, "*If* I were to move here, and that's a big if—I'm sure I'd have no problem finding work on the ships, or the tour boats or harbor work or something—I'm worried Lana will make an issue of it. Make me choose between the boys . . . or you."

Melora was both excited and a little scared he was already thinking about moving to Duluth, but she didn't want him to lose his boys. And she wouldn't want to see them taken far away from their mother. She hadn't seen Lana since their time in the U.P. eleven years ago. She didn't know how the woman might be different now. But if she were anything like the old Lana, she could be selfish, captivating, and spoiled. In other words, the opposite of what Melora thought was true of herself.

"I hope she won't do that," Melora said. "That would be awful for everyone."

"Unfortunately, I can totally imagine it." Drew sighed again, but then turned on his side to face her. "Let's not think about that right now." He put his hand on her hip and started moving it in slow circles. "If I'm not mistaken, it's your turn for satisfaction. I'm sorry I couldn't wait any longer."

Her own fulfillment was the farthest thing from Melora's mind at the moment. She was thinking about two little boys and the possible battle that may lie ahead. "You know, Drew, although your hand feels good—I mean really good—I think I've had enough for now." Drew's hand stopped its circling. "I love that you are thinking of me, but we have time. I'll still be here in the morning . . ."

Melora caressed his face with her hand, and Drew hugged her to him. The two of them drifted to sleep in each other's arms.

* * *

Sunday, April 30

Demetri looked over the side of the *Pilgrim Soul* as the cold waters of Lake Superior slid effortlessly along it. They—his mama, Trevor, and he—were cutting through the water of the lake just outside the Superior entryway on a Sunday morning. Demetri had delighted in seeing the bright red roof on the white lighthouse at the end of the pier for the first time. It was such a happy red against the patchy blue sky above the water. The weather was partly cloudy with a cold, light wind—good for sailing, or so Trevor said. Demetri could feel a rumbly unease in the sky. It was far away for now, but it worried him. He didn't know what it meant, so he kept quiet.

Demetri sat in the back of the white boat with the blue-gray trim, behind the big wheel that Trevor used to steer. His mama was helping Trevor with the ropes, running here and there as he instructed. Demetri wished he could help, but this was his first time on a sailboat. His mama and Trevor said he should just "enjoy the ride." So he was. His lifejacket and windbreaker kept him warm, and the radio beside the door to the cabin played the local college station, which Mama liked to listen to sometimes besides the classical music station. At the moment, it played jazz, which seemed to fit the movement of the water along the boat.

Mama came from working with a rope and sat beside him. "What do you think?" she asked a little breathlessly. "Isn't this fun?" The breeze caught her long hair and swirled it around her shoulders.

"Yes." Demetri spoke in all truthfulness. He liked that it was quiet, and yet there was music. And he liked being out on the water. It *was* fun.

"All right!" Trevor said. "I think we have a potential sailor on board." He hesitated. "And I don't mean just you, Samantha." Mama smiled at

Trevor. "We'll sail out into the lake a bit more, then we'll have some lunch." Trevor kept his eyes forward on their path.

As they traveled, Park Point got ever smaller behind them, but Demetri wasn't worried. The breeze felt like a playful sprite—messing with his hair, brushing his cheeks. It made him not worry so much about the sky. He giggled, which made Mama look at him funny.

Soon they came to a spot along the south shore of the lake where a creek entered. Trevor said it was safe and shallow enough to stop for lunch. He dropped anchor and then went below to get the cheese, crackers, and smoked fish they had brought along. When he came back on deck, he put the food and some utensils on one of the unoccupied benches and handed Demetri a juice box. "Thank you," Demetri said, taking the box from him.

Mama began cutting the cheese into little squares that would fit on the crackers.

"Oh—forgot something!" Trevor went below again to retrieve paper plates. Then Mama put some cheese squares, crackers and lake trout on each plate and handed them to her "men," as she put it.

"Ah, this gouda you brought is great!" Trevor said between chews. "What's in it again?"

"Garlic and rosemary," Mama answered.

Demetri liked just plain old yellow cheese better, but he wasn't going to argue. He picked up a cheese square from his plate, placed it on a cracker and took a bite. It had sort of a spicy taste to it, but it was all right.

Mama glanced over at Trevor. "Thanks for asking us out on your boat."

"It's great to have company," Trevor said. "The boat's too large for me to handle by myself anyway."

"How big is it?" Demetri asked.

"Thirty-two feet." Trevor gave him a smile.

"Is that big?" Demetri wasn't sure.

"Too big for one person," Trevor said. He had given them a tour of the boat before they left the dock, and Demetri had been impressed that there were beds in the cabin. He had asked all sorts of questions about whether Trevor ever slept on the boat. Trevor said he did sometimes on nice summer nights or if he was out on a sailing trip for several days. Demetri asked, "Could I sleep on your boat sometime?"

Trevor shot his mama a quick look, then his gaze returned to his plate. "Yeah . . . sometime . . . that might be fun. We could have a sleepover."

"I've never been on a sleepover before," Demetri said.

"Well, I think you're almost old enough," Mama said. "We'll see."

This sounded all right to Demetri and he continued eating his lunch.

Mama asked Trevor, "Do any of your relatives ever come out on your boat?"

"No . . . they aren't much for sailing." As if it explained things, he added, "They live on the Iron Range, so I see them sometimes, but not very often."

"Do you have any brothers or sisters?" she asked.

"Three brothers and two sisters. I'm the middle one," he said. "One of my sisters lives with my parents and the others are scattered across the country."

"Any nieces, nephews?" Mama asked, taking a bite of her cracker.

"Just getting started on that. My oldest sister—she's out in Colorado—she has two girls."

"Girls, yuk!" Demetri said. Both Trevor and Mama looked at him with such shock on their faces that he giggled. Then they laughed. They knew he wasn't serious.

"Goodness, Demetri," Mama said. "That's so unlike you. And what about your friend Christine?"

"Yeah, what are they teaching you at that preschool?" Trevor teased.

"I don't know. Just heard it somewhere."

"Well, you might change your mind once you get older." Trevor gave him a wink. Demetri noticed his mama's cheeks starting to get red.

"How about you, do you have any relatives around here?" Trevor asked Mama.

"No, they're all on the East Coast. I have two older brothers. My parents are deceased."

"Oh, sorry. Sometimes I wonder how long mine will last . . . what with all the drinking." Trevor said the last part of this more softly.

Demetri could tell his mama was having a hard time deciding what to say. *He* didn't know what to say about it. He wasn't sure why drinking was a bad thing. Finally, Mama said, "I'm sorry to hear that."

"I think that's one reason why I got into my line of work," Trevor said. "The land . . . the animals . . . they don't let you down. Not the way people do, anyway."

"That's very true." His mama put her hand on Trevor's knee.

"But you don't have to worry about that with me. I don't drink. I don't like how it changes people. I don't want to know how it would change me."

Demetri looked at his juice box. "Am I different now?"

The two grownups looked at him in surprise. Then Mama started to laugh. "Oh, sweetie, we weren't talking about drinking good things like juice or milk, we were talking about drinking alcohol."

That didn't help Demetri one bit. His mama said, "You've heard of beer or wine, haven't you?"

Demetri nodded. He remembered that Melora drank wine at the symphony.

"Well, they're drinks for adults that have alcohol in them. Alcohol is something that makes some people act differently than usual, especially if they drink too much. And that can be dangerous sometimes, so that's why only adults can drink it."

Melora hadn't seemed different when she drank the wine. Although he had been playing with his friend Sam for most of the intermission, when he and Melora sat back down in the auditorium, he hadn't noticed anything unusual about her. Well, maybe she had been quieter. Yes, she was quieter.

Demetri shrugged and took a drink from his box, then asked, "How come you named your boat *Pilgrim Soul?*"

Trevor put his hand to his chin for a moment. "There was this poet born in Ireland. His name was Yeats—William Butler Yeats. He's one of my favorite poets. He was in love with a woman named Maud Gonne. He asked Maud to marry him more than once, but she kept turning him down."

Demetri noticed Trevor look at his mom again, as if he couldn't help it. Then he looked back to Demetri and continued, "I'm not sure, but I think after she married another man, he wrote a poem out of frustration where he said that some day she would be old and she would think back on the men who loved her 'moments of glad grace,' and loved her 'beauty with love false or true,' and that she would regret how she spurned the love of a man who 'loved the pilgrim soul' in her and loved the sorrows of her changing face.

"I think of a pilgrim soul as a soul that's adventurous—willing to leave everything behind in search of a better life. It's Maud's true self, and Yeats was the one man who understood her." Now Trevor was turning red for some reason. "Anyway," Trevor said dismissively, "that's how I like to think of my sailboat. Every time I'm on it is an adventure, and it makes my life better."

Demetri didn't get it, but Mama said, "That's beautiful! I didn't realize you were so romantic."

Trevor fidgeted with a cracker on his plate. "Normally, I'm not, *really*. That poem just got to me."

After lunch, Trevor winched up the anchor. As they set sail again, Trevor kept looking over one shoulder. Demetri followed his gaze and saw dark clouds. Mama came from doing something with a rope and sat beside him. Demetri pointed to the clouds. "A storm's coming, Mama."

She saw the clouds and turned to Trevor. "What do you think?"

"I think it's coming our way. Better get Demetri below."

Mama helped him off the seat, and they went through the hatchway and down the short, steep stairway into the cabin. Demetri liked it down there. It was cozy, like a playhouse. His mama sat him on one of the benches by a small table. The bench was covered with a cushion that had fabric with tiny sailboats all over it. "You stay here, okay?" Without waiting for his answer, she looked around the cabin as if searching for something.

She walked over to the small kitchen, or galley, as Trevor had called it, and took something off a shelf. She handed him a deck of playing cards. "Play some of your favorite games."

Demetri clutched the card box.

Mama kneeled in front of him and put her hand on his arm. He saw worry in her eyes. "I have to go help Trevor with the sails. You keep your life jacket on and stay down here no matter what. It might not be safe for you to go on deck because of waves and the wind. Trevor or I will come get you when it's safe. Understand?"

Demetri nodded. "Yes, Mama." She was starting to scare him.

"All right. I'm going up now. Remember, stay here." She stood and walked up the small stairs, closing the hatchway door behind her.

Demetri took the cards out of the box and started to sift through them, but he couldn't think of anything he wanted to play. Sometimes he liked just looking at the faces on the cards and making up stories about the kings and queens, but he was too worried for that. He put the cards on the table and looked around. He could see the sky through a row of small rectangular windows along the wall across from him. Demetri got up and climbed on the bench below the windows. The clouds were getting closer, and they were looking blacker. Above him, he could hear the thuds of his mama's and Trevor's feet as they ran around, working with the sails and ropes.

This couldn't be good. Demetri had seen movies on television of boats caught in storms. Someone was always getting washed overboard. And sometimes the boats were attacked by giant octopuses with lots of suckers. He didn't want that to happen to his mama or to Trevor, even though at lunch they seemed to almost forget he was there when they were talking with each other. And although Demetri still missed his daddy, he was starting to like Trevor.

Demetri thought of the rain he had brought to his house. Not only his house, but he had been able to spread it for several blocks on either side. A small smile came to his face as he remembered Christine twirling around under the raindrops. He had half expected the rain to be salty like his tears, but she had assured him once they were inside the house that the rain was regular. The smile stayed on his face as he thought about how surprised everyone had been to see all the flowers in the front yard when Christine and her mom walked through it on their way to their car. Christine had given him the biggest smile when she saw the flowers. He knew she knew.

He had done that. And if he could bring rain, maybe he could make the rain stay away.

Demetri left the bench and looked around for a good place to do his flying. Then he remembered—what had Trevor called it? The head. Funny name. It would be a good place. It was small and sheltered. No one would be able to see him.

Demetri walked over to a low, skinny door, opened it, and stepped into the small space that was surrounded by thin, wood-paneled walls. He sat on the toilet seat lid. The boat was starting to rock more now, and he put a hand on the edge of the seat to steady himself. He could still hear the muffled footsteps of Mama and Trevor over his head.

Demetri pulled his legs up onto the toilet seat and crossed them. He closed his eyes, keeping his hands on the edge of the seat for balance. He became quiet on the inside and raised his face toward the ceiling. The vision inside his head followed, rising through the deck of the boat until it was outside. He watched for a moment as Mama and Trevor worked frantically to get the sails down. They were both wearing life jackets now, too. Then he saw the clouds. They formed a large black wall with a flat bottom like a huge shelf that spread across the lake. There was no doubt; a storm was coming toward their sailboat.

Demetri felt himself gulp. The clouds were so large. How could he ever make them move? But he had to do something or his mama and Trevor would be in trouble. He did not want the lake to take them like it had his daddy. Quick. He needed to think of something quick.

He could feel the wind buffeting him from more than one direction. Then he thought, *What if I blow back?* So simple. If crying could make rain, maybe blowing could make the clouds move.

Demetri faced the clouds with the boat at his back, and blew. Nothing happened. The wind and the clouds behaved just as before. He blew harder. Still nothing. The clouds were getting closer, and the boat was rocking harder. In desperation, Demetri raised his hands to the sides of his mouth as if he were shouting to someone. He blew again, as hard as he could.

The wind stopped. Demetri took a deep breath and blew again. Now the clouds stopped moving. Again, he blew—he was getting dizzy—but the wall of clouds started to retreat. When the movement of the cloud wall slowed, Demetri blew again. Soon, he was well out over the lake. He looked back, and the clouds were far away from the sailboat. Mama and Trevor had stopped their frantic scrambling and were standing still, looking at the cloud bank, their arms at their sides.

A wind from the side started pushing the clouds toward Duluth. Demetri thought it was okay to stop blowing. It seemed like the *Pilgrim Soul* was out of trouble now. As he watched, Mama and Trevor turned to each other and started talking calmly. Then he saw Mama open the door to the cabin. Quickly, Demetri started flying back to the sailboat. He made it there in time to see Mama opening the door to the head. He saw himself, still wearing his lifejacket, sitting on the toilet cross-legged with his head thrown back, the whites of his eyes showing. Mama screamed.

Chapter Fourteen

MELORA AND DREW MADE their way down the hill on Drew's motorcycle. Melora wore Drew's extra helmet, and she hugged him tighter as they negotiated the steep incline. She loved the pungent smell of his black leather jacket and the faint scent of his cologne. Old Spice—she had seen the bottle on her bathroom counter.

The weather was warm, with a light breeze from the south. Earlier that day, a fierce squall full of lightning, hail, and sheets of rain had hit the city. Melora wondered if it was the same storm Drew had experienced on his ride across the U.P., although the weather usually didn't come from the east. Lately, it seemed not to follow usual patterns. She wondered if it was yet another sign of climate change.

They were on their way across the lift bridge to Samantha's house for dinner. Melora brought a bottle of wine in the backpack she wore. She and Drew had enjoyed a lazy morning, waking up late and . . . Drew had done wonderful things with his hands. Since sleep had distanced her thoughts from his boys, her body had responded to his touch. Waiting until her head and heart were linked had been a good idea. Before her conversation with Georgina, Melora might have felt obligated to try and force her satisfaction, but she knew now, and from her past with Charlie, that it would have been a bad idea. The memory of their morning together made her tingle all over.

Melora inhaled Drew's scent again as he slowed the bike to rumble across the bridge. The grid work of the decking caught the tires of the motorcycle and made it feel unsteady, but Melora trusted Drew to get them safely across. Over the back of his shoulder, she could see the expanse of the lake and then the narrow column of waves that made their way through the ship canal. The waves must be much smaller than during the squall, but they still seemed to retain some of the storm's energy as they sloshed against the canal walls. On the St. Louis River side of the bridge, the water was dirty brown with sediment washed down the hillside from the storm. The brown water flowed through the ship canal and out into the clearer water of the lake—the fingers of the river sister reaching out to her lake sister.

Before she knew it, they passed the Park Point Recreation Area sign and were nearing Samantha's driveway. Except for a short conversation to arrange the dinner date, she and Samantha hadn't talked since the concert, and Melora wondered how things were going with Demetri and Trevor. Samantha said Trevor would be at dinner, so Melora guessed things must be going all right between them. Melora recalled the tension of Drew's and Trevor's last meeting when they had been on the beach with Samantha and Demetri—the pause before the two of them shook hands. It would be interesting to see how things panned out tonight, given the changes in everyone's lives during the past few weeks.

Drew turned the bike into the driveway and cut the engine. Melora slid off as he put down the kickstand. She removed the helmet and shook out her hair. Drew smiled at her. "You look like you were made to ride a 'cycle," he said, "like you're in some damn commercial."

"I'll take that as a compliment." Melora smiled and handed him the helmet so he could store it in the space beneath the seat. As they walked up to the door of the Tudor house, Melora noticed Samantha's flowers were in full bloom. She hadn't remembered seeing flowers that far along in anyone else's garden during the ride. She rang the bell.

Samantha answered, hugging them both. "Nice to see you again—Drew, I'm so glad you made it back!" She led them inside where Trevor and Demetri waited. They were sitting on the couch, trying to piece together a large wooden jigsaw puzzle on the coffee table. In the adjacent dining room, the table was set. Demetri jumped up, trotted over to them, and wrapped an arm around one of Melora's legs, and the other around one of Drew's in a hug. His soft cheek nestled into Melora's thigh. "Hi!" he said.

Melora tousled his hair. "Hi, Demetri. Looks like you're having fun with that puzzle."

Trevor gave a wave from the couch. "He's way better at this than me." He looked back down to the puzzle.

Melora took the wine out of her backpack and gave it to Samantha, who took it into the kitchen, saying, "The lasagna just came out of the oven, so you're right on time. Just hold on a minute and I'll have it on the table."

Melora scanned the living room for a seat. A chair sat at either end of the couch. She didn't want to infringe on Trevor and Demetri, so she guessed she and Drew would have to sit separate from each other. Funny, how that bothered her a little, but there was no other choice. She moved to sit in the nearest chair and Drew sat in the other.

They watched Trevor and Demetri work the puzzle. Melora could tell that Trevor was acting confused on purpose about which piece went where, but if Demetri caught on, he gave no sign. In fact, they seemed much more comfortable with each other than they had at the symphony. After a moment, Trevor looked up. "I heard the bike." He nodded at Drew. "Did you ride it from Michigan?"

"Yeah, had a good trip except for a storm that delayed me," Drew said. "If I didn't know better, I'd say it was the same storm that blew into Duluth today—lots of hail, wicked wind. I had to hole up under a bridge a couple of times."

"That *was* an unusual storm," Trevor said.

Demetri looked up from the puzzle, drawn in by the grownups' conversation. He watched Trevor as he continued his description.

"Black clouds, large flat shelf on the bottom. We've got quite the story to tell about it, but I think it should wait until dinner."

Demetri started squirming. Melora didn't have much time to wonder about him before Samantha called them to the table. The meal looked and smelled delicious—lasagna, salad with black olives, cheese garlic bread, and green beans. Melora and Drew had gotten out of bed so late, they'd only had one meal that day, and Melora's stomach was letting her know it wasn't enough.

Samantha directed them to chairs where they could sit next to each other, across from Samantha and Trevor. Demetri slipped into the seat of honor at the head of the table. Without ceremony, other than an appreciative glance at the steaming dishes, the group started to eat. The conversation flowed as they caught up on each other's lives, but Demetri seemed less talkative than usual.

Samantha passed around the green beans for the second time. "Trevor took us on his sailboat today for the first time." Her statement held a mixture of enthusiasm and caution.

This piqued Melora's interest. "How was it?"

"It was wonderful—we had lunch by the South Shore and I learned a lot about the ropes and things," Samantha said.

Trevor dished out some more beans and put the bowl back on the table. "We had some excitement, though, with that storm."

"What happened?" Melora looked from Trevor to Samantha.

"It almost caught us." Trevor's voice trembled a little. "We were racing away from it, back to Superior when it was like the storm stopped and changed direction." He exchanged a look with Samantha that Melora couldn't read.

"So it missed you?" Melora asked.

"Just barely." Trevor ran his hand through his black hair.

Samantha chimed in. "I was so scared. I was sure it was going to rip the sails to shreds, and us along with it."

"And where were *you* during the excitement?" Drew looked over at Demetri.

Demetri appeared about to speak, but Samantha answered for him. "He was below, in the cabin. We didn't want him to get hurt."

"It was scary," Demetri added.

"I'm so glad you guys didn't get caught in it," Melora said. "What an introduction to sailing for you!"

"They did great, though," Trevor said, nodding to Demetri and Samantha. "If I'd been out there alone, who knows what might've happened."

So that's what the difference was, Melora thought. The three had been through this harrowing experience together. *Nothing like a little trauma to promote bonding,* although she still sensed something was off with Demetri. Maybe he remained shaken up about it. And because Trevor and Samantha were more comfortable with each other now, Trevor seemed hardly to pay attention to Drew.

From there, the conversation switched to the plovers, and Melora gave them an update. Of course, Demetri was disappointed the monitors didn't know if the birds had laid eggs yet. Melora assured him she would take him and his mom, if she wanted, to see the plovers as soon as she knew for sure.

"And I'm sure Trevor told you the FAA wants to cut a bunch of the old white pines at Sky Harbor for safety reasons," she said to Samantha.

"Safety for what?" Demetri asked.

"For the planes," Melora explained. "The trees are in the way of the planes that land there, so the FAA wants them removed."

"What's a FAA?" Demetri asked.

Melora paused a moment, thinking of the best way to explain a large federal bureaucracy to a four-year-old—even a gifted four-year-old. "It's a big organization that tries to keep the people who fly in airplanes safe."

Demetri just blinked at her, processing her answer.

"Trevor and I talked about the issue," Samantha said. "I hope they don't cut those pines."

Trevor grinned and looked at Melora. "Not if Melora and I have anything to say about it."

"Me, too!" Demetri chirped. "I like those trees."

Melora felt herself melt a little. "I do, too, Demetri."

"So you won't let anything happen to them?" Demetri's big blue eyes were trained on her.

"We're doing everything we can," Melora said. "We even have the mayor working with us."

This seemed to reassure him. After a dessert of homemade vanilla ice cream, Demetri excused himself to his room to color in a dinosaur coloring book Trevor bought him. With a mixture of worry and wistfulness on her face, Samantha watched him walk down the hall. Melora wondered if she should ask what was going on. She wasn't sure it was her place to pry now that Trevor was in the picture.

They sat around the table in silence. Finally, Melora couldn't stand the tension. She turned to Samantha. "Is everything all right? Demetri seems a little off."

A flicker of worry passed through Samantha's eyes. "He's all right . . . now," she said.

Trevor put his hand on hers, which rested on the table top. "You can tell Melora," his voice was low. "Maybe she can help."

"Well . . . when we were sailing—once the storm passed, I went into the cabin to check on Demetri." Samantha paused as if the memory were difficult. "I found him sitting in the bathroom on the toilet cover with his head up and his eyes rolled back." Her voice shook and she fidgeted with her napkin on the table. "I called for Trevor, but by the time he came down it was like Demetri snapped out of it. He was sitting there just like normal."

Melora exchanged a puzzled glance with Drew. "Did Demetri say anything about it?" she asked.

"I asked him if he was okay, and he said he was. He also said . . . that he had been 'flying' and working to keep the storm away from us."

"Flying?" Drew asked. "What do you think he meant?"

Samantha spoke as if she were processing the words as she said them. "He said that he flies every few days, and that he helps the animals and the plants when he does it. He can fly from our house and around the city, and he can see everything. He thinks someday he'll even be able to fly across the lake. I don't know what to make of it."

Trevor added, "I heard it too. Demetri said it so matter-of-factly, which was even more frightening than the storm to me. At least with a storm, you know what you're dealing with, but this . . . this is something I don't understand."

"Do you think he could have been having a seizure?" Melora took a sip of her remaining wine to mask the worry she felt. Samantha and Trevor were already worried enough. She didn't want to fuel it with her own.

"I don't know," Samantha said. "I've never seen anyone have a seizure. Don't they move around a lot when that happens? He was just sitting there, *so still*."

"I think it depends on the type," Melora said. "It might be a good idea to get him checked out by his doctor."

Samantha sighed. "You're right. I thought of that, but of course, the office is closed today. I'll make an appointment as soon as I can on Monday. But, there are other things, too."

Melora wasn't sure she wanted to hear any more even though she was curious about what was going on with Demetri. Her heart was breaking for this little boy who had come so recently and unexpectedly into her life. She couldn't bear to imagine anything bad happening to him.

Drew was braver and asked, "Like what?"

Samantha took a deep breath. "You know Christine, Demetri's friend from preschool? She and her mother came over this weekend for a play date. Everything was fine . . . I mean, Bella—Christine's mother—was interesting to talk to and the kids had a good time—but there was a sun shower while they were here so we all went inside. Then when Bella and Christine left, the front yard was full of flowers."

Melora remembered noticing Samantha's garden. Her heart began to beat faster.

"What's wrong with that?" Drew asked.

"Demetri and I were weeding the garden when Christine and Bella came. No flowers were blooming then. They were hardly even above the ground!" Samantha put her hand on the table, palm down, for emphasis, as if she were trying to push plants back into the ground.

"I noticed how pretty your flowers were when we arrived," Melora said. "Nobody else's flowers are even blooming yet."

"That's the thing," Samantha said. "They *aren't* blooming. It's impossible for flowers to grow that fast. Yet . . . they did."

Trevor had been sitting back in his chair, his mouth a straight line. "That, coupled with what Demetri told us on the sailboat, has us wondering if *he* did it somehow."

"Have you asked him about it?" Melora's heart was racing full-tilt now.

Samantha lowered her eyes. "No. I'm not sure I'm ready for that. And then there's another thing."

Melora felt like pushing away from the table. *Another* thing?

Samantha spoke without waiting for anyone's permission. "Maybe you've noticed the begonia I have in the kitchen?" When they nodded, she said, "It keeps almost dying and then coming back to life. I thought I was just overwatering it. But now I realize that, when Demetri's upset about something, it turns brown. When he's happy, it blooms."

"So what does this mean?" Melora asked.

"We think it means that Demetri might be telling the truth," Trevor said. "He might indeed be able to influence at least plants and the weather. Possibly animals, but Samantha hasn't seen any evidence of that yet."

"It's just . . . so many things are starting to make sense now." Samantha looked briefly over to the table in the living room where the jigsaw puzzle sat, pieces scattered about. "So many things that have nagged the back of my mind have all come together."

The group was silent for a few moments. Drew spoke. "Well, you should start with a doctor's appointment, to rule out anything physical. If it's something more than that—" he gave Melora a quick look, "—we might have some ideas, but need time to think."

"I'm sorry to lay this on you," Samantha said. "It's just—you were so helpful with getting Demetri to accept going to preschool. I know that's nowhere near the scope of this, but Trevor and I have just been butting our heads against the wall thinking about this, and getting nowhere."

"You've got to admit," Trevor said, "it's not your usual kid-related problem. And I'm not that experienced with kids—even normal ones." He shot Samantha an apologetic look, but her expression was forgiving.

"You know, when Drew and I first met Demetri—when he ran away—we were very impressed with his knowledge about nature," Melora said.

"It seems like he's in touch with things most people aren't," Drew confirmed, "especially for a four-year-old."

Melora gave him an appreciative glance and turned back to Samantha. "If we rule out physical reasons, then it makes sense to look at spiritual ones."

"What do you mean?" Samantha's voice wavered. She took a drink of water.

"I've got some ties to the Native American community. My friends might be helpful with something like this."

"Are you thinking about Georgina?" Drew asked.

"Yes." Melora gazed at Samantha. "Georgina is a member of the Grand Portage Tribe. She was very helpful to me when I asked her about . . . a different matter. I bet she'd have some good insights into Demetri— if you're okay with me sharing information about him."

"Yes, yes," Samantha said. "If his doctor doesn't give us any ideas, I'd be okay with that."

"Is preschool still going all right for him?" Drew asked.

"His teacher, Ms. Monroe, says so. Demetri pretty much sticks around Christina, but his teacher has noticed him branching out to play with some of the boys, too. So far, so good." Samantha shrugged.

"That's wonderful to hear." Drew reached over and put a reassuring arm on Samantha's shoulder. From there, the conversation returned to more trivial topics. Soon it was time for Melora and Drew to go. They visited Demetri's room and said goodbye to him before they left, and then rode the motorcycle to Canal Park. The evening was still calm—a good time for a stroll on the Lakewalk.

They parked the bike behind Melora's office building and walked past the hotels to the boardwalk. They found a bench near Uncle Harvey's Mausoleum, where they decided to sit and watch the lake. The sky was beginning to turn a bluish-purple as the sun started to set. A light breeze wafted off the water.

Melora had been thinking about Demetri the whole time. When they sat, she couldn't help but ask, "So do you think Demetri's a werewolf?"

Drew gave a short laugh. "He's definitely *something*, but not a werewolf. So, you have any idea how to get a hold of Georgina?"

"I've got her cousin's phone number. I'm sure I'll be able to track her down that way."

Drew put his arm around her shoulders. "Good."

They sat for a few moments, watching the still water. Melora leaned her head into his shoulder, musing about Demetri. "So what kind of being can control plants and animals?"

"What's the name of that half-goat, half-man creature?" Drew asked.

"You mean a satyr, like Pan?"

"Yeah, Pan—god of nature and sheep or something. Maybe he's some sort of Pan."

"I hope not," Melora said. "I'd hate to see him start growing goat legs."

Drew chuckled. "Right. That doesn't quite fit."

"And the way he said he does things—by flying, even though his body stays on the ground—do you know what that's called?"

"Astral projection. It's when a person can project their spirit outside of their body. I've heard the idea is common in many religions and in people who've had near-death experiences."

"And they meditate to do it, right? Or go into some sort of trance?"

"That sounds like what he could be doing. But the question is, why?"

"Yes, indeed," Melora said. "I sure hope Georgina can help us."

* * *

Saturday, May 13

Demetri crawled into the entrance of the dark tent all by himself. The gray-haired Indian man, who had gone in first, told them they had to go single file. His heart was beating fast as a bird's, but he felt better knowing Mama was already in there. Drew and Melora would follow behind him. He made his arms and legs keep moving even though they didn't want to, so that no one would notice he was nervous. He didn't want a pile-up of people behind him.

From the outside, the tent looked like a dome covered in some sort of animal skin. It was about the same size as the tent he and Mama camped in, or the space he had under the cedars. When they had been standing around in the evening light by a small lake, listening to the Indian man, Mama told him how important it was to keep quiet until he was inside. Then he was supposed to say what the others said. He had walked through the woods past a fire on the way to the tent entrance. Demetri noticed a bunch of round rocks about the size of a grown-up's hand were among the branches in the fire. His mama had put some dried leaves into the fire as she passed before him. On the shore of the lake, she had told him it was tobacco, but that he didn't have to put any in. He had also passed something Mama told him was an altar. It was a small low table that had rocks, feathers, and what looked like a flute on it.

Just before Demetri ducked inside the tent, a young man who was holding a smoking bunch of sticks wafted the smoke in his direction with a big bird feather. Demetri closed his eyes so the smoke wouldn't sting them and scrunched up his nose in anticipation of the smell. It wasn't as bad as campfire smoke, though. If a smell could be soft, this was—and earthy.

Once inside, Mama motioned what direction he should go. He did, crawling around the edge of the tent, and sat beside her, cross-legged. From the light coming in through the door, he could see a stranger and the old Indian man sitting next to Mama. They greeted him and he said, "Hi," back. He looked around. The tent frame was made of long bent branches that reminded Demetri of ribs. In front of him was a shallow pit. A bucket with a ladle sat next to it.

Mama had told him they were going to a sweat lodge ceremony. It wasn't hot yet. But he was a little sweaty just from being around all the strangers and not knowing what would happen next. Mama said Melora's friend Georgina thought the ceremony would help them figure out why he could fly and what it meant.

Demetri's doctor had done all sorts of tests on him, plus he'd sent him to see some other doctors. They'd stuck him in this machine where he had to lay down like he was in a tight tunnel—it had been way smaller than the sweat lodge. And the machine had banged a lot. They told him it would do that, so he wasn't surprised. But he'd had to lie still for so long. The only thing that helped was the classical music they let him listen to on some headphones. The doctors had even stuck wires to his head, but Mama said they hadn't found anything bad. He was "perfectly normal." So Mama had decided to try the sweat lodge ceremony.

Demetri had met Georgina when she came with Melora to talk to Mama about the ceremony. He liked her. She was calm and friendly. She had given him a leather pouch to play with. She said he could keep his favorite things in it. He had the pouch with him now, tied to the belt loop on his shorts. His fingers felt the bulges of the agates and marbles he had filled it with.

Georgina was at the ceremony, too, but he wasn't sure when she would come into the tent. The place smelled smoky, and the air was stuffy. Trevor wasn't here. Demetri wasn't sure why he didn't come, but it didn't bother him.

Now Melora entered. She was wearing a skirt and a T-shirt, like all the other women. Demetri was wearing shorts and a T-shirt. Once she was inside, Melora said, "All my relations." Then she came over and sat by Demetri. Demetri felt bad. He hadn't said, "All my relations." No one had told him he was supposed to. He didn't even know what a "relation" was. He looked around at the Indian man and the stranger, but they didn't seem to be mad. The group greeted Melora like they had him, and he chimed in.

The process was repeated as Drew crawled in and sat next to Melora. Then Georgina arrived. Because there was only room for one more person, she sat next to Drew and the door. Then the young Indian man entered carrying something with oven mitts on his hands. He put the thing into the pit, and Demetri saw it was a rock. It was about the same shape and size as the rocks he'd seen in the fire outside. His mama told him that was how they made the lodge hot.

The young man came and went several times, bringing more rocks. As he worked, the gray-haired Indian man began singing. Demetri couldn't understand the words, but he noticed that the beat of the song matched the beat of his heart, which wasn't going as fast as before. Mama rested her hand on his knee.

After the man placed the last stone, the singing stopped and the gray-haired Indian man said, "If it gets too hot for you, you are free to leave. But before you leave, you need to say 'all my relations.' He looked around the circle of people to make sure they understood. Demetri nodded. Then the man swept his hand in a circular motion. "You need to leave in a clockwise direction, the same direction you were going when you came in. Because we have a special guest today—" he nodded at Demetri "—we are going to keep the ceremony shorter than usual, so I hope that will make it easier on us all. But, we should still have enough time to do what needs to be done."

Then he spoke words Demetri didn't understand to someone who must have been standing outside of the lodge. The door flap closed and the group was plunged into darkness. As his eyes adjusted, Demetri could make out the small pile of stones, glowing red.

"Let us be silent," the man said. After a few minutes, a drumming sound started, and Demetri could just make out that it came from the same man. The drumming was replaced by a hissing sound. The man was taking the ladle and putting water on the hot stones. In the next instant, a wave of hot air enveloped Demetri. It made it hard to breathe. He tried to keep calm, but before even thinking about it, he put his hand on top of the one Mama had on his knee. The hissing and steaming happened three more times.

After the air had stilled, the man spoke again. "Oh, Grandfather, we search for you along this great road you have set before us. Oh, Grandfather, we thank you for this world, for our life. We ask for your blessing and your instruction.

"Grandfather, put our feet on a path that leads to you. Give us strength to lead ourselves and our children past the darkness. Teach us to heal ourselves, to heal each other, and to heal the world. Let us begin now. Help us find the answers to our questions. Help us to walk the great road in peace."

With the rock's misty red glow, Demetri could see the Indian man pick up a stick with some feathers on it from the dirt floor beside him. He brushed a lock of long gray hair away from his face. "This is a talking stick. I will start passing it around to each of you. Please, introduce yourself, tell us where you are from and why you have come to this ceremony. If you are native, please tell us your clan. In case you missed my introduction outside, I am Slow Turtle. I live on the Fond du Lac Reservation near Cloquet. I am of the Loon Clan. It is my purpose to guide you through this ceremony and help you find the answers you seek. I am glad you are all here today."

He passed the stick to the man who sat next to him. The man said his name was Jared, that he was from Cloquet, and that he was of the Bear Clan. He was doing the sweat to gather strength to fight an addiction. "I have hurt a lot of people," he said. "I ask for their forgiveness and for guidance from the Creator."

Next came Mama. By now, the heat lay like a heavy blanket upon the group. Demetri removed his hand from atop hers, but her hand remained on his knee as she spoke. "My name is Samantha. I live in Duluth. Sorry, but I don't have a clan. I am here—" she tightened her grip on Demetri's knee "—to find out more about my son, Demetri, who is beside me. We'd—I'd like to know . . . what he is, and . . . why he is like he is. He is very special and I need some guidance."

She passed the stick to Demetri, whispering, "Do you want to say anything?"

He took the stick. He could feel sweat start to drip down his forehead. In a clear voice, he said, "My name is Demetri. I live in Duluth. I can fly and I want to know why so it doesn't worry Mama. I like helping the animals and the plants. I guess that's it." He shrugged and passed the stick to Melora.

She introduced herself and said she was there to support Samantha and Demetri. Drew said the same thing. Georgina said that she was from the Grand Portage Ojibway Tribe and the Fish Clan. She was glad to introduce her friends to the native ways and was there to help however necessary.

She passed the stick to Slow Turtle, who said, "Grandfather, hear our requests." His voice was deep and strong. "Help us to understand our place in your world and give us the ability to listen to your instructions." He began beating the drum again and singing more words that Demetri didn't understand. Demetri was starting to get used to the heat, but breathing was still hard and he had to work to calm himself so that he didn't stand up and run from the lodge. He was grateful when Slow Turtle stopped singing and said, "Now it's time for a break. We will leave the lodge for a few moments, and you can swim in the lake if you want." He called some instructions to the person outside, who opened the door flap. Light flooded the small space and Demetri could see the pink cheeks and damp skin of everyone who sat around the stones. A whisper of cool air reached him and he felt like he had been swimming underwater for a long time. He opened his mouth and gulped it in.

Slow Turtle left first, then Jared and everyone else, one by one. When Demetri emerged, he blinked and rubbed his eyes. Mama was waiting for him. She took his hand and walked him to the shore of the small lake. Everyone else was already in it, not caring that they were getting their clothes wet. He didn't care, either. He and Mama walked slowly into the cool water, stopping when it reached his chest.

"Feels good, doesn't it?" Mama asked.

He nodded. The sun was setting and an orange glow lit the sky, reflecting on the water. "Do we have to go back?" He looked hopefully at her. The water felt good and he couldn't imagine going back into the dark, hot tent.

"Yes, Demetri, we do," she replied. "We don't have the answer to our questions yet."

"But I don't have a question," he said.

"Don't you want to find out why you can fly?"

He didn't, really. He knew what he was supposed to do, and was only doing the sweat lodge to help make Mama less worried. He thought about what he should say. "It's okay, Mama. I already know why I can fly. It's to help the plants and animals. That's what I keep saying." As he finished, he noticed Slow Turtle watching them from a few yards away where he stood in the water.

Mama drew closer to him. "Well, I'd like to hear what Slow Turtle thinks about it."

They didn't talk any more until it was time to go back to the sweat lodge. "C'mon sweetheart." Mama took his hand and led him from the water.

Chapter Fifteen

MELORA SLID UNDER THE WATER and then stood up and let her head break the surface. Water dripped from her face and hair. Makeup was not allowed in the sweat lodge, so she didn't have to worry about it stinging her eyes. The pores on her face tingled from the temperature change of the spring-cold lake water. There were a few moments when she wasn't sure she could take any more of the sweat lodge's heat, but now she felt refreshed and ready for whatever else was in store.

"You still look like a mascara model even though you're not wearing any," Drew said, reminding her of their swimming race in a lake on Isle Royale. Afterwards, they had kissed for the first time. She had won the race but that paled in comparison to later winning his love.

She smiled mischievously and shook her hair for effect. "First you think I'm a motorcycle model, then a mascara model. Maybe you want to be dating someone in a magazine, not me!"

"You're the only kind of model I need." Drew leaned in and she kissed him, loving how his lips felt so soft and alive at the same time. She could have stood there, kissing him in the orange rays of the setting sun for much longer, but out of the corner of her eye, she noticed people leaving the water. She broke the kiss. "Guess we'd better go." Drew took her hand and they worked their way to the shore, the lake water pulling at their legs as if to keep them. In a way, she wished it would. Drew had been with her for almost two weeks and in four days, it was time for him to go back to Michigan. She didn't want him to go.

Once on shore, they toweled off and held hands as they walked back to the sweat lodge. Her wet skirt slapped against her legs. Melora supposed the water in it would heat up in the lodge and make it even hotter for her than before. But she thought she could take it. It was some of the other, more spiritual things, she was unsure of.

She and Drew walked by the fire pit, and each took a pinch of tobacco from Slow Turtle's outstretched hand. He was standing beside the fire, which was still burning bright. As they had done at the beginning of the ceremony, they sprinkled the tobacco into the fire in offering.

Then they ducked into the open flap of the lodge, Melora following Demetri in the same order as before.

"All my relations," Melora said as she crawled to sit next to Demetri and Samantha. Georgina entered and Slow Turtle came in last. Once he was seated, the door closed behind him and darkness enveloped them in velvety silence. Slow Turtle broke the stillness by chanting as he ladled water on the stones. The old stones must have been replaced with new hot ones because they hissed with more ferocity than before.

A wall of heat hit her face, and Melora fought an impulse to gasp. Her skirt clung to her legs and became hot. She imagined it must be steaming. Now Slow Turtle was silent. The pause stretched out until it almost became unnerving. Then he picked up the talking stick and set it in his lap.

"What I am going to say might sound funny, but I mean it in all seriousness." He paused. "What happens in the sweat lodge, stays in the sweat lodge—just as if you were in Las Vegas."

Melora suppressed a chuckle.

"The things I am going to say to you all are deeply personal and sacred. You need to respect that, and the other people who are in the lodge. This is a safe space, and we are bound by friendship and reverence inside it." He passed something to Jared. "Show me that you understand this by placing the sage onto the stones. Do it with your left hand."

Jared took a sprig and then passed the bunch to Samantha, who repeated the process. Once everyone had some sage, Slow Turtle nodded at Jared, who placed his onto the hot stone nearest him. Immediately, the pungent smell of the plant permeated the lodge. Everyone took their turn. Melora was impressed by how solemnly Demetri placed his sage, and how he didn't seem afraid of getting close to the heat of the stones. His actions gave Melora more courage than usual. She placed her sprig with a deliberateness that surprised her. The sweat returned to her skin and she could feel it running down her chest beneath her shirt.

Slow Turtle began drumming and chanting again. The beating of the drum reminded Melora of the piping plover ceremony and she felt she could hear the heartbeat of the Earth inside the sound. After a few minutes, he stopped and sat still. Then he picked up something and shook it.

"The noise of this rattle represents creation," Slow Turtle said, "the creation of life and the creation of the universe. When nothing existed, this sound was the *thought* of creation. It also reminds us we are the creator of our own lives. As such, we should think before we act. It is our responsibility to live in a good way—a spiritual way. Think upon what I am about to tell you . . . and then act in a spiritual manner to bring things to pass. The worst thing you can do after this ceremonies is not act on the information I give you."

He stopped shaking the rattle and passed it to Jared. "Keep this in your lap while I am speaking to you. Once I am done, you may pass it to Samantha."

"I will." Jared's voice was low with a little tremble.

"Jared, you are trapped inside the desires and cravings of your body. It is your challenge to resist the instruction of your body and listen instead to the instruction of your spirit. The body is not bad, but in this case, it is unwise because it has been abused. It is not strong enough to get well by itself. Your body and spirit must join in a common battle to defeat your addiction. You must make use of all the resources available to you—you know there are many offered by the tribe, yes?"

Jared nodded.

"But you must be ruled by your spirit and let it lead the way. As a member of the Bear Clan, you have a strong instinct for survival and healing. You must make use of these talents to fight your addiction."

Slow Turtle's calm, clear voice made Melora shiver despite the heat. She was sure if she were outside the lodge, the hairs on her arms would be standing on end.

He continued, "People look up to you to keep them safe. Your addiction will persist in letting them down. Your addiction will lower you in the eyes of your people unless you gather strength to fight it. Let this ceremony provide you with that strength. Know that you can call on me if you need, and I will do what I can to help you." Then Slow Turtle drew out something from a fold in his robe. As he held it out to Jared on the flat of his palm, Melora could see it was a black stone with several lumps on it.

"There will be times when you are alone. There's no way around this. And it will be those times when your own resources will be most important. Keep this with you for those times and draw strength and purpose from it. It is one of the weapons in your fight."

Jared held out both his hands and Slow Turtle dropped the stone into them. "Thank you, Slow Turtle," he said. After a moment, he passed the rattle to Samantha.

Melora would have loved to get a closer look at Jared's stone, but she couldn't during the ceremony. She supposed it was none of her business, but she couldn't help being curious about its shape.

Slow Turtle directed his dark, inscrutable gaze to Samantha. "Samantha, your boy is special. He is linked to the Creator more closely than most of us. That gives him the ability to speak with animals and to feel what the plants need. You must understand this and let him do his work. It is important. He was placed on Earth to right the wrongs we humans have done to it—to reverse the damage to the climate." He paused as if to let his words sink in. Even in the dimness, Melora could see Samantha take a big swallow.

"Demetri is just starting on his journey," Slow Turtle said. "As he grows, so will his powers. You must not let them scare you. They are of the Creator and for the good of humankind and the Earth. He is a climate changeling, if you will."

Melora gave a start as he said *climate changeling*. Of course! Why hadn't she seen that? She had been around enough people with the ability to change into something else—although Demetri changed his consciousness instead of his form. The idea excited her and scared her at the same time. She watched Samantha to see how she was taking the news. Samantha sat very still.

Slow Turtle continued, "You must guard him and protect him. Most people will not understand, so you must take great care to keep knowledge of his abilities within your circle of family and close friends. You must also counsel him as his powers grow. Someday, he will have great abilities and will need your guidance. But feel free to return to me if you need to. Georgina, I'm sure, will also be willing to help. You are not alone."

After a long pause, Samantha's voice quavered, "Thank you, Slow Turtle." Hesitantly, she passed the rattle into Demetri's lap.

The heat had settled around them now in full force. Melora fought to keep her breathing even and calm.

Slow Turtle began with a question. "Demetri, you have kept your abilities secret, yes?"

The boy nodded and said, "Well, except for Christine, and well . . . Mama and Trevor, but that was an accident." He thought for a moment. "I guess now everyone here knows, too."

Slow Turtle chuckled, a deep low sound. "Keep it that way. It is enough to have these people know." Then he took a long breath. "You bear a heavy burden, but it does not have to be that way. There is also great joy. Feel the love the Earth has for you, take care of it, and you will have a lightness of being you never thought possible. Keep eating and sleeping and growing. One day you will have the ability to change a great many things and you must do so wisely and with consideration. Do you know what consideration means?"

Demetri shrugged.

"You must think about your actions before you do them. Don't just try to impress your girlfriend." Slow Turtle chuckled again. "Your family and friends are here to help you. You do not have to bear this alone. Fly and keep flying. The Earth needs you."

Slow Turtle was silent for a moment, his eyes closed. When he opened them, he said, "Know that your father loved you even before you were born. When you help the Earth, you are helping him, since he is part of it now."

"Thank you, Slow Turtle," Demetri's tone was matter-of-fact, as if he already knew everything Slow Turtle had just told him.

Melora couldn't help but shake her head at his *chutzpa*. She wouldn't have been surprised if he did know it all already. Demetri handed her the rattle. She feared what Slow Turtle would tell her. His disclosures about the others had been surprising and deep, and somehow very true. What did he see in her?

"Melora," he began. "I know you said you are only here to support Samantha and Demetri, but you should know that you are like a bird— flitting here and there, never alighting for long. You know this is not good for you. You want commitment, but you are afraid. You can see the possibility of it, in your personal life and professional life. You need to overcome your fear and trust in the people and community around you."

Melora felt like he had taken her heart and turned it inside out. The next part, she swore he said with a twinkle in his eye. She almost wished the lodge was not so dark so she could see better.

"You are almost there. You need to trust that this time . . . things will work out for the best." He closed his eyes again and was silent. After a few moments, he opened them and said, "What I am about to say might only make sense to you and one other in this room."

As he waited to make sure she understood, Melora noticed everyone was looking sideways at each other as if wondering who Slow Turtle was referring to.

At her slight nod, he continued, "There was a reason you could not change—not become something other."

Instinctively, Melora knew he was talking about her decision not to become part of the wolf pack on Isle Royale. She felt Drew give her leg a light squeeze.

"It is because you are aligned with the birds. To us, birds are spiritual leaders. They are intuitive and can communicate with all levels of the senses. In common terms, they are known to have ESP. Their vision goes beyond the horizon, even into the spirit realm. For you to become something other would have been going against your basic nature. You must remember this and not regret it."

Slow Turtle's words were a great comfort. Melora had often grieved not becoming part of the wolf pack even though, as the alpha wolf had told her, it would not have been possible anyway. The alpha wolves could not join with more than one other human, and the pair of wolves were already joined with Lana and Drew. There had been nothing left for her.

But she wished she had fought more for Drew—not left him in the forest to become a family with Lana. They had lost so much time.

Melora realized that Slow Turtle had stopped talking several moments ago. Quietly, she said, "Thank you, Slow Turtle," and passed the rattle to Drew.

Slow Turtle looked to the lodge's low ceiling for a few moments, sweat dripping down the sides of his face, before his gaze fixed on Drew. "You also said you are here to support Samantha and Demetri, but I know that, although you deny it, you are close to the forest in a way few men are. It calls to you so loudly, sometimes you want to run into it."

Melora could feel Drew stiffening next to her as Slow Turtle's words sunk in. She recalled the conversation she and Drew had in the basement café after his return, when she asked half in jest, half seriously, *So you're sure you're not going to turn into a werewolf again and run away into the forest?* He had chuckled and replied, *No, Melora. You don't have to worry about that.*

Now it was her turn to stiffen. She felt betrayed. She had not sensed any desire in him to return to the forest. How could she have been so blind? All at once, the heat in the lodge became suffocating. It was all she could do to keep from running out.

Slow Turtle continued, "Although Melora is aligned with the birds, for you Drew, she is your anchor. She understands who you really are. Be patient, things will work out and fall into place as they should. Don't give up hope. Your time in the woods is over. Work on the water so that the call is not so great. You have helped your friends in the forest. Your place is here now, with people, and with your children. You must make peace with this or regrets will haunt you, much more than the call of the forest haunts you now."

His words made Melora feel better. She took slow, shallow breaths.

"Your children look up to you," Slow Turtle said. "As Melora is with the birds, you are with the wolves. Wolves are the scouts of the clan—the protectors. You need to make the way safe for those under your care. They are counting on you."

Drew bent his head into his hands, rubbing his forehead, hiding his eyes. "Thank you Slow Turtle," came from his lips slowly, his voice quavering. He passed the rattle.

Melora thought it fitting that Drew was of the Wolf Clan. However, at his obvious discomfort, she couldn't help but give his leg a squeeze in return for the support he had shown her.

"Georgina, my old friend." Slow Turtle's voice was full of warmth and the echo of times shared. "Thank you for bringing your friends here. It was a wise decision. You know that as a member of the Fish Clan, you can predict change and warn the rest of the community."

This made sense to Melora—when the wolves were in trouble on Isle Royale, it was Georgina who was drawn to the island. She told Melora she had felt called to it.

He continued, "Your good memory serves as a living record for the tribe. I'm sure it causes you to be impatient, at times, with others who don't remember for as long or as well as you do. But it is necessary that someone remembers the stories and can pass them on." Slow Turtle paused a moment, taking a towel to wipe the sweat from his eyes. "You must be sure you do this, Georgina—pass the stories on. Have you found someone worthy?"

Georgina nodded. "A girl from my clan."

"Good," Slow Turtle said. "Gaze into the stars that you know so well and share our history." He paused for a moment, eyes closed, hands resting on his thighs. "Demetri's coming is significant. It proves that the climate is changing and that the Creator needs our help to undo the wrongs done to the Earth. Warn your people, Georgina, as I will warn mine. We are on the cusp of great changes—unimaginable ones, even with Demetri's help. We need to support him as much as possible. Please be sure you visit with Demetri regularly, and Demetri—" Slow Turtle turned to the little boy. "Please come visit me every six months to begin with. I'd like to hear all about your adventures. And I'm sure you will have questions—lots of questions. I will do what I can to answer them."

Demetri gave him an emphatic nod.

"Georgina, it gives me great pleasure to see you again. May you walk with Kitchi Manitou, the Great Spirit."

Georgina passed the rattle to Slow Turtle, who shook it in the four directions. Then he put it down and started drumming. As he drummed, the men outside began to sing.

Chapter Sixteen

DEMETRI SKIPPED ALONG the sand, his hand in Melora's. The plovers had finally laid their eggs, so he was going to see them today. In person. Not flying. His mama was teaching a viola lesson, so it was just him, Melora, and Drew. They had ridden in Melora's car to the parking area by the airport and were making their way to the nest.

Demetri loosened his hand from Melora's to go look at something in the sand. He picked it up, cupping it. "Look, a ladybug!" He ran over to the grownups.

"That's cool, Demetri!" Melora bent down to get a better look. "I think that's the first one I've seen this season."

"Ladybug, ladybug, fly away home . . ." chanted Drew.

Demetri didn't like that song. They'd sung in it in preschool. The poor ladybug's house was burning and her children were gone. It just seemed mean. He closed his hands over the ladybug so it couldn't fly away. Then he opened his thumbs a sliver to look inside. "This ladybug's a boy. He's tired."

Demetri could not have explained how he knew this. Just from looking at the bug he sensed it was a boy. Then the image came to him of the ladybug flying over the water, along with the feeling that the water was a desert—a dangerous desert—because if the ladybug landed on it, it could drown or get eaten by a fish. All this he knew in an instant.

Melora looked at him and opened her mouth like she was going to talk. Then she closed it. She asked, "He's tired—how come?"

"He flew across the lake. It's a long way." The ladybug rested in his hands. He closed his thumbs and looked back to Melora. "Do plovers eat ladybugs?"

She looked thoughtful for a moment. "Well, they do like to eat beetles, and ladybugs are beetles, so I suppose so."

Demetri opened his hands and in a flutter of black and red the bug flew away. "We'll let the plovers eat some other ladybug, not you." He watched as it crossed the expanse of sand and landed near the water. He took Melora's hand again and kept walking.

"I'm sure the plovers will find other bugs to eat." Melora smiled at him.

Soon Demetri could see the log that marked the boundary of the site. Once they got to the log, Melora led him away from the water and closer to the dunes. She patted the two pairs of binoculars hanging around her neck. "We'll watch from back here. That way we won't scare them."

"Okay." Demetri ran ahead, excited to see the birds when he was with other people. Away from the beach, the bases of the dunes were covered with long grasses. The feel of the blades on his skin was both itchy and ticklish at the same time. Breathless, he turned to see where Melora and Drew were. They were walking slowly. He'd better wait. He didn't want to get into trouble like when he ran away.

Demetri scanned the beach for the nest. He thought he saw something move by the water, but he wasn't sure. While he waited, he crouched in the sand, picking it up and letting it flow through his hands. Demetri thought about what Slow Turtle had said during the sweat lodge ceremony—the thing about him being a climate changeling. That seemed to have both made Mama less worried and more worried, if that was possible. She treated him differently now, like she was more sure of him— she wasn't hovering over him so much or so nervous about how he did things. Then he would catch her looking out the window with sad eyes. It was as if the weight he sometimes felt after flying was also on her.

Demetri thought climate changeling was kind of a cool phrase. He had never heard those words before. Although he had gone through the ceremony for Mama, it did make him feel better to know there were words that fit what he did. He'd done his best the last few days to eat all his food and get good sleep like Slow Turtle had said. And when Demetri went to the cedars, it was nice not to have to keep it a secret. But the thing Slow Turtle had said about his daddy puzzled him. Mama had told him his daddy knew she was pregnant, but Demetri had often wondered if his daddy really knew about *him* since he died before Demetri was born. He had the feeling it was a mystery he'd never solve, but he liked the idea of the things he did for the Earth helping his daddy.

Melora and Drew were coming nearer. What Slow Turtle had said about those two hadn't surprised Demetri one bit. It had been obvious to him from the start that Melora was a bird person and Drew a wolf person. He didn't understand why everyone at the ceremony had been so impressed by that news. He could tell the same things about many of the kids who went to preschool—like Christine. She was a deer person, very caring and gentle. Good at art. Maybe someday he'd tell her about herself.

Plus there was something more that connected Drew with wolves. Demetri wasn't sure what it was—more like a feeling that Drew was joined with wolves somehow—almost like he was a wolf. It wasn't obvious from how he moved or acted, it was what Demetri sensed when he was around him.

Melora was approaching and Demetri noticed a distant look in her eyes. He guessed it was because Drew was leaving again tomorrow. Demetri wanted to see her smile, so he stood and jumped up and down a few times. "C'mon you guys, let's go see!"

"Sorry, Demetri," Melora said, "but you have to wait for us old folks to catch up!"

Demetri already felt like he had been waiting forever.

They walked farther into the dunes. Melora turned toward the lake and scanned the beach. "This is a good spot." She took one set of binoculars from around her neck and crouched near Demetri. She held the eyepieces up to his eyes. "Let me adjust these so you can see." She squeezed the ends together as far as they would go and held them on his nose so he could look through them. "Will that work?"

"Yep. I can't see the birds though, just a bunch of sand."

"Patience, patience, I'm just getting you set up." Melora removed the binoculars and stood. She walked a few paces and sat down. Demetri followed. Drew stayed standing, took the binoculars off his neck, and looked through them.

Melora gazed through the binoculars and turned a dial, then handed them to Demetri. "Look right there. You should be able to see the plovers."

As Melora removed her hands, Demetri parked his nose under the eyepieces and held the binoculars. He saw one plover sitting down in a cage-thing and the other was scurrying about nearby, looking for bugs. "I see them!"

"All right!" Melora said. "It's early for them to lay their eggs, so we're lucky to see them this time of year."

Demetri asked her about the cage and Melora explained it was the exclosure she had told him about before.

"How long do you leave it on?" Drew asked.

"Until the chicks hatch. Then it's not needed for protection anymore."

"Can the birds get out of it?" Demetri was doubtful, but before Melora could respond, the bird sitting on the nest got up and easily stepped through one of the wire squares of the cage, joining the other one. "Cool." Demetri said. "I don't have to worry about protecting them then."

"What's that?" Melora lowered the binoculars. Her gaze fixed on him.

Demetri couldn't believe he said that. Then he remembered they knew about him. "Uh, one time a fox was hunting the plovers. I stopped it."

"So *you're* the source of the mysterious force field! I should have known." Melora was quiet for a moment. "But then that means this *isn't* the first time you've seen the birds."

"No, but it is the first time I've had you with me to answer questions."

"Fire away," Melora said.

Demetri asked her more questions, like how long does it take for the babies to grow, will they leave for the winter like their parents, if they do, how do they keep up with them when they fly? Melora answered every question, except for, "Do plovers name their babies?"

"What do you think?" she asked.

Demetri was quiet for a moment. "Everyone names their babies, even animals."

"See?" Melora smiled at him. "What are you asking me for?"

* * *

Melora and Drew walked along the beach toward Duluth. They had dropped Demetri off at his house and had some time before they went to the Portage Café for dinner. Melora was glad for the opportunity to talk. They needed to clear the air, and she hoped it would make this last dinner together before Drew left less awkward.

It had taken more than a day before either of them had the courage to bring up what had been said during the sweat lodge ceremony. They'd had a conversation on Melora's couch over wine, and it hadn't gone well. It was as if the enclosed room had narrowed their thoughts and made their emotions small and petty. Talking in the open with the lake by their side was much better. The lowering sun cast its light on puffy clouds scattered across the sky.

They had ended their discussion on a stalemate. Now that she thought about it, Melora realized this was their first argument. She guessed it was about time, but wished the topic had been something more trivial and easily solved, like who should do the dishes. Neither of them had yelled. Somehow the topics were too serious for that. Melora almost wished they had yelled, maybe thrown a few things. It would have given her more release than this restrained respect she felt for him.

Drew was worried about Melora's commitment to him. If he uprooted his life in Michigan, how could he be sure she wouldn't dump him and "flit" away to some other man?

For Melora it was an issue of trust and of fear. Why didn't Drew tell her the forest still called to him? How could she trust him if he didn't tell her things like that? And what if the forest won like it had in Michigan and he left her? Melora didn't know if she could survive a separation like that. Not now.

She had hoped the ceremony would bring clarity about Demetri and bring their group of friends closer together. She didn't expect it to divide her and Drew. She had tried explaining to him that the men she dated after her divorce weren't serious affairs. They had all been poor substitutes for him, and that's why nothing lasted. She didn't deny she was afraid of her feelings for him and about their future. But she trusted him more than anyone else. That's why it was hard for her to understand why he didn't tell her about the forest. She wanted with all her heart to trust him, but she didn't know if she could.

Drew had admitted that Slow Turtle was right—the call was still there. That's why he had been so upset at the end of his session in the sweat lodge. "I guess I had buried it for the sake of my boys," he had explained. "But now I realize that, yes, all right, the call is still there. I enjoyed being a wolf—leading the pack instead of following someone else's orders. That is all still appealing. But there's no purpose in going back. The alphas are dead. The pack is safe. It would be pure selfishness to go to the pack now. Besides, I want to be with you. I wouldn't have come to you as soon as I could if that weren't the case. It was intentional, not just some whim."

His explanations had rung true, but they didn't make Melora feel any more secure. She noted that neither of them had mentioned the issue of her not becoming a werewolf—perhaps because there was no more to say. Slow Turtle's words helped Melora be at peace with it, and besides, it was so long ago. It was time to move on.

Drew reached for Melora's hand and gave it a squeeze. "It was fun to see how excited Demetri was about the plovers."

Melora turned to him. "Yeah, you'd think he never saw them before. That little stinker, he must not have been able to wait, so he flew to them."

"Good thing he did, though," Drew said. "He saved them from a fox."

Melora agreed, "But it's just that I wanted to be the first to show them to him." She sighed. "Oh, well, I guess that's just vanity on my part."

They continued walking, hand-in-hand, for several more steps. Drew ventured, "Have you had any new thoughts about us—our situation?"

Melora couldn't look at him. "No—no magic solutions have come to me. I did figure out the main questions we need to answer for each other, though."

"And what are those?"

She glanced over at Drew and found him looking at her intently. She couldn't handle the strength of his gaze, so she looked forward again. "I love that you came back here to spend more time with me. It's spoiled me. I wish you weren't leaving. But I understand you have to. Maybe this separation will give us the time we need to answer these questions." She paused for a few steps. "So the question I feel I need to answer for you is: what can I do to prove my commitment to you?"

Drew thought a moment. "Yes, I think that's the heart of it, except I'm not sure you can do anything. It might be one of those things only time will show."

"That very well could be," Melora said. "But will you use our time apart to think about it?" She gave him a ghost of a smile. "I'll think about it, too."

"Agreed," Drew said. "Now what's my question?"

Melora took a deep breath. She didn't want to spell out the situation. It felt selfish to her somehow—to ask this of him. But she had to. Their future depended on it.

"The question you need to answer for me is: how can you prove that you won't slip into the woods again? Like you were saying, maybe time will tell, but we each need some sort of proof from the other person to feel secure—to feel like we can trust each other."

"You're right, my lady," Drew said. "These are good questions. They'll give us something to think about besides how much we miss each other."

"Tell me about it," Melora said. "I know it's my turn to visit you. I'm not sure when. It depends on how the plover project goes. The eggs should hatch in a few weeks. I probably shouldn't leave until the chicks are partially grown. That might be until the end of June or so—a little over a month."

"That seems like a long time," Drew said.

Melora squeezed Drew's hand. "You got that right."

They strolled back to Melora's car. During their dinner at the café, Steve visited their table. The good food and conversation had helped the mood between them, but enough strain remained that once Melora and Drew returned to the duplex and went to bed, they both just lay looking up at the ceiling.

Drew took her hand and raised it, bending his elbow against the mattress. He moved his hand around hers, which was still.

"I don't want to go," he said, "especially with things like this."

"It's all right," Melora said. "We need time to think, to sort things out."

Drew's hand stilled. "Yes, but I'd rather we did it together."

"Me too," Melora said. "But what can we do? We both have jobs and lives. There's always the phone, you know."

"It's not the same." Drew's voice was low.

Melora turned toward Drew and hugged him. "I know, but it'll be all right. I have faith we'll figure something out."

You know that I love you, don't you?" Drew whispered.

Melora loosened her hug, so surprised she almost sat up. It was the first time he had ever said it to her.

"No." She blinked a few times. "Say that again."

Drew cleared his throat. "I love you, Melora."

Melora couldn't help the small squeal of happiness that escaped her throat. She resumed the hug and said, "I love you, too."

Chapter Seventeen

Monday, May 22

MELORA TYPED A FEW WORDS on her computer keyboard. She was composing an update about the plover project for Peg, which would also serve as a quarterly report for the project funders. She needed to get it to Peg today, and marveled that her brain was working well, unlike the first days following Drew's departure. Those had been filled with a mixture of euphoria over their shared love, loneliness, and confusion about their situation. All those feelings lingered, but they had boiled down to more manageable proportions.

One of the tasks she had been able to complete was working with the mayor on the letter to the FAA. After a few minor tweaks, all the partners had signed off on it, and the letter went into the mail with days to spare. She hadn't heard if the mayor had any response yet, but assumed no news was good news. He had been busy with press conferences and ceremonies for a new maintenance base for the local airlines.

The plovers were still attending to their nest. The monitors had managed to count three eggs. Several other plovers had visited the area, but none had stayed to nest. Melora sat back and tried to remember what a group of plovers was called. People had such funny names for flocks of birds. For crows, it was a "murder," for eagles, a "convocation." Oh yes, she remembered now that plovers were called different things depending on whether they were flying or not. A group of plovers on the sand was called a "congregation." A group of them flying was called a "flight." She hoped someday she would see flights of plovers over Park Point. She leaned in and started typing again.

Melora, focused on her report, barely noticed when Trevor entered her office. He settled in the chair next to her desk, a lock of his hair falling over his eyes and across the bump on his nose. "Hey, Melora, how's it going?"

Melora sat back. "Good—just working on the report for Peg."

"It's too bad none of those other plovers stayed." Trevor pushed the hair out of his eyes. "But at least we have one pair nesting. Do you realize how depressing it would be otherwise?"

"No kidding," Melora said. She hadn't had a chance to talk with Trevor about anything but business. "So how are things going with you?" She smiled and added, "And I don't mean just work."

Was it a trick of the fluorescent lights, or was Trevor blushing?

"Samantha's great. Since the sweat lodge ceremony, there's been a real change in her. She seems more relaxed. What did you think of the ceremony?"

Underneath the blush, Trevor looked relaxed, too, and happy. Melora didn't feel like it was her place to divulge anything that occurred during the ceremony—after all, what happened in Vegas stayed in Vegas. She kept her reply vague. "It was quite the experience. It changed us all to some extent."

"I know. I sure wish I could have gone, but I didn't feel it was my place," Trevor said. "My relationship with Samantha is so new." He paused. "It just didn't feel right to go."

"I totally understand," Melora said.

"She told me everything, you know."

Melora started feeling panicky that Trevor knew hers and Drew's secrets, however, he quickly added, "Samantha told me about Demetri . . . and herself. She told me what Slow Turtle said only about them."

"Then you know about the whole climate changeling thing?"

"Yeah, what the heck?" Trevor leaned forward and drew his hand through his hair. "It's crazy, but yet makes sense. Samantha and I have him to thank for changing the storm's course when we were sailing, I guess."

"And we have him to thank for saving the plovers from a fox." Melora waited for the light to dawn in Trevor's eyes. It did.

"Whoa." Trevor said. Then his look changed to thoughtful. "Sometimes I wonder if this is better or worse than something medical. At least a medical thing is explainable. This—"

"—is not explainable." Melora finished.

The two sat in silence for a while.

Melora decided to dive right in. "Are you ready to be involved with a woman whose son is a climate changeling?"

Trevor's reply was a question. "It fits in pretty well with the rest of my life, wouldn't you say?"

"I would!" Melora laughed.

"So how did Drew take the ceremony?"

Melora hesitated. She chose her words carefully. "It made him see some things he was blind to. We're still working it out."

"If you don't mind me being even nosier, how are you doing without him?"

Trevor's gaze was compassionate. Melora gave into it. "It's not easy being apart. I feel like something necessary—like air or water—is gone. I hate it, but I just can't see how I can visit him until the plovers have started to grow."

"If you feel that way, you shouldn't let the plovers stop you," Trevor said. "We can hold down the fort here without you."

"I know, I know," Melora sighed. "But I'd feel too guilty leaving so soon. I wouldn't have any fun."

"You're *way* too dedicated," Trevor said.

"Look who's talking," Melora shot back.

Trevor just shrugged. "You know—I figure I owe Drew."

This surprised Melora. In the past, Trevor seemed to think of Drew as a rival. She was curious what sparked the about-face. "How's that?"

"Without his trip here, and you two going to the beach together that first evening, you might not have ever met Demetri. If you didn't meet Demetri, I wouldn't have ever met Samantha."

Melora took a moment to follow his logic. "I guess you're right. But it seems to me if two people are fated to meet, it'll happen one way or another. Sometimes it just takes more time."

Trevor gave a little nod. "I guess that could be true. All I know for sure is that it was set in motion by his visit, and for that, I'm thankful."

Melora grappled with an urge to hug him. "That's a sweet way of looking at things."

"That's me, Trevor the sweet!" He gave her a self-deprecating smile and got up to leave.

"Hey, wait a minute," she said.

Trevor sat back down.

"You haven't heard anything about the FAA letter, have you?"

"Nope. Only that it got sent off. Today's the deadline, right?"

"Yes," Melora said. "It's just making me nervous we haven't heard any sort of confirmation yet."

"I'll give the mayor a call and see what's up."

"Thanks."

About fifteen minutes later, Trevor popped his head into her office. "There's nobody at the mayor's office who can confirm they've heard back from the FAA. Everyone who can is involved in the aircraft maintenance base ceremony."

Melora looked at the clock, which read four. "Shoot, I bet they won't be back in the office after the ceremony. Did you leave a message?"

Trevor nodded.

Melora debated a few moments about the wisdom of usurping the mayor's authority by contacting the FAA directly. She decided it was too big an issue not to contact the FAA. "Try and call our friend Bob, why don't you? I need to finish this plover report for Peg, and I don't want to be worrying about the letter all night."

"Will do."

A nagging voice in Melora's head was beginning to question her earlier confidence in the functioning power of her brain. Why hadn't she been more on top of this? What if something happened to the letter? An acquaintance who worked in the postal service told her that letters got lost more often than people realized. They were jammed in machinery, labels went missing or got caught on other letters, and mail was misrouted.

She sat back from her computer and put her head in her hands, massaging her temples. This couldn't be happening. She hoped Trevor would come back soon and tell her everything was copacetic.

He didn't. Instead he said, "Bob's gone for the day. He'll be in tomorrow."

Shit. It was going to be a long night after all. "Got any ideas what else we can do?"

"Well, I suppose one of us could go to the ceremony and ask the mayor. Or we could send Seth to do it."

"Do we know where it is?" Melora tried to keep sounding calm. She wasn't sure she was successful.

"No, but I assume it's at the maintenance base. I'll find out."

"Maybe call the mayor's office or something. I'll think about who should go."

Trevor turned heel and zipped back to his office.

In any other circumstance, Melora would send Seth. But she felt responsible for this—had too much at stake. She'd better be the one to go. Melora closed out the document. This was one of those times she wished her organization was hooked up to electronic mail. It was a couple years old and just beginning to catch on, but The Nature Conservancy hadn't sprung for it yet. It was the sort of thing that had to come from the national office, and their computer people weren't up to speed. She suspected the ability to use electronic mail might have avoided a problem like this. But then again, maybe there were just as many things that could go wrong with it.

Melora started putting her things away so she could leave. As she did, she wondered about faxing—that was another alternative. Had the mayor faxed a letter in addition to mailing one? She doubted it. They had days to spare after the letter was finished. Why would the mayor fax it?

Just as she finished packing up, Trevor came back. "The ceremony's behind the international airport, up on Stebner Road."

Melora nodded. "I got it. I'll let you know what I find out. If you're gone by then, I'll try you at home."

"Sounds good," Trevor said. "Good luck!"

Melora left the office at a jog.

* * *

Tuesday, May 23

Demetri soared over the trees through an overcast early morning. Before he flew anywhere else, he wanted to check on the plovers like he usually did. As he approached Sky Harbor Airport, Demetri heard the rumble of large machines. As he passed over the airport hangars, he could see them—two bulldozers and another large yellow machine he didn't know the name of. The bulldozers were crawling along on their belted tracks from the end of the runway to the white pine forest. The other machine just sat by the last hangar. He couldn't see a driver in it.

Demetri hovered a few moments to see what the bulldozers were doing. His curiosity turned to fear and anger when the first bulldozer lift its shovel and rammed into one of the beautiful large trees. The impact made Demetri's body double over, as if he were the one hit by the bulldozer.

He couldn't believe this was happening. Hadn't Melora said at dinner the other night that people were working to save the trees—even the mayor? That the trees would be left alone? The tree that was hit was still standing, but it had a big dent and the bark was scraped off. The other bulldozer wasn't far behind. It veered off to the side, heading toward another tree a few yards away.

Something must have gone wrong with Melora's plan. Demetri knew the noise from the bulldozers and from trees falling would scare the plovers off their nest. And he liked those trees. This could not happen. He had to do something.

Demetri spun around in the air, looking for something, anything, to help. Finally, he stayed still, looking over the lake instead of the trees, because they were upsetting him too much to think. The rumble and scraping sounds of the bulldozers continued. He guessed the second one must have hit the tree it was aiming for.

He thought about the force field he had used on the fox. Demetri wasn't sure he could make one big enough or strong enough to fend off a bulldozer. And now wasn't the time to experiment. His attention on the lake was interrupted. Off to the side, Demetri noticed a big fat bug flying toward him—a bumblebee. He wondered what it was doing up so high. Usually, they kept low to reach the flowers. Then it came to him—wasps. They could help solve this problem! He had seen a wasp nest in the forest, not too far from the dozers.

He flew as fast as he could to the nest, hovering outside it. The yellow-and-black insects were coming and going, a little more slowly than usual since it was still morning and the air was cool. Demetri enfolded himself around the nest. The sensation was unlike any he had ever felt before. He could feel the energy of several hundred wasps crawling around inside. It seemed as if they were crawling around in his stomach. It was creepy but he had to be brave to help the trees.

Demetri focused his thoughts on the nest and addressed the wasps. "Hello, friend wasps."

Immediately, he felt the insects stop moving. He supposed that was good.

"I'm here to let you know some bad men have come to hurt your forest."

Now he could feel some of the wasps jerk a little bit, like they wanted to fly and do something about the bad men.

"The men are driving big machines." He pictured the bulldozers, hoping the wasps could see them through him. "They're hurting the trees."

Now more wasps were jerking. A few had begun to fly out of the nest. He'd better say the next part of his message fast so he could be sure they did what he wanted.

"Don't hurt the men. Don't sting them. Cover their machines. The men will run away and stop hurting the trees. Just sit on their machines. Please?"

The wasps resumed crawling and a line of them started coming out of the nest. Demetri withdrew and started flying toward the machines to make sure the wasps knew where to go. But he needn't have worried. They seemed to know right where the bulldozers were.

Demetri sped over to the site. Already a few wasps were sitting on top of the roof of the cab. "Go inside, go inside!" Demetri instructed them.

The wasps on the roof flew under it and landed above the driver's head. Intent on backing up to ram another tree, the driver didn't notice. The first tree he had struck now lay toppled on the forest floor.

Soon, dozens of wasps came and started lining the sides of the cab. Demetri looked over to the other driver, who was skinnier than the first. The wasps had reached his bulldozer, too, although he didn't seem to notice either. However, when the insects started landing on the steering wheel, the driver stopped. Demetri could see him looking down, trying to brush them off the wheel with a gloved hand. He knew this would make the wasps mad.

"Don't sting the drivers!" He reminded them.

Then he saw both drivers look around their cabs at the writhing mass of yellow-and-black insects. The first driver turned off his engine and yelled to the other, "Holy shit! Let's get out of here!"

The skinny driver didn't wait to turn off his engine. He jumped from his machine and ran. When they were several yards away, the two men stopped and looked around, as if trying to figure out why no wasps were chasing them. They turned around and looked back at the bulldozers. The tops of the bulldozer cabs were now completely covered in wasps.

The bigger man scratched his head under his hardhat. "What the hell? You think one of the trees had a nest?"

"Could be," the other man said.

The big man looked around. "Let's wait over there." He pointed to a rock at the edge of the forest. "Maybe they'll leave after a while."

"Should I try and shut off my engine?" the skinny man asked.

"Be my guest."

Then the two looked at each other and burst out laughing. They walked over to a large rock and sat in the shade.

"Hope they leave before I run outta gas," the skinny one said.

Demetri twirled around in the sky. "Good job, friend wasps. You did it! Don't leave yet, though—stay until the men leave the forest." That took about an hour. By that time, the second dozer had sputtered and died. The loggers, disgusted, had walked to the hanger. Demetri heard them say something about making a phone call.

Demetri had not flown for this long before. His body felt heavy, and he knew he would need to go home soon. And he could feel the sharp impatience of the wasps to get back to their hive.

"Thank you, friends. You did a great job. The men are gone. I don't know if they will stay away. But the forest is safe for now." Demetri tried to share a feeling of gladness and thankfulness through his words. "You can go back to your hive. Please be sure and visit my home. There are lots of flowers for you." He sent them an image of the garden in his front yard.

The wasps left the bulldozers several at a time. Soon, they were gone.

Demetri flew back to his house and re-entered the grove and his body. He sat under the trees for a few moments, breathing deeply and stretching his arms and legs. That flight had taken a long time. He wasn't sure when he'd be able to fly again to check on the trees. He'd better tell Mama what happened so she could tell Melora.

He stood up and walked a few unsteady steps. Then he bent over so he could avoid the branches above the entrance to the grove. When he walked into the house, Mama was in the kitchen getting him a bowl of his favorite cereal, Captain Crunch. She looked at him and asked, "What's the matter?"

Demetri explained how he had been flying over the seaplane base when he noticed the bulldozers ramming into the trees. "You've got to tell Melora," he said. "Something's not right."

Mama put the cereal box on the counter and hurried to the phone.

Chapter Eighteen

MELORA WANTED TO REV the engine on her idling Prelude, squeal the tires and jump the empty expanse of water over the shipping canal. Who cared that five other cars were in front of her in Canal Park, waiting for the aerial lift bridge to lower? Maybe she could use them as a ramp to gain air.

She could *not* believe it—of all times to get bridged. She tapped her foot and pounded the steering wheel with the flat of her hand. She needed to get to Sky Harbor at the end of the point and find those loggers. Samantha had said they were stopped for now, but they could return and start the job again.

Her worst fears were being realized. After a fruitless search for the mayor yesterday—arriving at the airbase maintenance ceremony too late—she'd gone home to a fitful night's sleep, only to be woken this morning by Samantha's phone call about the loggers. Samantha had also mentioned something about Demetri and wasps, but Melora hadn't totally understood that.

That bastard Bob was no doubt smiling. She wouldn't have been surprised to learn that, even if the mayor sent the letter, Bob found some way around it to log the trees. Before she left home, Melora had made a quick, also fruitless, call to Trevor. She'd left a message for him, explaining about the logging and pleading for him to find the mayor and tell him what was up.

A ghostly gray ship Melora recognized as a limestone carrier crawled like a slow skyscraper under the bridge toward the harbor. It seemed like it was going extra slow just because it knew she was in a hurry—like the cosmos was conspiring to give her a heart attack.

She looked around on either side of the bridge. Where was that mythical Park Point Tunnel when you needed it? Residents liked to joke there was a secret tunnel only they had permits for, which allowed them to drive under the ship canal and bypass the bridge. It was a favorite April Fool's joke to post "Park Point Tunnel Permits" in their windows, just to make people wonder. Melora would have gladly paid two hundred dollars for such a permit now. Heck, make that five hundred.

The stern of the ship slid past her line of view, disappearing behind the Paulucci Building with its blue-and-white sign that proclaimed its name. Melora knew it was owned by Chun King Chinese food empire builder and local businessman Jeno Paulucci.

It would take a few more minutes before the bridge bell rang and the span lowered. Melora banged her head against the steering wheel. When she'd had enough, she looked in her rearview mirror. An elderly couple in the car behind her were looking at her like she was nuts. *Well, maybe I am. I'm a tree hugger bird freak on a mission. Cut me some slack!* She adjusted her view in the mirror and saw a red mark across her forehead. Her hair was disheveled. She hadn't taken time to brush it or shower before she pulled on some clothes. As she ran out of the house, Spencer had watched her with his head cocked.

Okay. She had to get it together. She should be using this time to think about how she was going to approach the loggers once she got to the airport. Try as she might, the only strategy she could imagine involved running in front of their machines and blocking the trees with her body. Or, all one hundred and twenty pounds of her could jump into their cabs and try to pull the men out. *Yeah, like that would work.*

Maybe she should meditate, sit here in the car and calm down, play some classical music.

The bridge alarm bell went off and the structure started to lower. She knew this meant another kind of torture was in store for her once the cars began moving. She predicted that this morning, for some reason, all of the cars in front of her would want to obey the fifteen-mile-per-hour speed limit going over the bridge. They would also obey the thirty-mile-per-hour speed limit the entire five miles of road to the airport. She gritted her teeth.

171

After what seemed like forever, the traffic light turned green and the gate arm rose, allowing the cars to pass. As she feared, the cars in front of her went the speed limit, but miraculously, after a few blocks, they either turned into driveways or onto side streets.

Melora gunned the accelerator, then laid off it until she was going a steady forty miles per hour—above the speed limit, yes, but at least the ticket wouldn't be too expensive. She figured it was worth the risk to save her sanity and the trees. She also figured it would be just her luck this morning to get pulled over and have to spend precious minutes explaining things to a policeman. She was gambling it was too early for them to be on traffic patrol.

After coming to a complete stop at the single stop sign on the road, she reached the airport in a few minutes. Normally, she would have parked in the lot outside and walked in, but she didn't want to waste time. As she had seen pilots do, she pressed the button on a pole outside the airport fence and a gate opened, allowing her entrance. She knew the gate would close automatically, so she gunned the engine and sped past the hangars. Once she was past the last building, she could see the bulldozers. She drove as far as the pavement would allow and then abandoned her car.

As she jogged toward the dozers, she could see two men standing beside one, talking. They weren't facing her, so she called out, "Hey, hello! Hello!"

The men turned and watched as Melora approached. The thinner of the two leered at her.

Melora swallowed and slowed her pace. She was just a few yards away from them. "I think there's been some sort of mistake here."

"You lost, missy?" the thin man said.

The other man whacked him in the chest with his plaid-covered arm. "What's up?" he asked.

"These trees aren't supposed to be cut," Melora said. "We sent a letter to the FAA outlining a different plan that the FAA agreed to when we met with them here."

"Well, that ain't our problem," the thin man said, drawing his hand through his sparse sandy hair. "We were told to cut these trees, and we are gonna cut 'em. No cutting, no pay. It's that simple."

The heavyset man looked her over. "Who you with?"

Trying in vain to smooth her hair, Melora told them she represented The Nature Conservancy and that she had the mayor's backing to save these trees, along with the airport's and other community groups. She didn't dare bring up the plovers. She suspected that argument would get nowhere with these two, elevator message or not. "Is the airport manager, Mark, here? He'll tell you." Melora stopped to catch her breath.

The thin man stepped toward her. "He ain't here yet. It's too early."

Melora took a step back. She looked around to see if anyone else was nearby who could help her if things got ugly. She couldn't see anyone. What she did see was one pine tree down and another with a big gouge into its bark.

Although Melora suspected the heavyset man would keep the other man in line, she couldn't be sure. She needed to invoke the name of someone more important to persuade these guys, so she said, "The mayor's on his way. He's not going to like this."

The thin man looked over to his buddy, then back at Melora. "Why would he care about a bunch of trees?"

"I told you, he's been part of the discussions about them. He's the one who's been dealing with the FAA."

The larger man raised his hands, exasperated. "Lady, we've had a delay this morning and we're behind schedule. Until we hear from the FAA, you're going to have to get back in your car and leave. We've got trees to cut."

"The mayor's coming," the thin man mocked Melora in a high voice. "Yeah, I bet." He walked toward her again. This time, Melora stood her ground as the man continued, "You think you can scare us? It'll take more than you and a bunch of bees to do that." He was close enough now that Melora could smell his rank breath—see the tobacco stains on his teeth. She didn't back down.

A car door slammed and all three of them turned. Melora's spirits rose at the sight of Seth making his way across the grass. It was all she could do to keep from running to him and giving him a hug.

Seth stopped in front of them. "What seems to be the matter, gentlemen?"

The heavyset man cleared his throat. "This lady here was just telling us not to cut these trees. But what's it to you?"

Seth took an instamatic camera out of his pocket. "I care because I'd hate to see you guys on the front page of the newspaper doing something this community doesn't want."

The men looked from the camera in Seth's hand to his face. Their complexions paled under their hard hats.

"My name's Seth. I'm from The Nature Conservancy."

"Now look here," the heavyset man said. "Why'd you have to go and take pictures?"

Seth paused, enjoying seeing the men squirm. "Let's just say it's for insurance."

The thin man's eyes darted. Melora wouldn't put it past him to make a grab for the camera. She stepped nearer to Seth so they presented a united front.

"What do you say you guys just hold on for a while until the big guns get here? You'll have your answers soon enough." Seth's smile was slow.

"Shit," the heavyset man rubbed his hands together as if shedding responsibility for the situation.

Just then, the crunch of gravel alerted them to another vehicle nearing. Trevor's Jeep pulled up next to her Prelude and Seth's car. Melora was glad enough to see that, but her happiness quotient tripled when the mayor stepped out the passenger side door. Trevor and Stewart walked over to the group.

"Gentlemen, I think you're familiar with Mayor Starkweather," Seth said, "and along with him is our co-worker, Trevor."

The men shook hands. The heavyset man introduced himself as Phil and the other as Stan.

"There's been a misunderstanding," Stewart said. "These pines aren't supposed to be cut."

"Well, sir," began Phil, "all I know is we were ordered by the FAA to begin cutting the trees today because they're a hazard for the airplanes."

Melora jumped into the conversation. "I told them about the agreement, but they wouldn't listen." She tried not to sound whiny, but wasn't sure she succeeded.

"I'm not sure what the problem is, but you need to stop this—" the mayor swept his arm to encompass the tree carnage "—until I get to the bottom of it."

Trevor didn't talk. He just stood by, smiling at the logger's discomfort.

Stan threw down his hard hat and began to walk away. "Whatever," he said.

With a bewildered look, Phil watched him go. He turned back to the mayor. "You're the boss," he said. "We'll stop until we get further orders. But you'd better call the FAA and explain, or we'll be out a day's wages."

"Thank you," Stewart said. "I appreciate it, and this community appreciates it. You should be hearing something soon."

Phil nodded and followed Stan.

After the logger was out of hearing distance, Trevor clapped a hand on the mayor's back. "Way to go, Mayor."

"Well, it's not over yet," Stewart said. "I don't know what happened. I sent the letter we wrote days ago. I guess I should have sent it certified, but I didn't think there was any need . . . I'll figure it out, that's for sure."

The group walked over to the downed tree for closer inspection. Melora reached out and touched one of the gouges in the trunk. It oozed sap like clear, sticky blood. She wiped her hand on her pants, but the sap was too thick. It stuck to her.

In his low and authoritative voice, Seth said, "It's too bad this tree got knocked down, but at least they didn't get any others."

"That was brilliant of you to take pictures," Melora said.

A sheepish look came over Seth's face. "Uh, the batteries are dead. You looked like you could use some help, so I grabbed the most threatening thing I could find in my car."

"That's even more brilliant!" Melora beamed.

"Those guys were giving you a hard time?" Trevor asked Melora.

"I was holding my own," she said. "But I was sure relieved to see you all. I'm so glad you got my message, Trevor. Thanks for coming on such short notice."

"Like I said, I'm going to find out what went wrong, and I'm going to give the FAA a piece of my mind. It might even be time to get our federal legislators involved." The mayor paused a moment. "Trevor wasn't clear about who reported the cutting. Can you tell me how you found out?"

Momentary panic. Melora looked from Seth to Trevor, then back to Stewart. No answers were forthcoming from their eyes, and there was no way she could tell the mayor that an astral-projecting little boy let her know. "Uh, one of the neighbors familiar with the project gave me a call this morning."

Trevor gave her a quick smile, letting her know it was a good answer. It was true, after all. Her reply also seemed to satisfy the mayor, who looked to Trevor and asked, "Can we head back?"

Trevor snapped to attention. "Yes, no problem." They turned and started walking toward the cars.

Melora wasn't ready to leave just yet. "I'm going to check on the plovers," she said to Seth. "I want to make sure this didn't scare them off."

"You want company?"

Still shaken from her encounter with the loggers, Melora agreed. She and Seth walked through the forest to the beach. The sun was higher and the air was warming. It looked like it was going to be a blue-sky kind of day.

"I wasn't getting anywhere with those guys," Melora confessed. "I'll have to remember that camera trick, or something like it if I'm ever in that kind of situation again."

"Well, Trevor called me, so I thought I'd see what I could do. I dealt with all types of people when I worked for the park service. You'd be amazed," Seth said.

Not for the first time, Melora silently gave thanks for having someone with Seth's experience on their team. "We'll have to get you out of the office more often."

Seth chuckled. "Nice hair, by the way."

Melora reached up and tried to smooth her hair down again. "I was a little rushed this morning."

Inspecting her, Seth said, "It probably scared the loggers as much as the mayor did—some wild banshee coming at them, trying to speak for the trees . . ."

"Well, the technique didn't work." Melora was tempted to tell Seth about the wasp attack the men had experienced, but decided it would bring up too many questions she couldn't answer.

They reached the edge of the trees and stopped to get their bearings. The plover site was just a short way farther down the beach. They kept to the tree line as they walked. Melora didn't have her binoculars, but she could see the exclosure without them. They stopped and watched for a few moments, letting out a collective sigh of relief when they saw both plovers running along the waterline.

"I'm so glad they're still here," Melora whispered.

* * *

BACK IN THE OFFICE later that morning, Melora took a phone call from the mayor. He said Bob claimed never to have received the letter. The mayor's office faxed him a copy of the original. That, combined with threats of a visit by one of Minnesota's legislators who chaired the national transportation committee, convinced Bob to relent. "But he didn't sound happy about it," Stewart said.

"What's that guy's problem, anyway?" Melora asked.

"Lord only knows," the mayor replied. "But we have our reprieve. They're going to remove the equipment and the downed tree as soon as possible. The trees are safe again."

Melora was relieved to hear the machines were gone, but she was still fearful for the trees. She didn't trust Bob, and neither did her peace radar. Well, that wasn't anything she could solve right now. Her mind jumped to the news media, who she knew would be interested in a story like this. "So what do we do if reporters get wind of the cutting?"

"Good question." The mayor was silent as he thought for a moment. "I don't think we want to issue a release or anything. I'd rather not call attention to it if we don't have to. But if you get any calls, refer them to me. I'll tell them there was a miscommunication with the contractor that's been cleared up now. Could you call Mark and Karen to make sure they know what's happened in case they get questions?"

"Sure," Melora said.

"And thanks for getting out there so soon this morning. Who knows how many trees saved."

"Well, it wasn't all me. I'm just glad we found out in time." Melora couldn't help the secret smile that appeared on her face.

"I need to go," the mayor said, "but we'll be in touch."

"You got it." Melora hung up just as Trevor came into her office. He closed the door behind him. They had an open-door policy, so this made Melora curious.

"Did any of the guys mention the wasps?" He sat in the chair near Melora.

"One of them mentioned something about a bunch of bees," Melora said. "But that was all. We didn't have a lot of time to talk before Seth came, and they weren't exactly the type of guys I wanted to have a long conversation with."

"I hear you there," Trevor said. "That skinny guy was a hothead."

"So what was the deal with Demetri and the wasps?"

Trevor explained how Samantha described Demetri's flight and seeing the men cutting the trees. "She said he knew he needed to stop it somehow, and the only thing he could think of was to get the wasps to help him. He told them they needed to land on the machinery to scare the men, and they did it. They didn't even sting them."

"So he can control animals then." Melora shook her head in amazement.

"Yeah, crazy, right?" Trevor ran a hand through his hair.

"Yeah, but I guess we shouldn't be surprised."

Trevor asked her if she told Seth about the wasps. "No. It would've raised too many questions, so I didn't bring it up."

178

"That's wise," Trevor said.

After they discussed Melora's conversation with the mayor, Trevor left so Melora could make calls to Karen and Mark so that they knew what had happened. She knew she should feel a sense of relief now that the plovers were safe, but she didn't. There were still so many things that could go wrong.

Chapter Nineteen

Wednesday, May 24

MAMA PUT A PLATE of homemade macaroni and cheese in front of Demetri. He loved mac and cheese, especially his mama's. Sometimes she cooked the box type but it tasted rubbery. Demetri blew the steam away, and it reminded him of how he'd blown away the storm clouds when they'd been sailing. Of course, he didn't blow as hard now as he had then. A small pile of green peas sat on his plate alongside the macaroni. He was wearing the leather pouch that Georgina gave him. It was tied onto one of the belt loops on his pants. He rubbed the outside of it, feeling the small lumps of the marbles and stones inside.

Mama sat opposite him for supper. Since they didn't have company, they ate at the small table in the kitchen, where they often ate breakfast. The radio played Mozart piano music in the background, exacting and soft.

"You make good mac and cheese, Mama." Demetri took a bite.

"Thank you, sweetheart." Mama picked up a fork full.

She had spent the day teaching lessons and Demetri had spent the day at preschool. Demetri liked how being away made him feel a little like a stranger in his own home. It made him enjoy things at home even more than usual.

Mama asked him how his day went and he told her about how they were trying to grow beans with wet blotter paper placed in drinking glasses. He didn't understand how plants could grow without any soil. Mama got this look in her eye like she was remembering something from long ago. "I did that in elementary school. It does work, you know. The beans will grow. But I never got to see how big they could get. I think school ended for the summer before they were done growing."

"Maybe I'll be able to tell you," Demetri said. "My school doesn't stop in the summer does it?"

Mama looked at him kindly. "No, Demetri. It goes all year."

"But when I go to regular school—that ends during summer, right?"

Mama told him it did. The two ate in silence for a while. Demetri admired the long strings of cheese that hung off his fork. He twisted the tines around to roll the cheese onto it. As he did, he thought about the loggers and the wasps. He asked, "Mama, is what I did with the wasps okay?" With his free hand, he rubbed the pouch again.

Mama stopped eating and looked out the back window. When she turned back to him, she said, "Yes, Demetri, I think it was okay. You stopped the loggers and you didn't hurt anyone."

"But I didn't think about it before I did it." At her curious look, he said, "Slow Turtle told me I need to think about things before I do them. I didn't think about it. I just did it. I saw a bee flying past and it gave me the idea. I just *did it*."

Mama extended her arm and patted his hand on the table. "It's all right, Demetri. You saw that the trees were in trouble and you saved them without hurting anyone." A slow smile came over her face. "You scared the men, yes, but that's the only way they would stop. As long as you don't hurt anyone on purpose, it should be all right." She removed her hand and looked at him, waiting for his reply.

Now Demetri knew he could hurt people if he wanted. He could have made those wasps sting the men to scare them instead of just covering their machines. He could see the men, running screaming away from the forest, welts rising on their skin. That might have been funny, but he could imagine how much it would hurt. Demetri didn't want to hurt anyone, ever. There was too much suffering around already. He thought of the wounded sparrow he had saved from the cat in the city. He wanted to do more things like that.

The piano music swelled. Demetri imagined the player's fingers moving fast over the keys. He took a bite of his macaroni and chewed. When he was done, he said, "I promise, Mama, I'll try not to hurt anyone."

"I know you won't, sweetheart," she said.

* * *

MELORA HAD SETTLED in for the evening. She sat on her couch and dialed Drew's number. Her heart beat faster in anticipation. They hadn't spoken in a few days, so Drew hadn't heard about the logging fiasco. Melora still felt responsible for it in some way. Maybe that was why she hadn't called him yesterday when it all happened.

"Hello?" His low voice soothed her nerves, but her heart still raced.

"Hey," she replied.

"Ah, Melorahhh. It's good to hear you."

"Same here," she said. Spencer jumped up on the couch next to her. Melora started petting him absent-mindedly.

They talked about mundane things. Then Melora got into Demetri's flight and the loggers. In addition to the wasp "attack," Melora had learned the loggers each suffered cases of poison ivy they claimed to have picked up on Park Point.

She and Drew laughed about that. Otherwise, he didn't seem as concerned about the trees as she had been. In fact, he seemed downright distracted. His voice kept trailing off. Melora asked him if anything was wrong.

"I've had my boys with me since I returned. Lana hasn't told me when she wants them back at her place," he said. "They're sleeping now, so I can talk about it, but the situation is starting to worry me."

Melora's heart started a slow ache, for both Drew and his boys. She saw how spending so much time together could be both a good and a bad thing—good in that they were with each other, bad for the uncertainty it created. She let Drew continue.

"When I asked her about it earlier today, she wouldn't answer. She just kept talking about all the things keeping her and her boyfriend busy. They're going here and there, doing this and that. I just let her go on, knowing I wasn't going to get an answer."

"You sound sad," Melora said.

"Well, I am for the boys, but also . . . I was hoping that the next time we exchanged them, I could feel her out about sharing Jason and Tony if I moved. Now, I don't know when that's going to happen. It's no huge deal. It's just frustrating." He paused. "I'm just trying to get some clarity about my life, and she's making everything muddy."

"That's what exes seem to be good at." Melora wasn't sure her attempt at consolation was working. Part of her thought maybe it was a good thing Lana didn't seem to want the boys back, but she suspected this was not the right time to bring that up.

"I'm just so afraid we won't be able to work something out—that she'll want to keep them here and I won't get to see them."

She tried again to console Drew. "You just have to have faith things will work out. You'll get to talk to her in time. She's selfish, yes, but not unreasonable. I've heard that when parents split, it's best if the kids still get to see them both somehow. If you go into it thinking about the kids and not so much about yourself, you guys might be able to work it through." Melora paused a moment. "You might have to remind Lana not to think so much about herself, though."

That got a small laugh out of Drew. Melora continued, asking him how his boys were doing. He brightened, talking about their personalities and quirks. "Tony, you know, the youngest—he looks like me." Melora thought she detected a note of pride in his voice. "He can be timid sometimes, but he's curious—and that always overcomes any hesitation he feels in situations that are new to him."

"And what about Jason?" Melora asked.

"He looks more like Lana—red hair, green eyes. He's a good big brother to Tony—always sticks up for him when he needs to. But he can be a little lazy sometimes. I have to remind him about his chores more than I do Tony."

"I can't wait to meet them," Melora said, and she meant it. She would adore seeing these little pieces of Drew someday. Eventually, the conversation came back to the plovers, and Melora told Drew about the trouble she was having believing the birds were safe from logging in the future. "I don't know what else I could do besides camp out on the beach," she said.

It was Drew's turn to console her. "You have Demetri looking out for them, and the monitors. If anything else happens, they'll let you know."

"Yes, but will they let me know in time?"

"I wish I could answer that," Drew said. He asked her how the birds were doing, and Melora told him about the latest reports from the monitors. Later in the conversation, they both admitted to thinking about their stalemate questions.

"You have any break-throughs for your question?" Drew asked.

Melora sighed. "No, sorry. I've been wracking my brain, but I don't know how I could prove my commitment to you." Her voice lowered, "I mean, I love you, and I want to be with you. Other than saying it . . . what more can I do? How about you—have you learned anything new about your question?"

Drew sighed as well. "I wish I could say I did, but I haven't." He sounded defeated. It felt like one unsolvable problem was starting to stack up on another.

Even though their conversation was frustrating, Melora could feel an undercurrent of love and respect running through it. After hanging up, she gazed at the city lights twinkling out her window. She and Drew needed to hang onto that love; it was what would see them through these problems and others that arose in the future. If their love was one of the lights below, which would it be? She gazed for a while and chose a bright white light by the harbor. It shone strong and clear, larger than the lights that surrounded it.

But Melora knew how ephemeral love could be. All it took was for one of them to have a change of heart or mind, and it was over. All it would take was one well-aimed rock to knock out that light by the water. How could she open herself up to that? *Not this old argument again*, she thought.

Melora sighed and laid her head on Spencer's shoulder, remembering the sweat lodge ceremony. It all seemed like a smoky dream now. Hadn't Slow Turtle told her things would work out for the best this time? They'd had a potluck supper after the ceremony, and although everyone enjoyed each other's company, there was a look of rawness in everyone's eyes. All their secrets had been laid bare. She felt that way now: bare, exposed, raw. Why in the world had she told Drew she loved him?

Because she did. And he had said it to her first in the dark in her bed. It was only polite to respond in kind. But she wasn't just being polite. It was real. She wouldn't say those words unless she meant them. She was in big trouble.

Spencer whined and licked her cheek.

Chapter Twenty

Monday, June 19

MELORA PARKED HER CAR in the lot by the Sky Harbor Airport and started along the beach to the plover site. It was evening. A mist had hung in the air for most of the day, but it burned off late that afternoon, and the sky was a clear turquoise blue. The warm, still air caressed her as she strolled alone through the sand.

The plover chicks were a few days old. This was Melora's first opportunity to visit since their hatching. Normally, she would be hurrying in anticipation, but she was tired. It had been a long work day and she missed Drew. They had talked on the phone again last night. Although there was no change in their stalemate, there were new developments with the boys.

Lana had announced to Drew she was moving to Australia with her boyfriend. She said that Drew could have the boys, but she intended to visit them or bring them to visit her several times a year. Drew got the impression Lana's boyfriend wasn't into children, and the boys disliked him. Lana was working on documents giving Drew full custody. So the boys would be his to take where he pleased.

This was a great relief. Although Melora suspected the lure of Australia was just more exciting than Michigan to Lana, part of her hoped the woman had seen how torn Drew was over the situation and that she decided to give him a break for once.

Lana wasn't moving for a few weeks, so she could take the boys if Drew wanted to make another trip to Minnesota. And he did, although Melora protested that it was her turn. But Drew knew how important the plover project was to her, and how worried she was something else unexpected would happen, so he wouldn't hear of her leaving Duluth now. Melora was grateful for his understanding.

Melora could see the boundary log coming up. She knew the plovers could be ranging outside the site with their chicks, so to avoid them, she started traveling inland toward the dunes. But before she left the water's edge, she turned to the lake and let her gaze settle on the flat horizon. She closed her eyes and took a deep breath. Spontaneously, she raised her arms to shoulder height, as if to hug the lake. Energy seeped back into her. A sense of freedom and well-being surrounded her. It was so peaceful. Melora lowered her arms and opened her eyes, becoming self-conscious. She looked around, but did not see anyone pointing and laughing at her.

She chuckled and turned inland. The sand was still warm from the afternoon sun. It sifted soft and gritty between her toes in her sandals. Melora kept to the low spots between the dunes, the grasses whispering her passage. She tried not to step on the thin strands of greenery since she knew the grasses were rare and easily disturbed.

Seth had spoken with her earlier that day. He had contacts in the Twin Cities who knew FAA Bob and had shed some light on the man's motivations, or lack thereof. Seth said that Bob used to date an environmentalist. The woman had worked for one of the nonprofit groups active in Minneapolis. Their relationship ended on a bad note, so to exact a strange sort of revenge, Bob had it out for any projects that carried the faintest whiff of environmental preservation.

That must be why his eyes were so flat during my descriptions of the plover project, Melora mused, *and why my peace radar was buzzing an alarm.* She felt sorry for him, but really, a failed love affair was no reason for him to interfere with projects his former girlfriend wasn't attached to. Or any projects she *was* attached to, for that matter. It would have been like

Melora hating all wolves after Drew had decided to live with them. And, of course, she didn't. *Men. Some men.* It was too bad.

During the past few weeks, Melora had watched Trevor and Samantha grow closer. Samantha often stopped by the office to visit, and she had seen them at musical events or sailing the *Pilgrim Soul*, sometimes with Demetri, sometimes not. Melora was happy for them, and perhaps a bit jealous, too. She wished she and Drew could see each other as often.

Melora sighed and paused at the water's edge, scanning for signs of the plovers. Seeing a blur of orange legs, she took up her binoculars. The tan and white plumage of a plover filled her view. She watched a few moments. Then, wanting to be closer, she walked through the dunes. From her research and the reports of the monitors, she knew they weren't as skittish now that they weren't nesting. The chicks could run almost as fast as the adults, and she guessed that made the parents less wary.

When she was about twenty-five feet away from the water, Melora stopped. She watched for a while without the binoculars, not wanting to have the artificial device between her and the birds. She marveled at the three chicks. They zoomed around the adults like brown-spotted cotton balls on little stick legs. She felt a grin of delight cross her face. She couldn't believe how small and fast they were. The monitors had removed the exclosure. Now that the chicks were off the nest, the plovers didn't need its protection. Soon, the monitors would catch the chicks and band them—putting light-weight colorful strips of aluminum around their legs. Once the chicks grew and migrated, the bands would help plover monitors in other parts of the country identify them.

The chicks reminded Melora of Demetri. She supposed it was because he was a little chick of a human. And it was partially thanks to him this small family had survived. One recent evening after work, Melora had been mingling with the tourists at the ship canal. She'd seen Demetri waving with Samantha from the stern of the *Pilgrim Soul* as Trevor piloted it under the lift bridge and between the piers, out into Lake Superior. Demetri seemed to be thriving.

Such a burden he carried—the burden of the entire planet. Since the sweat lodge ceremony, Melora had been researching climate change—what was known about it, what was being done. She was puzzled her own organization, The Nature Conservancy, wasn't doing anything about it yet. She'd have to see if she could change that. Only international organizations like the United Nations seemed to be tackling it. Yes, the problem was global, but there were things that could be done in the U.S. to affect it. Perhaps car manufacturers could produce cars with better gas mileage. Maybe changes to fossil fuels could minimize carbon emissions. More trees could be planted—something, anything. Although Melora couldn't quite grasp what climate change would mean for her hometown of Duluth, she knew it was a vital issue, now more than ever since Demetri's purpose had come to light.

The plover chicks still scooted here and there on the sand. Melora moved closer, almost without realizing it. What would climate change mean to birds like this? Would it make it harder for them to migrate because of more storms? Would the beaches they needed for nesting be wiped out by wave action and higher lake levels? Would the bugs they ate become scarcer as temperatures changed?

She wished she knew. It comforted her that Demetri was here. It meant that God, the Great Spirit, the Supreme Being—whoever—was aware of the problem and was going to set it right, despite the ignorance of most humans. The one thing she knew for sure was that she would help that little boy however she could.

One of the plover parents called to the other, "Peep-lo, peep-lo." Its song was so melodious and light, Melora's thinking jumped to past changes that had occurred on the Earth. That birds might once have been dinosaurs was a concept as challenging to grasp as climate change. How could the plover's song have evolved from a heavy, roaring dinosaur?

But maybe paleontologists and movie producers had it wrong. Perhaps dinosaurs didn't roar. Maybe their voices were light and sweet all along and their bodies just grew into shapes that better matched their songs. She liked the idea of flesh conforming to sound. What adaptations might birds develop to cope with climate disruption—if they could adapt fast enough? She knew that the levels of carbon dioxide in the atmosphere were rising faster than ever before. How could anything adapt to that?

And what if birds couldn't adapt fast enough and became extinct? What difference would that make? Melora remembered the Hawaiian Shirt Man who had criticized the plover project. It had been hard enough to come up with a response to his criticism about protecting shorebirds. What if someday they needed to justify protecting all sorts of birds? Melora mused for a while about why birds mattered. She supposed arguments could range from the amount of revenue bird watching brought into communities, to maintaining the web of life, to their beauty, to what they could teach us about flight, to pest control, to dispersing seeds, to things humans couldn't even imagine yet.

It bothered her even to have to think about justifying a species' existence. It smacked of hubris. Birds mattered because they were here. If they were here, they were important.

Melora walked nearer to the plovers until she was out of the dunes and onto the broad expanse of sand. She watched as both parents worked together to feed the chicks and look for predators. Demetri had said the plovers named their babies. She wondered what the chicks' names were.

Her approach didn't seem to bother the birds, perhaps because her movements had been so gradual. Waves gently lapped the shore. Sometimes the plovers got their feet wet, other times they didn't. She couldn't see any rhyme or reason to it.

She stifled a laugh as both the male and female brought an insect to one of the chicks at the same time. The chick just stood there as both parents tried to feed it. Finally, the female realized the technique wasn't going to work. But instead of going to find the other chick, she waited until the beleaguered chick had eaten the offering the male had, and then she fed it.

The scene caused a pang in Melora's heart. One parent was not flitting away, doing its own thing. Both were engaged in taking care of the chicks. There was no question about their commitment to the chicks and to each other. There could be no other way, it seemed. Melora wasn't sure she would have noticed these things before her experiences of the past few weeks—with Drew coming back into her life and making her think about commitment, with meeting Demetri and Samantha, and from hearing the revelations by

Slow Turtle. If she didn't know better, she'd say she had grown. She had started to care about things beyond herself—to learn to call another's name more than her own. And the plover project was her way of giving back to the community as well as giving back through supporting her friends.

It seemed like everything was coming together—like she'd been part of a great circle that was missing a large section. Now that section was sliding into place, smoothly and quietly but with purpose. If her head and heart were not linked yet, they were well on their way.

The sun was beginning to set over the Duluth hills, the sky changing from periwinkle-blue to a pinky-red, and the underside of scattered clouds glowing. The plovers made their way closer to her until they came within a few feet. She could make out the individual speckles on the chicks' backs—see their shiny dark eyes. She stood motionless, almost afraid to breathe. Now the parents approached, treating her as if she were nothing more than a rock or a log on the sand. One caught a fly and fed it to a chick. Such a never-ending job, this caring for the young; would it be like that for her if she ever had a baby?

If it was, she sure hoped she would have help. Drew seemed like the type to stick around. He already knew what taking care of children was about. She remembered their first night together after so many years apart. Hadn't he been the one to bring up the idea of having children? He had been half-joking, but she could tell from his eyes there was seriousness to his statement, too. Would she be able to handle having a family? What if the demands became too overwhelming and she bolted—handed Drew the baby and said, "I'm outta here"?

Deep down, she knew she'd never do that. Her innate sense of responsibility wouldn't let her. But she'd have to stay with Drew if they were to raise a family—stay with him for a long time. No flitting away. Could she handle that? And there were Jason and Tony to consider. She'd have a ready-made family if she and Drew continued their relationship. She hoped to meet the boys soon, and see how it felt to be with them.

Melora looked up from the sand and saw the sun's rays shining over the crest of the hill, spreading across the sky in multi-color beams, tracking patterns in the water. The birds continued to mill about her feet as if she were a rock, or better yet, one of them. The brightness seemed to enter her eyes and go directly to her heart where it spiraled and spread through her ribs, to her shoulders and down her arms. She wanted to lift her arms again like she had before at the water's edge. She hesitated, not wanting to scare the birds. But the feeling seemed to demand it of her.

Slowly, she raised her arms to shoulder height, unbending. She didn't want to take her eyes off the light. She let it infuse her. Sensing the birds were not skittish, she continued to raise her arms over her head. She held them there, half expecting light to shoot out through the tips of her fingers as if she were a conduit. If she opened her mouth, the light would shoot out from it, too, like she was some supernatural character in a novel.

Melora stood, arms straight up, for several minutes. Then she closed her eyes and lowered her arms. She looked down at the birds and they were standing around her in a half-circle, facing her, watching her. She dared not breathe, much less speak. A wisp of a breeze broke the spell and the plovers scurried away on bird business, as if nothing unusual had happened.

Chapter Twenty-One

Saturday, September 2

REW AND MELORA STOOD at the bow of the *Voyageur II* watching the waves. Drew stood behind Melora, his muscular arms and a Hudson Bay wool blanket wrapped around her to ward off Lake Superior's chill. Only a few other hardy souls had joined them in the elements for this initial open-water part of the crossing to Isle Royale. The rest of the passengers, who were tourists or Melora and Drew's friends, crowded into the cabin or the more protected outdoor seating area in the stern.

Melora grinned into the bow wind, feeling the spray on her face. Her heart felt full to bursting. They were going to the island to be married. Drew had asked her "the question" at the end of his third trip, figuring out it was the best way to answer both of their stalemate issues and would allow them the opportunity to prove their commitment to each other. He wouldn't go running off into the forest and would pledge himself to her. She would face her fear and not flit off to some other man.

The symbol he presented to her was an Isle Royale Greenstone ring. It was a large trapezoidal stone with a distinctive green pattern like the back of a turtle shell. Greenstones were only found on the island. The stone was set in thick gold with three diamonds nestled next to it. Melora couldn't keep from gasping when Drew pulled it out of a velvet pouch he retrieved from his jeans pocket, and got down on one knee.

The spot he chose was on the rocky shore of Lake Superior near Uncle Harvey's Mausoleum on the Lakewalk, close to where they had talked when he arrived in Duluth on his first trip.

Looking up at her, Drew began.

"You know, when I first came here and saw this mausoleum—" he cocked his head toward it "—I was worried it meant my idea to come here would be a failure. I thought my feelings for you were so strong, just like this place is strong. It's withstood the wind and waves for so long, yet it turned out to be a bad plan. I was worried you wouldn't need me—didn't want me after so long."

Melora remembered having some of the same worries during Drew's first visit—that he wouldn't want her after so long. And of course, Drew was so misguided in his fears she wanted to protest. Before she could, he began again, speaking words she would never forget.

"Slow Turtle was right. You're my anchor. You understand who I am. You're my rock. Since we met on The Rock, I thought it appropriate that I present you with a piece of it to prove—" he faltered and took a deep breath. "—to prove that I love you and I want to spend the rest of my life with you."

Melora felt the blood rushing from her head. She swayed.

Drew's eyes were shining. "I want to take care of you and be with you. Melora St. James, will you marry me?"

Unable to stand any longer, Melora fell to her knees. She hugged Drew and whispered in his ear, "Yes, Drew," and then louder, "Yes, I'll marry you."

They stayed together for a while, feeling the eyes of passing tourists upon them. When they parted, Drew clasped her left hand and brought the ring near.

Melora was curious to see if the ring would fit. She made a move to reach for it. But before she could try it on, Drew said, "Here, let me." He gently held her ring finger and slid the ring on. It fit perfectly.

Melora held out her hand to admire it. "Oh, it's beautiful!" She hugged him again. "I love you!" She wanted to hold onto this moment, and Drew, for as long as she could. Finally, she said, "I'll have to get you one!"

"Me, a ring?" Drew pulled away from her, seeming puzzled. "I don't need a ring, not until we're married, anyway."

"But I want to get you one! I want everyone to know you're promised to me."

"Possessive, are you?"

"And you're not? Why am I wearing this ring then?"

"Oh, all right, if you think you must."

The next day, she had bought him a greenstone ring with a stone a bit larger than hers, surrounded by gold. He didn't want any diamonds, though. He said those were too froufrou. They decided to wed as soon as they could—they didn't want to waste any more time. Once they were married, Drew would move to Duluth with his boys, and he'd try to find work on the water.

In the convening months, Melora managed to visit Drew in Michigan and met Tony and Jason. To her relief, the visit had gone well. When she first saw Tony, Drew's son who was about the same age as Demetri, there was no mistaking Drew in him. His eyes were the same luscious brown, his hair dark chestnut. He had struck her as pleasant—a little timid sometimes, but all boy—into trucks and cars, and anything that could get him muddy.

Jason, the six-year-old, had Lana's red hair, fair skin, and green eyes. He always seemed to be watching and gauging people's reactions. There was something calculating about him, but he liked telling jokes and seemed to be constantly moving.

The boys got along well together and seemed to enjoy Melora's company during the outings Drew took them on among the hemlock pines on the Old Mission Peninsula, a long spit of land outside of Traverse City that reached into Lake Michigan. She felt she could grow to care for them and welcome them into her life. Melora had always suspected Drew was a great father, and it was nice to see it confirmed. The two of them had discussed how to break the news to the boys about all the changes about to take place. They had decided it was best to reveal one thing at a time—first the engagement, then the marriage, then the move to Duluth, and their mother's plans to move.

After seeing how well everyone got along together, on Melora's last day with them, Drew told them about their engagement. Jason thought it was "cool," and soon his excitement brought Tony around. They were also excited to hear that Melora had a dog. Tony had always wanted a dog, but complained his mom wouldn't get one because, as he said, she didn't want the "'sponsibility." Melora had left them with hugs and promises they could visit her in Duluth and meet Spencer.

That meeting had taken place yesterday, when they arrived with Drew by car. Spencer and the boys got along so well together that Melora and Drew had to take them outside to romp, so they wouldn't break anything in her house. The dog treated the boys like they were puppy playmates—running with them, nipping their legs, rolling together on her small lawn. To the boys' delight, Spencer loved playing catch, and they spent a good hour doing that once they discovered he knew this particular skill.

Watching the boys play with Spencer had done much to dispel any doubts Melora had about how they would adjust to their new lives when the time came. Drew had told her later that the paperwork was almost complete for his full custody, so it was becoming a reality.

Under the blanket, Drew's hand caressed Melora's waist, breaking her reverie. Melora put her hand over his, feeling the ring on it. Another wave of happiness rose in her. On impulse, she turned and saw that both Georgina and her captain husband Ben were in the pilot house. Melora waved to them. Georgina waved back, and Ben gave a short blast to the *Voyageur*'s horn, which made them both jump and laugh with surprise.

They were about halfway to the island, headed for the western end and the Windigo Ranger Station. There they would take on new passengers and let others off. Their destination at the end of the six-hour trip was Rock Harbor, on the far eastern part of the forty-mile-long narrow band of land in Lake Superior. The ship would follow close to shore, paralleling the island and tucking into several protected bays to pick up hikers and drop off mail and groceries for any lingering summer residents and commercial fishermen.

The boat trip would be shorter than usual because there were fewer fishermen and residents. Some had lost their motivation to continue their businesses in the face of government bureaucracy or lost their life-leases for property with the death of a family matriarch or patriarch. Also, it was the end of the season and many had fled the oncoming winter.

On board with them were Demetri, Samantha, and Trevor; and June and Steve, who were in the cabin taking care of Drew's sons. Dogs weren't allowed on the island, so Spencer was at a boarding kennel. Melora and Drew had timed the trip to coincide with the exit of most of Rock Harbor Lodge resort's employees. The lodge was still open, operating with a skeleton crew. The last time Melora and Drew had been on the island, they had stolen the resort's tour boat to help the wolf pack escape. Even though time had passed, they didn't want to take any chances on being identified. June and Steve had made discreet inquiries among the friends they still had working at the resort to make sure hardly anyone would be left who knew Melora and Drew.

After standing in the bow and hugging for a few more minutes, Drew said, "We'd better go to the stern and socialize, before I ravish you." Melora laughed and Drew slid the blanket off, giving it to her. They soon found Samantha, Trevor, Demetri, and Tony sitting on the cushioned seats that lined the low wall along the stern.

"Where's Jason?" Drew asked.

"He's in the cabin with the others," Samantha said.

Melora watched Tony and Demetri, who were sitting next to each other. They each had a small metal race car, and they were driving them along the cushion and atop the gunmetal-gray wall. They'd race them as far as their arms could reach, leaning across each other, then reverse directions, driving over Trevor's leg when necessary.

"Come sit by me," Samantha motioned to Drew and Melora, patting the empty cushion beside her. Drew sat closest to Samantha and Melora sat next to him. Melora spread the blanket out over their laps.

"This is going to be so fun," Samantha said. "So tell me about the ceremony. The plans happened so fast, we haven't had time to talk. Who will do it, and where will you have it?"

"Technically, since I have my boat captain's license, I could do the ceremony," Drew said. At Samantha's surprised look, he added, "No, no, that's just a myth, and it would be self-serving. But it happens that Ben is both a captain and licensed to perform marriages, so he's agreed to do it for us."

"It's so wonderful someone you know will be doing the ceremony," Samantha said. "That'll make it more meaningful."

Although Melora didn't think they knew Ben that well, when she had mentioned the wedding to Georgina during a phone call, Georgina had insisted. Melora didn't have any ties to churches, so having Ben do the ceremony seemed fitting, and Drew liked the idea of being married by a ship captain.

Drew just gave Samantha a nod. "We decided to have the ceremony tomorrow afternoon. That'll give us time to settle into our rooms, have a good sleep, and show you and the boys around the compound before the ceremony."

"I've heard so much about Isle Royale, but I've never been here. I'm looking forward to seeing it in person," Samantha said.

"It means a lot to us to show it to you," Melora said. "We're going to have the ceremony on the *America* dock—it's near the lodge, just down a short nature trail. The dock was a great place to sleep outside when Drew and I worked there, and everyone should fit on the main section of it. Plus, we wanted to be close to the water."

"It sounds lovely." Samantha leaned against Trevor and took his arm.

"Uh-oh," Trevor said. "*Some*body's getting ideas!"

Samantha's tone was one of mock innocence, "Who me?"

"We could always make it a double wedding, you know," Drew teased.

Samantha and Trevor looked at each other.

"Um . . . we're not quite there yet," Trevor said, gazing into her eyes.

Samantha finished the thought, "But maybe. Maybe someday."

"Definitely maybe," Trevor said.

Melora hoped he wouldn't change his mind about that.

Demetri had stopped playing. He looked at his mother and Trevor. Melora couldn't tell what he was thinking, but it didn't seem negative, at least. More like he was just observing the two love-struck grown-ups.

Tony made a car noise and Demetri was quickly distracted.

Samantha let go of Trevor's arm and addressed Melora. "So you'll have me for music . . . did you bring anything along to decorate the dock?"

Melora felt abashed. "I didn't even think of it. Plus, I'm not sure the Park Service would like that. The dock is a historic structure of sorts. I think it'll be pretty enough with the lake and the sky, anyway."

"True," Samantha said, "and so romantic. Let's hope the weather holds."

Melora noticed Samantha glance at Demetri as she said this, and guessed she was thinking that, if the weather didn't cooperate, he could change it, but Demetri was engrossed in playing with his car.

They stopped talking for a moment, listening to the roar of the engine and the slosh of the waves against the boat. This ceremony would be so different from Melora's wedding to Charlie. That had been in his family's church. She'd worn an expensive dress with a long veil, they'd had organ music—the works. She guessed a traditional wedding was no guarantee a marriage would work. It hadn't done hers and Charlie's relationship any good. She trusted the simplicity of this service, and it was more her style.

Trevor asked, "Have either of you been back to the island since you left?"

Melora and Drew looked at each other. "No," they said in unison.

"So you're seeing it again together." Samantha sighed. "How doubly romantic."

Demetri stopped playing cars again and stared at Drew. "Aren't you worried about the wolves?" he asked.

Drew looked back at Demetri. A moment passed, then two. Melora started to get nervous.

Drew shook his head. "No, Demetri," he said. "It will be all right."

Trevor looked confused. Melora felt a chill run through her. Demetri was talking about what Slow Turtle had said to Drew. But of course, poor Trevor didn't know everything that occurred during the ceremony.

Demetri gave a little smile and turned back to Tony. Trevor looked like he was going to ask something, but Samantha touched his arm again, leaned in and whispered something in his ear that seemed to satisfy him for now.

Shortly afterwards, Melora and Drew went into the cabin to see how Jason, June, and Steve were doing. They found them mingling with the hikers, who seemed interested in learning that June and Steve had worked on the island. It wasn't long before they reached Windigo. Once passengers disembarked and embarked, the vessel followed the south shore of the island toward Rock Harbor. Although the lake was choppy, the waves were only about three feet, so no one was in danger of getting seasick.

Melora and Drew were sitting in the bow section again as the ship entered the passage into Rock Harbor between Caribou Island and Saginaw Point. They could see the crooked white tower of the Rock Harbor Lighthouse surrounded by stunted spruces.

A small thrill of excitement went through Melora at the familiar landmark. They were going back to Rock Harbor. And she was going to get married there! This journey was so different from when they had left the island under cover of darkness. She looked into the inky depths of the lake. The experiences she had the night they left eleven years ago had forced her to face her fear of the lake, which had taken hold when she was just a girl.

She had dived into the lake to save Drew's life by saving the drowning wolf that he was joined with. While she had overcome her fear out of necessity, she still didn't seek out the lake for pleasure swims, preferring instead any other body of water or swimming pool.

Melora grasped Drew's hand, thankful for his presence. Although the resort was still several miles away, she could tell from Drew's answering squeeze that he was excited by the journey, too.

Melora turned to him. "Are you sure you wouldn't rather camp than stay at the lodge?"

"No," Drew said. "We're getting married. We need a proper shower and a soft bed. There'll be plenty of other times for camping. Besides, we deserve this—to be tourists for once."

"It just seems so indulgent," Melora said.

Drew kissed her forehead. "We're worth it, my love."

"You're so sweet," Melora said. "It's just that I don't know if I can get into the right mindset while we're there. I'm so used to being the one waiting on people, not the one being waited upon."

"It might be hard at first." Drew grinned. "But I'm sure you'll get used to it."

Jason and Tony scampered down the deck to sit beside them. They had all sorts of questions about the lighthouse and when the ship would reach the resort. Drew answered them with patience and good humor. Melora joined the discussion, sharing her knowledge of the island.

The *Voyageur* made steady progress, passing an opening in the trees along the shore that Melora recognized as Three Mile Campground. A few colorful tents nestled among the pines. Then they'd pass Suzy's Cave, where Drew became a werewolf. Melora was glad the cave was set so far back. It wasn't visible from the water. She wasn't sure how Drew would react seeing it. That way, the boys wouldn't see it and ask questions that could stir up the past. During one of their many phone conversations over the past few months, Melora had asked Drew if the boys knew about his and Lana's werewolf past. He said no—it'd just confuse them. They could see no good coming from it.

The rocky point, the entrance to the harbor and the resort, came into view. Melora's heart beat faster. Guilt and apprehension mingled with her excitement. She still felt bad about stealing the boat eleven years ago, even though everything worked out all right, and even though she had disliked the resort manager at the time—Garner Stillman. June told Melora he had quit the next summer, citing personal reasons—but Melora suspected he just couldn't handle the isolation and demands that came with managing so many college-aged employees. However, she couldn't help but feel that the former manager would be at the dock waiting to punish them, his red-rimmed eyes staring at them like some baleful bull's from a Spanish ring.

As the ship rounded the point, the Rock Harbor Visitor Center came into view, a dark-red house-like building next to the marina and grocery store. Melora noted a new concrete dock had been built to receive visitors in front of the grocery store.

Jason peered over the side of the boat across the water at the buildings. He turned to Drew. "Is that where you and Mommy met?"

"Yes," Drew said. "And Melora and I met there, too."

"You knew our mommy?" Jason's eyes were big.

Melora fought to keep her comments as positive as possible. "Yes, your mommy and I used to waitress together at the restaurant here."

"Cool!" Tony chimed in, his chestnut hair blowing in the wind of their passage. The boat slowed, and Ben's voice came over a loudspeaker, asking everyone to sit until they were docked.

Slowly, the *Voyageur* sidled up to the dock. The deckhands scrambled to tie the lines. Then they opened the low door and put out the ramp. A small tractor with a trailer behind it appeared—one of the few motorized vehicles on the island. It was driven by a lodge bellhop in a white shirt reminiscent of a lab coat. Melora knew the trailer with its high railings was for transporting suitcases and packs. Drew squeezed her hand, then rose to help his boys off the boat. Melora followed, still holding his hand.

Once on the dock, Drew put his other arm around his boys as they stood beside him. "Welcome to Isle Royale," he said.

* * *

Sunday, September 3

T HROUGH THE SUN-DRENCHED FOG, Melora saw Drew waiting for her on the *America* dock. A breeze ruffled the sleeves of his dark-green silk shirt and tousled his hair. His black dress pants molded to the muscles in his legs.

Everyone else was already assembled for the afternoon ceremony. From the beginning of the gangplank that led to the dock, Melora's gaze scanned from where Ben stood, ready to officiate, at the head of the group near Drew. As best man, Steve stood next to Drew. As maid of honor, June stood near where Melora would go, holding her bouquet of wild-picked purple asters and daisies. Melora hoped the park service would forgive them this transgression against the local flora. Samantha stood to the side, playing a sprightly tune on her viola. Jason and Tony stood back with Trevor and Demetri.

Melora's gaze was arrested by three unexpected figures in their small party. The first was a big man wearing a white apron and a toothy grin. Jackson, the cook from when Melora worked at the lodge, gave her a thumbs up. She grinned at him. It was comforting to see another member of their old kitchen crew.

The other two were an older couple. The stocky man wore a plaid shirt and jeans with suspenders. The woman wore a flowered housedress. Melora recognized them as Davis and Emily Peterson, a commercial fisherman and his wife who lived on the other side of the island. She and Drew had met them during a canoe trip, and Davis had regaled them with Native American tales about the island and the wolves. Although Melora suspected Steve had a hand in Jackson finding out about the ceremony, she had no clue how the Petersons found out. Melora couldn't be mad even though she and Drew were supposedly there in secret. The Petersons were good people. She swallowed hard and looked at the wide gangplank that led to the dock.

She would take that walk alone. No father would give her away since her parents were deceased. But she didn't feel like anything was missing. Instead, she felt an odd mixture of exhilaration and peace. She tugged on the sleeves of the faded jean jacket she wore over a short white dress that had an intricate design of lace and embroidery on the front and along the hem—a high-low hem that rode above her knees in the front and dipped lower in the back. A heart locket dangled from a long gold chain around her neck. The necklace was a present Drew had given her just this morning, and it featured individual photos of his sons inside.

As she started to walk, she looked down, taking care that her sandal heels wouldn't get stuck between the wooden planks. It wasn't that long a walk—a dozen steps or so—but it felt like it spanned a great time and distance. Samantha stopped playing, so only the breeze through the pines and the waves against the shore accompanied her.

The fog was light enough for Melora to see the dock and the lake for several feet around it. Then it thickened so that the rest of the surroundings were a white blur. It felt like only this dock and this time existed—and Drew, waiting for her. His smile was wide as Melora stopped next to June and took her bouquet. June gave her a wink.

Melora turned to face Ben and the ceremony began. In a strong, clear voice, Ben recited the wedding vows. Before she knew it, Ben was asking Drew if he took Melora for his wife.

"I do," he said, his voice sure.

Ben asked Melora the same question about Drew. "I do," she said. As soon as she finished speaking, Melora heard a fluttering noise and watched in amazement as two tan-and-white blurs emerged from the fog and revealed themselves as piping plovers. The birds landed on the dock railing.

Afraid they were some trick of the fog, Melora looked around at the wedding party to make sure she wasn't the only one who saw the birds. Everyone was staring at the railing in rapt attention. The birds bobbed their heads, seeming to look straight at her for several moments, then with a small "peep!" they flew upward, tendrils of mist parting with their passing.

Everyone was quiet. Ben cleared his throat. "Somebody please tell me those weren't piping plovers."

Demetri's small voice said, "Of course they were!"

Laughter rippled through the gathering. Melora thought her heart would overflow. The appearance of the birds felt like a testament to all she and the others gathered there had done to help bring their kind back to the area. She was here with her love, with her people. Having the plovers visit, even for a moment, made her feel like everything was complete. She couldn't imagine anything that could make it better.

Once everyone settled down enough to listen again, Ben continued. "You are now husband and wife. You may kiss."

Drew came near to her. She could feel the heat of him, smell his spicy cologne. A familiar rush of sensations and anticipation filled her. In an unusual move, Drew brought his hands up and cupped her face. The warm smooth skin of his hands sent tingling waves through her face and down her neck. Melora closed her eyes and felt his lips on hers. The pressure increased, lessened, then came again. Melora couldn't help but lift her arms, bouquet and all, and start wrapping them around Drew. Time seemed suspended, and then he was gone.

Melora opened her eyes, dazed. Drew stood smiling at her. The crowd clapped while Melora thought how wrong she had been moments before, when she couldn't imagine anything better than the appearance of the plovers. She lowered her arms from Drew, laughing a little in embarrassment over her reaction to his kiss, and smiling for the world to see. Drew took her hand and they walked into their small crowd of friends.

Chapter Twenty-Two

I N THE RESTAURANT after the wedding, Melora scanned the dinner menu. She was amazed the choices hadn't changed since she waitressed at the lodge. They were even served relish and vegetable trays that featured the radish roses Melora had learned to make there. The resort still did not sell alcohol, so they had brought along their own bottles of champagne.

The waitress serving the wedding party was a short young blonde. She took their orders efficiently and delivered everyone's food correctly. *If only she knew my story*, Melora mused. Then she thought again, *Better yet, maybe she's in the middle of her own story*. Who knew what things might have happened already on the island to this typical college-age waitress.

When they worked at the resort, Melora and Drew had been long gone by this time in the tourist season. They had already gotten the wolves off the island and were living in the woods in Michigan's Upper Peninsula.

During dinner, Melora and Drew caught up with Jackson, who managed to stay out of the kitchen for once. Melora expected he had something to do with the delicious chocolate cake that arrived at their table once dinner was done. A large wolf gallivanted across it in blue frosting. Seeing the wolf caused several of them to laugh nervously. A gleam of mischief shone in Jackson's eyes, making Melora wonder just how much he knew about their connection with the island's wolves.

The Petersons told them they found out about the wedding from Georgina, and they didn't want to miss seeing the nice young couple they remembered sharing tea and stories with so long ago. The intervening years had been kind to the Petersons, but they admitted it was time to start thinking of staying on the mainland instead of coming to the island during summers. Like Jackson, they also seemed to know more about the wolves, Melora, and Drew than they let on. Melora didn't mind. They were all friends, and the conversation flowed.

After supper, Melora and Drew walked the paved trail to their room. Their unit was built right on the rocky shore, with balconies practically on top of the lake. A half moon, waxing toward full, glinted down upon them as they made their way under the spruces.

Melora and Drew walked up the stairs to the wooden porch that ran across the front of their lodge unit. The rooms were nothing special—white cement block walls, thin bedspreads and old carpet. But anything more than a tent was considered luxurious on the island. After they entered their room, Drew closed the door and stood with his back against it.

"Alone at last," he joked. "I love those people, but I thought they'd never let us go."

Melora walked toward him, stopping just inches away. "It's not too late to get Tony and Jason back from Samantha. Are you sure you don't want them to spend our honeymoon night with us?" She playfully trailed a finger down the front of his silky shirt.

In answer, Drew growled and reached for her. As he kissed her and tugged her jean jacket from her shoulders, the rest of the world fell away.

Later, they fell asleep in the path of moonlight that came through their open window. Melora slept for half the night until she was awakened by Drew groaning and moving as he lay on his back. His legs were straining and twitching in his sleep, like Spencer's sometimes did. She lay there, wondering what Drew was dreaming about, trying to interpret it through his movements and moans. All at once, his back arched and his teeth ground together as if he were in pain.

Alarmed now, Melora shifted and sat up, staring at him. Drew's breathing was ragged. She wondered if she should wake him, but she was afraid it might be too much of a shock—he might swing out at her, thinking she was whatever he was fighting.

She watched his face, outlined in harsh moon shadows. His mouth relaxed but his breathing was still rapid. His heavy brows drew together in a frown. Gradually, his back loosened and he lay flat on the bed. Drew's chest and arms were uncovered. Melora could see his biceps tensing, bulging in hard knots, like he was grappling with something or somebody. His fingers twitched.

Part of her wondered if he was reliving what it was like to change into a werewolf. She had seen it happen to him in the U.P.—both being freed of the Joining and then recovering the Joining after he realized being a werewolf was what he wanted. She felt like the island was exerting a spell on him, trying to cast him back to what he was before. But that was silly. It was just a dream, wasn't it? Maybe she should wake him.

Melora raised her arm and hesitated, ready to touch him on the shoulder. Drew's arms and hands flexed, and his legs began moving in rhythmic twitches, like he was running. Grunts issued from his mouth, matching the timing of his legs.

Melora couldn't take it anymore. She lowered her hand and gently touched his shoulder, applying more pressure.

Drew's intake of breath was sharp. His eyelids flew open. In the moonlight, Melora swore his irises were the tannish-yellow of a wolf's. At her small sound of distress, Drew's eyes changed color to chocolate brown, and focused. He let out his breath.

"You scared the crap out of me," he said.

"I could say the same for you."

"Why, what happened?" Drew asked.

"It seemed like you were having a bad dream."

Drew shook his head as if to clear it, and brought his hands to his temples. "I don't know what the hell that was."

* * *

Monday, September 4

T HE NEXT MORNING, Melora and Drew ate breakfast in the dining room at the lodge. Since their sleep had been interrupted, they rose from bed later than usual. They hadn't talked much about his "episode" last night. They had calmed each other, too sleepy to get into much more of a discussion.

On their way to the restaurant, they met Samantha, and Demetri, and Drew's sons, who had already eaten. The boys seemed content, although they greeted their father with big hugs. They were all going on a short hike to look at some old mine pits near the lodge.

Melora and Drew sat at a front-window table, enjoying the view of docks and harbor, waiting for breakfast. They planned to stay on the island today—explore for old time's sake—and take the *Voyageur* back tomorrow.

Drew had ordered a cheese omelet and Melora ordered toast and oatmeal. She didn't have much of an appetite. She had a bad feeling about Drew. She'd slept fitfully and woken with a knot in the pit of her stomach.

As foggy as the previous day had been, this day was clear and warm— an Indian Summer kind of day. Melora couldn't wait to get out in it— hiking to Scoville Point or somewhere else—hoping it would dispel her unease. As she and Drew talked about inconsequential things, Melora looked out the window, watching the tour boat that had replaced the one they stole, bobbing on the waves in the harbor. She realized Drew had stopped talking when he cleared his throat quietly to get her attention. When she looked to him, Drew was gazing at her.

"Melora, that dream I had last night was pretty intense," he said.

"I know. Are you ready to talk more about it?"

"Yes. I think I know better what it means now."

Melora waited, terrified about what he might say.

"I know it's a lot to ask of you . . ." He hesitated. "But I feel like I need to look for the wolves."

Melora felt like her world was collapsing. Last night, before Drew's dream, she had felt fulfilled in a way she never thought possible. During their lovemaking, they hadn't used any birth control. Melora hadn't felt the sensation of skin-on-skin inside her ever, and she had laughed with joy. She had her man. She had some inkling of what the future could hold. Marriage. Children. Her job. Her community.

Now, it seemed like she could lose everything. What if Drew went to find the wolves and never came back? What if he decided, like he had before, that being with a pack was more important than being with her? What if the wolves harmed him?

Melora felt tears invading her eyes. She willed them away and blinked. "Why?" she asked. "The wolves are doing all right now. There are twenty of them. It's not like they are in as much in danger as when we were here before . . . why?"

Drew took a deep breath and let it out. "It's hard to explain. It's not so much that I feel I need to help them again. I need to go out there—" he looked away from the lake, back toward the forest "—and make sure I made the right decision. Black Wolf's death broke the Joining before. I didn't have a choice, and then there was Lana and the baby . . . I need to make peace with it. I need to say goodbye to my wolf life properly."

Melora fought the urge to grab Drew and shake him. Why couldn't he have done this before the wedding? Maybe he was just scared. Maybe he had forgotten everything Slow Turtle told him. Maybe he was being an idiot. Or, maybe he felt safe enough to confront the issue. And coming back to the island had made it inevitable. Melora shivered as she thought of the way his eyes seemed to change when she woke him up last night. Whose bright idea had it been to get married here, anyway?

She pushed away all this mental chatter. "Drew." She looked at him steadily. "I need you. Your children need you. Remember what Slow Turtle said—you are our protector. Your time in the woods is over. Please, stay with us. You don't need to do this."

His gaze was sad. "But I do, Melora. I wouldn't ask it of you if I didn't feel I had to."

Their waiter brought them orange juice and coffee. Melora tore her gaze away from Drew and looked out the window again to hide her feelings from the server. He left quickly.

Drew sipped his juice. Melora went through the motions of adding sugar and cream to her coffee. It was taking all her power to try to understand. But she didn't understand it, not one bit. This was the day after their wedding. They were married. The plovers had even appeared. How much more symbolic could things get? She and Drew were supposed to be doing happy husband-and-wife things, like frolicking in the woods together, going on a tour boat trip, paddling a canoe. But no, her husband wanted to leave her alone to go run around in the forest with a bunch of wolves. *Wonderful, just wonderful.*

Now it was Melora's turn to take a deep breath. The tension was draining her. She remembered those tawny yellow eyes staring at her out of Drew's face. Something was going on here that was too big for her to fight. She needed to trust Drew—to let him deal with whatever this thing was.

"Go," she said. "Just go. Get yourself figured out. Make your peace. I'll spend the day with the boys. But then *come back to me.*" She almost hissed, "Remember, the boat leaves at nine in the morning."

The look Drew gave her was one of gratitude mixed with sorrow and a kind of hope. "Thank you," he said.

Melora couldn't eat anything. She stood. "I'm sorry, but I can't stay here and watch you leave."

"Melora . . ." Drew looked at her with pleading eyes.

She turned and walked away.

Chapter Twenty-Three

MELORA PERFORMED A J-STROKE in the water to keep the canoe on course. June paddled in the front and Jason and Tony sat in the middle compartments, their wavy hair blowing in the slight breeze.

"When will we get to the island?" Tony turned to her, his big brown eyes so serious. His look made Melora wonder if he was afraid of the water. She tried to reassure him, pointing to the pine-covered land mass fringed with long grasses about two-hundred yards ahead of them.

"See, Tony? That's where we're going. We'll be to Raspberry Island in no time."

"Are there really plants that eat bugs there?" Jason wanted to know.

"Yep—the island has some wetlands with lots of pitcher plants and sundews," Melora said.

"Cooool," Jason said.

"Why do the plants eat bugs?" Tony looked about as uncomfortable with this idea as he was about crossing the water.

"Because wetlands don't supply everything the plants there need to grow. The plants catch the bugs to get what they need to be healthy."

"But don't the bugs mind?" Tony asked.

This was becoming too existential for Melora to handle in her current state of mind. At her hesitation, June chimed in. "What do you think? Would you mind being eaten by a plant?"

"Yes," Tony said.

"I wouldn't mind," Jason countered. "I think that'd be cool. I can't wait to see them."

Melora didn't want the experience to be traumatic for Tony. She decided to show the boys how the plants were triggered by using a stick or something.

She corrected their course again, headed for the dock that poked out of the side of the island. She thought it would be a good place to bring the boys because there were lots of boardwalks to run on, and interpretive signs with pictures. Plus there were the strange plants. The island was in view from the resort, an easy paddle on a beautiful day.

After leaving the dining room, Melora had walked directly to June's lodge room—spilling out her disappointment and confusion about Drew. Ever the good friend, June listened with concern. When Jason and Tony came back from their hike to the mine pits with Samantha and Demetri and were looking for something else to do, June had agreed to spend the day with Melora and the boys, leaving Steve to socialize with the others.

After Melora had vented, she realized she didn't want to go hiking or do anything where there was a chance of running into Drew. So they had taken to the water, which offered the only means of escape—both from the island and from any questions the others might ask about where Drew was. When Jason and Tony asked, Melora and June told them Drew had gone for a hike and they weren't sure when he would return. Luckily, the boys accepted this without question.

When Melora nosed the canoe into the gravel by the dock, the boys clambered out. Before Melora or June could protest, Jason and Tony had started running down the trail. June looked at Melora.

"Just let them go. They'll be all right," Melora replied in answer to the questions in June's eyes. She finished pulling the canoe up onto the gravel far enough so that no rogue waves could float it away. As they walked down the trail, they were greeted with the scent of pine duff and dirt, fresh and musty. Soon they heard the clump of the boy's shoes on the boardwalk. They weren't too far ahead. Melora knew they were good kids and just needed to run off some energy. Besides, it wasn't like they could get lost since the island was small. About the worst thing that could happen was that they could fall into the wetlands and, well . . . get wet.

"So where do you think he went?" June asked. Melora knew who she was talking about.

She sighed. "I suppose he went to the old den site to see if any new wolves have taken it over. Or maybe he went straight to the neighboring pack's territory. Who knows how the pack boundaries have shifted now." But then she shrugged. "I really don't know."

"It'll be all right." The path was wide enough for them to walk side-by-side, and June laid her hand on Melora's shoulder.

Although Melora welcomed June's touch, part of her wanted to shrug it off. With an edge to her voice, she said, "You know what bugs me?"

June removed her hand. "What?"

"When we were in the sweat lodge, Slow Turtle told me—you're almost there. You need to trust that this time things will work out for the best. Ha!" Her short laugh was ironic.

"Well, you don't know it hasn't worked out yet," June observed.

"In a way, I feel everything is already ruined."

"I guess this isn't an ideal way to spend the day after your wedding, but you know what?"

"What?"

"I bet that if—" June corrected herself, "—when Drew comes back, nothing will ever make him leave you again. He's just got to get the last of this wolf stuff out of his system."

"But what if something happens to him?" Melora hated the whine she heard creeping into her voice. "Or what if he can't get it all out of his system in just one day?" She didn't think he'd try to become a werewolf again. That would take not only a willing alpha wolf, but the Devil's Club plant, which wasn't found on Isle Royale, but on an island a few miles away.

Melora's comment gave June pause. "These are all fears you have, Melora. They're all 'what-ifs.' A person can what-if things to death. I know Slow Turtle isn't your favorite man right now, but you've got to have a little trust in Drew and in your relationship. Maybe even a little trust in the magic of this place." She raised her hand to the silent trees and bushes that surrounded them.

"I suppose so," Melora said. "But it still pisses me off."

"You're just upset because things didn't go the way you think they should." June spoke carefully, watching Melora for her reaction.

Melora was taken aback by this soft rebuke. But why couldn't things go the way she wanted once in her life? She was expecting unicorns and rainbows, and what she got was wolves and gray fog. One of the reasons Drew wanted to marry was to prove that he wouldn't run off into the forest again. What was the first thing he did once they were married? Melora could feel the blood pound in her head. If she dwelled on it too much, the situation would drive her crazy. She just needed to have some trust.

"I suppose you're right," Melora sighed. They reached the boardwalk. She could see the boys ahead of them, crouched to look at something beside it. She approached them with June and saw that a group of plants was the object of their intense study.

"Good job, boys! You found some. Do you know what this kind is?"

They looked at her and shook their heads. The leaf that formed the base of each plant was oblong and rounded, with an opening that looked like a small gaping mouth. The leaves were red and green with stems that led to single dark-red flowers. The flowers had dried with age and each had five rounded petals. Several of the plants were clustered by the wooden walkway.

Melora directed the boy's attention to the veiny base. "See in here? The hairs point downward. It makes it hard for bugs to crawl out once they get in."

Jason lifted his green eyes to hers. "Is this a plants that eats bugs?"

"Yes, it's called a pitcher plant. It's like a trap. The bugs are attracted to the pool of sweet water in the base of the plant." She looked closer inside. "But I think these are all dried up. It's kind of late in the season."

Tony leaned over farther to peer into each plant. Melora held onto him to keep him from falling into the bog. He began to gesture excitedly. "I see an ant in this one!"

"Oh—poor ant," Melora said. "He's on his way to becoming plant food."

"How do they eat it?" Tony wanted to know.

"The plants digest the bugs in the pool."

"Cool," said Jason.

Tony leaned back and tugged on Jason's sleeve. "C'mon, let's see if we can find that other one!"

The boys took off running again. June laughed. Melora found herself laughing, too. They continued walking. Now that they were in the wetlands, the landscape had changed from trees to low shrubs and grasses. If it had been earlier in the summer, Melora knew they would have seen blue flag irises and the foliage would have been more lush. She reached down to touch the green wooly leaves of a Labrador tea plant. They were dry and brittle. Everything was changing with the oncoming fall.

Jason stopped on the boardwalk. Little Tony ran into him. "What's that?" Jason pointed to a small pool where a turtle disappeared with a ripple.

"Aww, you scared it away!" Tony complained.

Melora and June approached. Jason asked Melora, "What was that?"

"Looked like a turtle." Melora spied something next to the pool. "Hey, look boys." She crouched and showed them a cluster of short plants with round leaves on the ends of long stems, each leaf spiked with long hairs.

"Is that a Venus flytrap?" June asked as she bent to get a better look.

"Close," Melora said. "It's a sundew." She turned to the boys. "Guess what gets caught on those sticky hairs?"

"Bugs!" said Tony.

Melora ruffled his chestnut hair. "You are so smart. The bugs get caught and are stuck until the plant digests them."

"So just like that other plant, but different," said Jason.

"You are so smart, too," Melora said.

Melora's heart caught in her throat as she thought about what would happen to these sweet boys if their father didn't return. Drew didn't have full custody yet, and she hadn't adopted them, so she supposed they'd go back to Lana—a mother who was ready to give them up. She had to turn her head away for a moment so they wouldn't see the look in her eyes.

June distracted them. "Look, the turtle's climbing out over there!"

The boys left the sundews and trotted farther down the boardwalk, following June.

* * *

MELORA SAT IN A CHAIR on the balcony outside her room, watching the moon on the waves. She was alone, drinking leftover wedding champagne. Earlier in the day, she'd welcomed and needed the company of others, but after she and June brought the boys back from Raspberry Island, Melora knew she needed solitude. She had half-expected Drew to have returned to their room. He hadn't.

After dinner at the lodge with her friends, she had come to the balcony to brood. And drink. Lively champagne bubbles trickled down her throat. There were three bottles left from the wedding. She was starting on the second. Tired of worrying, Melora wished for oblivion. She wasn't a big drinker, but figured this was as good a time to start as any.

She laid her head on the back of the chair and closed her eyes in weariness. She tried to feel for Drew—see if she could tell where he was, what he was doing, from the air that they shared on this island. Hadn't Slow Turtle said she had ESP? His observation didn't surprise her. More like it confirmed something she'd always felt but never acknowledged, and never pursued. She'd always just experienced it as something in the background.

Maybe it was like her peace radar. Or maybe her peace radar was a type of ESP. It would be just her luck that like her radar, her ESP wouldn't work well on those she held closest.

Melora sat very still. She could feel a connection to Drew, like a thread that tugged and twisted gently. She remembered this same feeling when they were living in the forest in the U.P. And the connection had felt different depending on whether he was in human or wolf form.

She mused about how she would explain the difference to someone. That task required another sip of champagne. She closed her eyes again. Yes, the feeling of Drew in human form was upright. Tall. Straight. She couldn't explain it any better than that. The feeling of him in wolf form was lower, emotional, and she imagined a slight musty smell tied to it.

Right now, it felt like he was still human. But heck if she could tell what he was doing or where he was. It made her wish she could fly like Demetri. She had never tried.

Melora put down her glass of champagne and sat straighter in her chair. She crossed her legs and closed her eyes, letting her hands rest on her legs. The night sounds came to her: water lapping the rocks, a breeze through the trees. A loon called mournfully from nearby Tobin Harbor, making her feel even more alone. She tried to shut down the sounds and concentrate on lifting out of herself.

She felt the spinning of the chair from the champagne. Round and round she went. It was no use. No upward movement. Plus, it was dark. How did she expect to see Drew in the dark? Melora opened her eyes and gave up. She sat, drinking the rest of the bottle, before stumbling inside and into bed.

* * *

Tuesday, September 5

A BREAK IN THE CLOUDS allowed a shaft of sunlight through the curtains. The light fell across Melora's eyes, waking her. Her tongue felt like cotton, and she had to use the bathroom. She groped for the nightstand as she arose, noting from the clock that it was seven—enough time to get her act together before the boat left at nine. In the bathroom, she ran some water to drink and looked in the mirror at her bloodshot eyes. She groaned, then stood straighter as she realized what she needed to do.

She splashed water in her face and drank it from the faucet. She dressed and combed her hair, trying to make it presentable. Last night in her alcohol haze, she had decided she would wait for Drew this morning on the dock where they were married. The thought just came to her. Maybe it came to her from Drew, she didn't know. But it seemed right.

She dressed and went out. The sunlight that woke her was an anomaly in the overcast sky. Gray clouds packed together, hanging like a low ceiling. Melora hoped that didn't bode ill for the day. No one else was moving yet, although she saw lights in the employee dining room behind the restaurant.

A hush seemed to follow her as she walked on the trail, her footsteps silent on the cover of pine needles. When she reached the end of the dock, she paused, remembering all the thoughts and feelings that had run through her before the ceremony. Had it only been two days ago? There had been such excitement and hope. *Hope.* She clung to the tendrils of it that June and Slow Turtle gave her. Drew had to come back. He just had to. She didn't want to consider for a moment what would happen if he didn't.

Melora walked down the gangplank to the dock. A low bench was built into the side. She sat facing the trail, waiting.

Chapter Twenty-Four

EMETRI SAT ON A ROCK by the water just outside of the room he shared with Mama. The rock was cold from the night, but it was dry and flat. He looked up at the gray sky and hoped it wouldn't rain. Then again, if it did rain, he could do something about it, couldn't he?

But he didn't want to. Changing anything on this island seemed wrong. It was so wild and natural. He'd never been to a place before that had no roads and so many trees—so few people. He wasn't sure what he would find when he flew, but he wanted to, so he could see more of the island. He hadn't had time to fly since they came here, and this morning, they were leaving. It was his last chance.

Demetri crossed his legs and relaxed, closing his eyes. Just like at home, he could hear gulls and waves, but unlike home, there was a deep stillness instead of the background roar of cars. He felt himself lifting, and soon he could see the tops of the trees.

He and Mama had hiked to Tobin Harbor yesterday—the long finger of Lake Superior that lay a short walk from Rock Harbor. He had seen lots of different trees and cool rocks, but he wanted to see someplace else now. Demetri took off over the main body of the island, heading in the opposite direction of the harbor. He passed over the lodge and some cabins, flew over tents in the campground. People were cooking breakfast over fires. Then it was just trees. So many pines grew on the island, it was like a sea of green spikes.

Although Mama had shown him a map, he was surprised at how long and narrow the island was. He almost felt like he could touch the lake on either side if he spread his arms wide enough. Seeing anything through the canopy of trees was hard, so Demetri drifted toward the shore. He wanted to see some big animals. On the hike yesterday, they had seen a snake sunning itself in the middle of the trail, and a beaver swimming in the harbor, but he wanted to see a moose or a wolf.

It wasn't long before he was rewarded. A pack of four wolves surrounded a big bloody lump that looked like it could have been a moose. It had the right color hair on what skin remained. Demetri didn't want to get too close since it was so yucky. He circled around several times, watching the wolves eat. A big gray was tearing meat from the middle of the moose, while the other members of the pack lay around it. Demetri couldn't wait to tell Christine what he had seen once he got back home. He imagined her round eyes and how the freckles on her nose would wrinkle in disgust when he described the wolf kill to her.

On his third pass by the wolves, Demetri saw someone standing under a tree, away from the pack. He moved in for a closer look. Almost immediately, he recognized Drew by his curling brown hair. Demetri knew Drew had gone hiking yesterday, and began to wonder if his hike had lasted all night. Either that, or he had risen earlier than Demetri to come this far walking.

As Demetri flew closer, Drew crouched by the base of the tree. What was he doing there, so close to the wolves? He seemed just to be watching them.

Even as far up as he was, Demetri was glad the wolves couldn't see him while he was flying. From his seat on the rock back at the lodge, he felt a change in the wind direction on his face. Because he couldn't feel wind or anything while he was flying, he wondered if the wind had changed where he flew. He wasn't that far away from the lodge, maybe a mile or so. He watched the tops of the trees for a clue.

The reaction of the eating wolf told him all he needed to know. It lifted its head, nose to the wind. Demetri looked back to Drew. He seemed so intent on watching the wolves, that he didn't notice the wind shift. Demetri flew a little lower to see better. The big gray turned its head in

Drew's direction. Demetri went very still. He wished he could warn Drew. He knew he could talk to animals when he flew. He had never tried to talk to a person during a flight—he'd had no reason to. He worried he might not have time to try now. Things were happening fast.

The wolf gave a low bark. The three other wolves looked up at him and started to rise, turning in Drew's direction. Demetri saw Drew crouch lower, as if trying to make himself less visible, but it was no use. The wolves knew he was there. The gray wolf jumped over the carcass and ran straight at Drew, not waiting for the other wolves. From where he stood, Drew looked up into the branches of the tree, as if gauging whether he could jump into it and climb to safety.

Demetri decided not to wait to see if Drew could save himself. Back on his perch on the rock, Demetri formed an invisible ball with his hands. He pushed the ball into his chest and down through his body, then directed it with his hands toward the wolves. The energy ball traveled underground, unseen, except that Demetri could feel its motion. While flying, Demetri saw it come above ground and stop just in front of Drew. To him, it shimmered, but he knew Drew and the wolves wouldn't see it unless they ran into it.

By now, the wolf and its packmates were almost upon Drew. He stood, still and strong, awaiting his fate, as if he thought he could intimidate them with his stare and his wide-legged stance.

His posture didn't seem to effect the big gray, who bounded over a fallen log and kept running. However, when it was a few feet away from Drew, the wolf stopped, as if waiting for its pack mates. Growling low in his throat, the wolf stared at Drew. The other wolves fanned out on either side of the gray and stood still, as if expecting a signal. Drew remained standing, facing off with them.

Back on his rock, Demetri joined his hands and brought them up to his forehead. He stood, hoping that would make the ball into a shield larger than the one he had used to protect the plovers, and locked his forearms together and made a semi-circle. He held his breath as the gray wolf jumped up toward Drew's throat. Drew raised his arms as if to grapple the wolf.

The wolf hit a shimmering bubble wall and yelped as it bounced backward. Its pack mates, already launched mid-air in attack, did not have time to reverse course before they, too, hit Demetri's shield. They cried and writhed on the ground along with the gray.

Drew reached out a hand in wonder, gingerly touching the shield, before drawing his fingers back. By now, the lead wolf was standing. It approached Drew, sniffing the air. Drew crouched again and stared into the wolf's eyes. The wolf raised a paw and extended it forward, jumping back several feet as it hit the bubble wall. The other wolves were standing now and came to the side of their leader. Drew broke his stare with the wolf, looking up and around, as if searching for something. Demetri wondered if Drew was looking for him. He flew closer, until he was next to Drew.

Drew's voice was soft and reassuring. "Demetri, this looks like your handiwork. Tell the wolves I mean no harm. I thought . . . maybe they needed me, but I see that's not the case. Please, ask them to let me go."

Talking with wasps was one thing, talking to four large wolves was another. Demetri wasn't sure he could spread himself among them. He decided to concentrate on the big gray wolf. He floated over to him and surrounded him. The wolf took a few steps back, and the other wolves looked at him with their heads cocked.

"Friend wolf, this human . . . this person is a friend. Please don't hurt him." Demetri felt the wolf shudder at his words, and it looked around, wildly. Demetri was quick to reassure the animal. "It's all right. I won't hurt you, either. But you need to let the person go. Let him leave." On impulse, he added, "He used to be joined with a wolf, but he's not anymore. Let him go."

At this, the wolf startled and backed away. His pack mates looked at him and slowly followed suit. Demetri rose and hovered over Drew as the wolves went back to their kill, at least one of them always keeping an eye on Drew until they reached it. They sat in front of the dead moose, watching Drew.

On his rock, Demetri lowered his arms. A moment later, Drew put out a tentative hand again, as if to see if the shield was still there. His outstretched fingers touched empty air.

"Thanks, Demetri," Drew whispered. "Guess it's time for me to go." He backed away, his gaze locked on the wolves, until he was far enough into the trees that he was out of their view. Then he turned and headed in the direction of the lodge.

* * *

JUST TWO MORNINGS AGO, Melora had been on her way to the island, so full of hope and love. Now she sat, wondering if her husband was ever coming back. What would she say to everyone if they had to leave the island without him? No. Impossible. She wouldn't let it happen. She, his boys, and maybe one other person would stay here, and she would scour the forest and drag him out if she had to. Leaving her was one thing—leaving his boys, something entirely different. Maybe she could enlist Demetri's help to find him, if she needed.

Melora closed her eyes and leaned her head back against the dock railing. She could still feel the tug of Drew, but other than that, she could tell no more. She held on to that tug, tried not to let the hope die within her, tried to have some faith. It was hard, though, given everything that had happened in her life. Hope was a luxury she could barely allow. It was more painful than sorrow, more hurtful than disappointment because it represented a potential: the potential for happiness. If only her happiness didn't depend so much on other people, she'd be fine.

Eyes still closed, Melora smiled despite herself. She knew she had good friends with her here and to return to in Duluth. She had her job. Maybe she could be content with that, if she had to. Many people had it worse and managed to survive. If she'd learned anything over the years, it was that she was strong and resilient. She might go down into the depths for a while, but she would always surface again, kicking her way back to the top.

That thought made her open her eyes. From where she sat, she could see the tour boat dock—the same one she dove off of to save Drew's wolf from drowning. She had faced her fears head-on then; she would do it now, too. Melora inhaled and let her breath out slowly. She crossed her arms over her chest and turned to look at the trail.

The clouds were breaking up, with openings that allowed light through. Sunlight covered a spot in the trail about twenty feet from the end of the dock. She focused on it, willing Drew to appear. She closed her eyes several times, the light making lingering green blotches on the insides of her eyelids.

She was opening her eyes, fighting to see through the blotches, when she noticed movement on the trail, coming toward the light. At first, it looked low to the ground, like a gray dog or wolf, trotting fast. When it reached the sunlight, it stopped. Melora shook her head. The image before her now stood tall, straight and strong.

Melora's heart caught in her throat. She blinked again—just to make sure what she was seeing was real. Thick brown hair, broad shoulders— Drew smiled as he strode toward her. Melora stood and took a few steps in his direction, but started feeling light-headed and had to stop. Drew closed the distance between them, catching her up in a hug. She clung to him as he spun with her around and around.

"Don't you ever do that again," she whispered.

Drew's response was immediate. "I'm sorry I had to leave you, my love. The wolves—I should have known they don't need me. That was a mistake. I'm at peace with it. My heart and my life are yours."

Melora kissed Drew, dizzy with gladness, with relief, hope, and most of all—happiness.

* * *

Demetri rose away from the wolf pack, looking across the lake. He saw the big hills that formed what Mama called the Sleeping Giant. She told him the giant was in a different country called Canada. What would it be like to go to a different country? He could go there. Then Demetri looked at the expanse of water. It seemed like a long ways, but maybe that was just because it was so open. He wasn't used to flying all the way somewhere over water. But if he was ever to fly to the end of Lake Superior someday, this would be good practice.

Demetri decided to see how fast he could do it. He stretched out his arms in front of him like Superman and took off. Once he cleared the island, he was surprised at how clear the water was. He could see huge boulders deep beneath the surface. Once, he even thought he saw a large fish. A few boats were scattered about.

Before he knew it, he was hovering over the top of the giant. It was a series of bulging pine-covered hills that looked like a man lying down. It wasn't an island like Isle Royale, but like the island it was long and narrow. He saw some hikers walking along a ridge crest, and thought he would like to do that someday. Although flying was fun, he couldn't get a sense of a place like he could when he walked through it.

Demetri zoomed around for a while, seeing what Canada looked like. There was a city with roads and cars. It didn't look much different from his country. Then he started getting worried about time. He should be getting back. He stretched his arms and flew toward the island. He was about halfway there when something made him look to his left. A bright light was coming toward him over the lake. Demetri stopped, trying to figure out what it was. The light didn't seem to be connected to anything like a plane or a helicopter.

He kept hovering and the light kept getting closer. Just when he thought it might run into him, the light stopped. It was oval and large, about the size of a small person. It glowed yellow-white. Demetri squinted against the brightness and moved backward a few feet in surprise. Inside the light, he saw a figure.

It was a boy! He had brown hair, a blue-and-white-striped shirt, and tan pants. The boy, who looked like he was about the same age, gave Demetri and big smile and waved. Hesitantly, then with growing joy, Demetri waved back. He was not alone.

The End